DAREDEVIL®

PREDATOR'S SMILE

DAREDEVIL®
—PREDATOR'S SMILE—

Christopher Golden

Illustrations by Bill Reinhold

BYRON PREISS MULTIMEDIA COMPANY, INC.
NEW YORK

BOULEVARD BOOKS, NEW YORK

For more on Marvel books, see the World Wide Web site at
http://www.byronpreiss.com

DAREDEVIL: PREDATOR'S SMILE

A Boulevard Book
A Byron Preiss Multimedia Company, Inc. Book

PRINTING HISTORY
Boulevard edition / April 1996

All rights reserved.
Copyright © 1996 Marvel Entertainment Group, Inc.
Edited by Keith R.A. DeCandido.
Cover art by Matt Wagner.
Cover design by Todd Sutherland.
Interior design by Michael Mendelsohn.
This book may not be reproduced in whole or in part,
by mimeograph or any other means, without permission.
For information address: Byron Preiss Multimedia Company, Inc.,
24 West 25th Street, New York, New York 10010.

The Putnam Berkley World Wide Web site address is
http://www.berkley.com

ISBN: 1-57297-010-3

BOULEVARD
Boulevard Books are published by The Berkley Publishing Group,
200 Madison Avenue, New York, New York 10016.
BOULEVARD and its logo
are trademarks belonging to Berkley Publishing Corporation.

PRINTED IN THE UNITED STATES OF AMERICA

10 9 8 7 6 5 4 3 2 1

For Bob Tomko,
a genuine friend with an extraordinary heart,
because he'll appreciate it the most.

Special thanks to Lou Aronica, Ginjer
Buchanan, Ken Grobe, Ralph Macchio, John
Betancourt, Julia Molino, Stacy Gittelman, and
the gang at Marvel Creative Services.

Acknowledgments

First, as always, thanks to my wonderful wife and best friend, Connie Golden, and our son Nicholas. Thanks also to my agent Lori Perkins and my editor Keith R.A. DeCandido. And for opening a window into the world of comics, thanks to Meloney Crawford Chadwick, Scott Lobdell, Mike Mignola, and Evan Skolnick.

Finally, for the inspiration, very special thanks to the people who've brought Daredevil to life over the years, especially Stan Lee, Gene Colan, Dennis O'Neil, Klaus Janson, Ralph Macchio, David Mazzuchelli, and, of course, Frank Miller.

Author's Note

Daredevil is a unique character with a fascinating supporting cast and a rich foundation of relationships and stories. For first-time readers of the character, *Predator's Smile* is intended to act as an introduction. For those of you who are long time fans of Daredevil, and especially for you continuity buffs, however, this novel takes place between issues 233 and 234.

Issue 233 was writer Frank Miller and artist David Mazzuchelli's last, and featured Daredevil's final face-off against the crazed super-soldier known as Nuke, and had the Kingpin of Crime finally exposed as a criminal. Issue 234 took place at least one month later, after Matt Murdock and Karen Page had begun to settle into their new life together after the Kingpin had dismantled Murdock's previous life as a lawyer.

DAREDEVIL ®

— PREDATOR'S SMILE —

Prologue

I T WAS AUTUMN, YET IT WAS STILL QUITE WARM IN Venice. A band played, badly, on the patio of a trattoria in St. Mark's Square. The tables were packed, mostly with tourists and businesspeople, and a few couples danced on the cobblestones of the square.

It was a clear night, the tiniest of stars visible far beyond the brighter ones, and the moon hung casually, unobtrusively in the sky. A breeze with the slightest whisper of winter blew across the square, and tourists shivered briefly, then relaxed again as the warmth returned. The wine, no doubt, helped.

All the shops were long closed of course; Venice locked up early, except for restaurants and trattorias. The extraordinary face of St. Mark's Basilica loomed over everything in the square, and opposite it the open arcades led to other parts of the city, to alleys and canals. On either side of the square, shops and offices were dark, but the square itself had lights. Otherwise it would not be a safe place to be at night.

Thieves and assassins, you know.

If you walked down the steps of the Basilica and to the left, a wide section of the square lay open to the Grand Canal and the gondolas that bobbed there in the dirty water. Even the smallest waves sent seawater splashing across the stones by the docks, but there were no gondoliers there that late; there was no one to ferry through the night.

In the pitch-black moonshadow cast by the Basilica, a madman slipped from the water, the slick kevlar of his uniform drying almost instantly. He wore black, but his gloves and boots, his belt, and the wide circles around his neck were stark white. From a waterproof bag, he removed his Glock semiauto pistol, still in its white holster, and strapped it to his leg. He rarely used it, since it took the fun out of everything, but he valued insurance.

In the center of his forehead, in white, was a bull's-eye.

Dario Pennetta sat patiently at his table, suffering the disharmonious efforts of the restaurant's tone-deaf "entertainment" with tenuous restraint. Pennetta was not a man known for his restraint, nor his patience for that matter, and he was quickly tiring of waiting for the courier. It was a great discourtesy on her part, considering that Pennetta had never paid so much for the services of a courier, and as the moments ticked by, he was quickly deciding that he had paid too much.

Far too much, if she did not have the disc for him.

The band was taking a break, finally, but Pennetta suspected it would be mercilessly short. If the courier hadn't arrived by the time the music started again, he would leave. It was that simple. If she wished to collect the rest of her pay, the woman would have to use her vaunted skills to find him first.

The CD-ROM disc contained every bit of technology TakeshiCorp. had in the experimental stage, including all the schematics and technical specifications. They would take their time, confident of their command of the market, controlling the world's march toward the future. But Pennetta would not wait. He wanted that CD-ROM, and his lack of patience made it difficult for him to even consider waiting to receive it. His team was ready and waiting to complete the development and begin the manufacture of every product on the disc. By the time TakeshiCorp. realized what was happening, they would be hopelessly behind.

He sipped his Chianti and leaned back slightly in his chair.

"You are a wise man, *signor*," she whispered in his ear, and Pennetta nearly leaped from his chair.

She bent over him, her arms wrapping around him as she hugged tightly, kissing the balding area on the top of his head. Then she slid gracefully into the opposite seat.

She wore black stirrup pants and black high-top sneakers. A leather jacket hid her figure, but from the neck he thought she might be wearing some kind of body suit. Her hair was short, almost sheared off in the back, with a handful hanging over the front, partially obscuring her eyes. Her makeup was severe, black slashes accentuating her Asian features. "You are quite late, Yukio," he said quietly, though with a pleasant smile on his face.

"For a very important date," she agreed, flashing a disarming smile.

She was a very charming woman actually, which

was most certainly part of her game, one of the tools she used for her work. And yet, her personality could be abrasive. As far as Pennetta knew, Yukio had spent almost her entire life in Japan, and yet she seemed obsessed with Western culture, her every utterance some effort to prove that she had an American frame of reference.

"Are you prepared to conclude our business?" he asked.

Yukio nodded, but did not move to give him the disc.

"Well," he said after a moment. "Let me have it."

"Whoa, camel," she said with a smile. "Relax. You've already got it."

"What are you talking about?" he fumed, his voice rising. "I'm warning you, do not play games with me!"

"I'm terrified beyond the capacity for rational thought," she said dryly. "Run away, run away."

"Yukio . . ." Pennetta hissed.

"Pennetta, I told you. You've already got it. Search your feelings, you know it to be true."

It dawned on him then that she could be telling the truth. As inconspicuously as possible he patted the outside pockets of his suit, then reached for the inside pocket, as if going for his wallet. The disc was there.

Pennetta was not happy about being made to look a fool here in his home city, but he let it pass. Under the table, he used his foot to slide the soft black leather shoulder bag over to her chair.

"I trust," he said, standing slowly, "that we will never see each other again."

"Not unless you need me, sweetheart. And if you do, just whistle."

Yukio was going to say more, but Pennetta interrupted her. "Don't ask me if I know how to whistle," he snapped, frustrated. "I saw the damn movie."

Yukio just giggled. It was clear to him that she knew how annoying she could be, she'd mastered the art.

Pennetta huffed and reached for his wallet, planning to leave a few thousand lira to cover his drink. He looked up as he dropped the money on the table, but Yukio and the black bag were gone.

He hadn't heard a sound.

A constant lunatic rhythm echoed through Bullseye's brain, a rhythm produced to avoid thinking about *him*, the red-man. That was unhealthy.

The assassin had been shadowing Dario Pennetta through the weaving alleys of Venice, across canals and through open archways. He was completely silent, and yet he had to muffle a small chuckle.

Pennetta had four bodyguards with him. Two walked at his side, one slipped through the shadows far ahead, scouting for trouble, and the last hung back to trip up anyone who tried to follow. They'd been in the trattoria when the thief, Yukio, had delivered the disc, and the woman hadn't noticed them. But then, that wasn't her job, and she was too cocky to worry about not being able to defend herself. Bullseye admired her, in a way, and had no other quarrel with her, so he permitted her to leave the city alive.

But these jesters in Pennetta's court were another story. The man was wealthy, so his bodyguards were probably very good at what they did. But "very good" was dime-a-dozen common in their line of work, and Bullseye barely gave them a conscious thought. His confidence stemmed not from ego or arrogance, but from knowledge of his abilities. Still, he was a fair man, and he gave them a fighting chance simply by wearing the costume. He did, after all, have white on his hands, feet, and chest, which made him a target even in the dark. Hell, he had a bull's-eye on his head, inviting them to take their shot.

But they'd never even get a shot off.

Pennetta seemed more concerned about an ambush from the front, so he rarely glanced back to search the night for the guy batting the cleanup position on his team. Bullseye went for him first. He waited in the dark alley, barely fifty feet behind the bodyguard, who also sat in the pitch blackness watching Pennetta and his sidemen cross a moonlit bridge over a filthy canal, then disappear into the night on the other side.

When they were safely across and had already turned the corner of the alley ahead, the man slid from his hiding spot and walked with forced calm onto the bridge, muscles tense and alert, eyes searching. Though the bodyguard was smartly dressed, in

Bullseye's twisted vision he wore red, his face and eyes were masked, and horns protruded from his head.

They always looked like that just before he killed them.

"How's it goin'?"

The first word prompted the guard to draw his gun, and he spun back the way he'd come, aiming at the dark. He seemed unsure, probably thinking it was merely a drunk American trying to find his hotel. He took two steps back across the bridge and cocked his head to the left. He barely registered the gleam of silver in the moonlight as a sai—a razor-sharp dagger with pointed guards for use in close combat or to protect its wielder from the blow of another weapon—flew from the night and pierced his larynx, punching a hole through the back of his neck. The guard fell flat on his back, reaching to pull the sai from his throat, trying to scream but having no luck without a voice box. Bleeding profusely, the man got to his knees and reached for the gun he'd lost, perhaps thinking he might take down his own killer before he bled to death.

Then the other sai pierced his heart, and he fell to the pavement.

Grinning, Bullseye sprinted onto the bridge, withdrew the pair of sai from the corpse and wiped them on the bodyguard's wool suit. He returned the weapons to their sheath on his lower back, then lifted and tumbled the body over the edge of the bridge into the murky water below. In the morning, a gondola was certain to run across it, literally, but by then Bullseye would be long gone from the city.

He ran, then, not wanting to fall too far behind. He knew that he had to get to the roof of the building, but the thought made him uncomfortable. It wasn't his style. It was the red-man's. The crazy rhythm surged in his brain, trying to erase all thoughts of the red-man. He couldn't afford to be distracted, but the hatred welled up. He tried to push it down, eliminate the thoughts and images that visited him like malicious spirits countless times a day.

No, no, no! he told himself, and pushed away thoughts of the man who'd thwarted him so many times, who'd brought him to the brink of death twice, but refused to deliver on the promise of that oblivion.

He reached around to the small pack resting on his lower back and retrieved one of the many small weapons he carried there: bolos. This was his own variation, two steel balls linked by three feet of razor sharp monofilament wire. If it weren't for the kevlar in his gloves, he wouldn't even be able to throw the damn thing.

Bullseye smiled. He avoided thinking about . . . about him, until later. Instead, he pictured the death of Pennetta's point man even as he scaled the building next to him using every available window ledge and architectural conceit. He moved easily across the tops of the buildings. Often several in a row had been built so close to each other that there was no actual gap between them.

A quick glance told him he'd caught up to Pennetta and his sidemen, the man walking arrogant and unafraid, though his eyes continued to glance furtively ahead and to either side. He expected to get his money's worth from the men he paid. Fool. Bullseye slowed, pacing them, trying to get a glimpse of their point man, the one Pennetta seemed to be relying on most. He moved ahead a few paces, then stopped completely, crouching and narrowing his eyes as he stared into the darkness, watching for any movement.

He didn't have to wait long. Just a few moments and then, bang, there it was, plain as day. The guy may have been given point because he was the most skilled killer Pennetta could find, but he wasn't exactly Mr. Stealth. Bullseye, on the other hand, was.

He ran ahead to where the alley met an intersection. If the point man went straight, Bullseye would have to go down after him, left and he'd have him immediately below and out of sight of Pennetta's other goons. He went right, out of Pennetta's sight, but also moving away from Bullseye, who would never be able to leap the alley in either direction.

Not a problem. He'd just have to kill him from where he stood. The bolos had been wrapped tight around his gloved hand, but now he let them fall loose at his side. The point man had turned the corner and crept to the first doorway, where he stood waiting for an ambush, setting himself up. Guy figured he could handle anything.

He never considered death from above.

Bullseye swung the bolos above his head, trying not to let the monofilament wear on any one area of his kevlar glove. Eventually, it would cut even that. He waited, and about fifteen seconds went by before Mr. Stealth stepped away from the building into the darkened alley. He was perhaps fifty feet down, and sixty odd yards away when Bullseye spun the bolos toward him.

There was no whisking noise as the steel balls rushed toward their target, razor wire hanging behind like a dragnet . . . those effects were for the movies. This was real life, and in real life, weapons and those that wield them were silent, or ineffective.

The bolos were very effective. Bullseye's aim, of course, was perfect. The steel balls passed just below the point man's ears on either side. Maybe he had a second or two to think how lucky he'd been that the projectiles had missed him, but certainly no more. The monofilament sliced cleanly through the back of his neck, and likely partway through his spinal column, before snagging. The momentum of the bolos made the steel balls swing around his neck, slicing in from the sides and front much deeper than had been possible from the back. The balls clacked together behind his head, the only sound save for the thump of his body hitting the cobblestones.

''What was that sound?'' Pennetta snapped to his guards, motioning for them to check out whatever had happened around the corner.

Bullseye was in a hurry now. No time for fooling around. He walked to the edge of the building, the alleyway dark below him, and stepped off. The fall was nearly fifty feet, straight to the cobblestones, and when he hit, he crumpled up immediately, as if he'd landed with a parachute. Only harder. He tasted blood on his lip, but that was nothing. He knew he couldn't have broken anything major. Most of his bones had been broken in a fall, a fall caused by him, by . . .

Don't think that name . . .

He'd been paralyzed after the fall, shattered. But then he'd been taken to Tokyo, where a Japanese crimelord thought to buy his fealty by resurrecting him. His spine, and most of his major bones, had been reinforced with implants made from adamantium, an unbreakable metal.

He stood. He'd be bruised from this fall, but that was all.

"Who the hell is that?"

He was on his feet and leaping for a recessed doorway even as the gunfire began. Pennetta's remaining pair of bodyguards, unnerved by the death of their point man, had begun firing wildly. In the dark of the alley, they probably weren't even sure where he'd ended up, and of course, they were still counting on their backup man to show up with an assist.

"Stop firing at nothing, you fools," Pennetta hissed. "Go in and get him."

Bullseye shook his head, nearly sighing. Their firing blindly into the alley had been the only thing keeping the two morons alive. He stepped out of his hiding spot and swung his arms forward, flicking his wrists all in one smooth motion. Four shuriken, Japanese throwing stars, flew from where he'd gripped them between his knuckles. He dove forward to avoid gunfire even as the shuriken embedded themselves, two apiece, in the chests of the bodyguards.

They fired for a few more seconds, then fell to their knees, and finally slumped to the ground. The edges of the shuriken had been dipped in curare, a fast and deadly poison.

"Sandro!" Pennetta was yelling now, for his backup man. It was nearly a shriek. "Sandro!"

"The canal rats have him by now," Bullseye said, and then he cackled with glee.

Dario Pennetta had his gun drawn, but his hand shook.

"Bullseye!" Pennetta gasped as he recognized the costume.

He fired, knocking Bullseye off his feet and the wind from his chest momentarily. The assassin stretched, feeling tenderness already where the bruises would appear in minutes. Then he sat up. Stood up. Drew his own gun faster than Pennetta could see.

"The magic of kevlar!" Bullseye crowed. "It's a shame you're not wearing any, Dario. But let's make it fair. If you can put a bullet through one of my eyes, I'll die for sure. Go ahead, take a shot."

Pennetta didn't move.

"Bullseye, listen, I'll give you the disc. I'll give you

whatever you want. Just please don't kill me," he begged. "I'll pay you twice what you're getting for this job. Three times!"

"God!" Bullseye said, waving away Pennetta's words. "That doesn't even work in the movies."

Bullseye fired, Pennetta's gun flew from his hand and he clutched it tight to his chest, blood running freely down his arm.

"The disc," the assassin said, and Pennetta didn't argue. His good hand reached inside his jacket and produced the gleaming silver disk in a clear plastic case. Bullseye stepped forward and took it from him, removed it from its case and examined it.

"Tell you what," Bullseye said, slipping the disk behind him to the pack on his waist, not even looking up at his mark. "The contract didn't include your life. I just figured I'd kill you for kicks. But if you can answer one question, one easy question, I'll let you live."

"Yes, anything. I'll tell you anything," Pennetta gasped, hope surging in his eyes.

"What was Chekov's first name on *Star Trek*?"

Pennetta's eyes went wide with horror, he began to gibber something in Italian and fell to his knees as if praying.

"Come on!" Bullseye screamed, suddenly not caring if anyone heard. He was disgusted, infuriated by the sniveling fool in front of him.

"Come on!" he screamed again and kicked Pennetta in the side.

Pennetta looked up, and the utter terror on his

face made him look like a corpse already. Bullseye put the gun to his head.

"*Pavel!*" he shouted. "It's Pavel, you friggin' moron!"

He pulled the trigger.

Bullseye hated Europe. Once he'd been *the man* in New York, the bodyguard and chief assassin to Wilson Fisk, the Kingpin of Crime. A bimbo called Elektra came along and took that job away from him, but he'd taken care of her. Bullseye wanted his old job back; problem was, the Kingpin didn't want him. Mainly because the biggest thorn in the Kingpin's sizable butt was the red-man himself.

Daredevil.

There, I said it! Daredevil!

He was raking in millions on these foreign jobs, but he knew that one day he would go back to New York. He would kill everything that Daredevil loved, and then the man himself. Once that mission was accomplished, the Kingpin would have to take him back. New York, the city of dreams. It was waiting for him.

The name on the hotel register, and the credit card with which he paid for his room, was Dexter Franklin. He liked the sound of that and hoped he could use it for a while. He pulled on blue jeans and a black t-shirt, tightly tied his black sneakers, and ran his hands through his blonde hair instead of brushing it out. It would dry fine, as long as it wasn't in his eyes.

16

He wasn't comfortable in these clothes, not by a long shot, but he'd be headed to the train station soon—he had a meeting scheduled three days from now in Paris—and the Bullseye costume would be a little conspicuous while traveling.

There was a knock at the door, and Bullseye wasn't expecting anyone. He reached into his satchel and slid a sai from the sheath sewn into the bag . . . a bag that he made certain never went through customs, or metal detectors, or x-ray stations. He stepped quickly to the door.

"Who is it?" he asked.

"Room service."

"I didn't order anything," he answered harshly.

"Mr. Franklin? Dexter Franklin?"

"Yes?"

"It was sent to you by a Mr. Miller. Would you like me to bring it back?"

He thought a moment, realized he was hungry and was preparing to open the door when another voice came from the other side.

"Mr. Franklin," the voice said softly, "I am Klaus Miller. I have sent the man away, but the food is still here. You must be hungry after such a long day, and I thought you might want to eat something while I make you a proposal of employment."

Bullseye reached behind him and hooked the sai on his belt, then unlocked the door and swung it wide to admit Klaus Miller and a cart covered with silver trays. The man was repulsively average. About five foot eight, approximately one hundred seventy

17

pounds, perhaps a small roll of fat there, thinnish brown hair and dull brown eyes. He moved with the caution of an unarmed man in a showdown, which was only appropriate.

"What do we have here?" Bullseye asked, gesturing toward the trays in front of him. Miller stepped forward and began removing the covers one by one.

"Gnocchi and braccialitini for starters," Miller said, smiling grandly.

It was quite a spread, potato pasta, veal wrapped around prosciutto and cheese, salad, roasted peppers. The smells were mouthwatering. Still.

"Of course you know I can't eat any of this," he said to Miller, who merely continued to smile.

"Oh, yes, not yet anyway. I do understand," he said as he covered all of the dishes again. "Let's keep these warm shall we, while we conduct a little business?"

"And what business is that?" Bullseye asked, acutely aware of the sai at his back. He tracked Miller's every gesture, the motion of every part of his body, with the same mental acuity that gave him his extraordinary aim.

"A job, of course," Miller said, showing for the first time a hint of the cruelly arrogant core that lay under the smooth, businesslike veneer. "My client is already waging a, shall we say, campaign? Yes, a campaign to win a controlling interest in the, um, shadier American industries. My client wishes to unseat the incumbent, so to speak, and believes you might have a vested interest in his campaign."

The man was getting far too much pleasure from his allusions and political metaphors, and in the meantime, was confusing the hell out of Bullseye.

"Miller, speak your piece or take a hike," he warned. "I've got a train to catch."

"I have an assignment for you, the elimination of a certain American politician," Miller answered. "Consider this a . . . hmm, trial run, eh?"

"Trial run," Bullseye repeated, drily, not amused. Then he exploded. "Do you have any idea who you're dealing with here, little man?" He snatched the sai from his belt and pointed it at Miller, punctuating his words with it. "New York City trembled in fear of me when I worked for Wilson Fisk. I was the enforcer for the Kingpin of Crime!"

"Yes," Miller nodded, eyes downcast. "You *were*."

Bullseye could not believe the gall of this officious little nothing of a man, but he saw in Miller's eyes that the man realized the mistake he'd made.

"You're either out of your mind insulting me like this, or you're being paid far too much money."

He stood, staring at Miller, tossing the sai into the air and catching it by the blade, over and over again. It was calming for him, and likely near hypnotic for Miller, who waited to find out whether he was going to die. Seconds crawled by, and Bullseye just stared at Miller, who had begun to sweat noticeably and had developed a tic beneath his left eye. But he wasn't going to bolt for the door, which showed either intelligence, hopefulness, or resignation. He couldn't tell which.

"Who is your client?" he asked, walking to Miller and laying the flat of the sai blade against the man's face, its tip pointed at Miller's eye. "Who is this incumbent, and where is this 'trial run' assignment?"

"The first assignment is in Cairo, after which you would move on to New York for the more direct aspects of the campaign. My client is a man named Gary Wiezak. The incumbent, you have already named. Wilson Fisk."

Bullseye's mouth dropped open and hung there loose, as if at any moment his lower jaw might fall completely off.

New York! New York City! Home again, home again, jiggety-jig! His mind raced with the possibilities. It was time, finally, for him to meet with Daredevil again, maybe for the last time. Time to have his revenge and maybe get his old job back as he'd hoped, to prove himself to . . .

"Wait," he said. "The Kingpin? This weasel, or whatever the hell his name is . . ."

"Wiezak," Miller said, but Bullseye ignored him.

"This weasel wants me to help him take New York away from the Kingpin?"

"More or less correct."

Bullseye's mind was racing, several different voices having their say inside his skull, and he needed to shake some of them out so he could hear himself think. He needed to slow down.

Ignoring Miller, he uncovered the gnocchi, which was thankfully still hot, and sat down on the edge of the bed as he lifted a forkful to his mouth. As he ate, he considered his future. Many had tried to take the title of Kingpin for themselves, but you didn't get up in Wilson Fisk's face and expect to live. On the other hand, maybe hurting Fisk, reminding him that he wasn't invulnerable, was the way to make him realize he needed Bullseye after all.

Wiezak would pay him to put some chinks in the Kingpin's armor. And once Fisk was hurting, he'd have to outbid the competition for Bullseye's services. But the icing on the cake was that, while the Kingpin and this new pretender to the throne were warring, Bullseye would be back in New York, where he could finally have his revenge on Daredevil.

When the dish of gnocchi was empty, he put down his fork and wiped his lips with a cloth napkin.

"Klaus," Bullseye said with a grin, "you only live twice."

He bellowed laughter so suddenly that Miller jumped back.

"I'm afraid I don't understand," Miller said cautiously. "Does that mean you'll take the job?"

"Take it?" Bullseye shouted, leaping to his feet and holding an arm in the air like a politician preparing to lie. "Of course I'll take it!"

Miller began to give him the details of the job and his first assignment, a sanction in Cairo. But though he looked Klaus Miller directly in the eye, though he tried to pay close attention, he could hear only every other word.

Bullseye was going home.

Chapter 1

A FIRE BURNED IN HELL'S KITCHEN, AND DAREDEVIL was not pleased. This was his home, midtown Manhattan's West Side, and it had suffered far too much of late. Barely two weeks had passed since the insane super soldier known as Nuke had destroyed several buildings and dozens of lives. There had been fires then, as well.

Daredevil ran, danced, flowed across the rooftops of 8th Avenue. The night was crisp around him, colder than he'd expected, and he allowed himself the luxury of a selfish thought—*I should have worn the heavier costume.*

The smell of smoke was a beacon. In seconds, he pinpointed the fire, ten blocks north and three west, 52nd Street, flush between the West Side Highway and 11th Avenue. It was the furthest edge of Hell's Kitchen, but it was still close to home.

He'd grown up in Hell's Kitchen, motherless, his father a washed up boxer with vague mob ties. Battlin' Jack Murdock was poor and uneducated, like most of the residents of Hell's Kitchen, but he knew one thing for sure . . . his son was not going to be trapped in the same life. Jack wasn't going to let his boy, Matt, follow in his footsteps. With his father's urging, Matt studied constantly, and while the other boys taunted him, pushed him around, called him "daredevil" to make fun of his timidity, he let them.

Like most little boys, Matt Murdock thought his

father was a hero. He wanted Battlin' Jack to be proud of him. Perhaps that's why he didn't hesitate the day he shoved an old man from the path of an oncoming truck. That's what his Dad would have done, Matt figured. But while the old man was merely bruised, Matt's eyes were splashed with something toxic, something that shouldn't have been there. Something radioactive.

It blinded him.

After that, Matt had continued to study hard, and even worked out at the gym when his Dad wasn't around. He was fast and strong, a perfect student and a peaceful boy . . . but now he was blind. Lost. Not merely because of the blindness, but because in the moment of the accident his senses had opened up, almost exploded so that every stimulus, sound, touch, taste, and smell, was multiplied a thousand times. It was frustrating, maddening.

But then there was Stick.

Mentor, sensei, old warrior, Stick became Matt's salvation. With his help, Matt learned that, though he'd lost his sight, he'd gained much more in return—not merely enhanced senses, but a sixth sense, something like internal radar. A bat emanates sound, and from that it can determine its surroundings. Matt Murdock emanated nothing, except perhaps the inner peace of his mind. But within that, he could decipher the geography, the shapes and patterns, of his surroundings for 360 degrees.

If you could forget, for a moment, the blue of a spring morning, the orange of flickering firelight, the green of rolling fields, and the red of a candy apple; if you could forget what it was like to see love in another's eyes, the crinkle at the corner of a laughing mouth, the chocolate smeared face of a small child . . . if you could forget all that, the gifts Matt had been given were almost better than vision. And once in a while, Matt did forget.

One night, Jack Murdock was told to take a dive, or else. But Matt was in the crowd that night, and it didn't matter that Matt couldn't see; Battlin' Jack wasn't throwing in the towel with his boy there. Battlin' Jack Murdock took a bullet for his pride, but he died a winner.

A fire burned in Hell's Kitchen, and Daredevil, the neighborhood's protector, was not pleased. It was the tenth in a series of similar blazes that had occurred in the past week. New York had no amusement park. To some, arson was the next best thing. He'd been searching for the arsonist for two nearly sleepless days and nights, always a step behind. Daredevil was exhausted.

"This was no friggin' accident!" a fireman yelled to his lieutenant over the roar of hungry flames, the hiss of water exploding from high-pressure hoses, and all the background noises of the city.

To a normal man, these sounds would have blended into an ever-widening maelstrom of noise. But seven blocks south and two east of the burning warehouse, it was effortless, almost instinctive, for Daredevil to separate those sounds, to pull out the voices, hearing them all, focusing on the one vital bit of information. Another arson fire. Big surprise.

Daredevil's movements were far too fluid to be called running, too varied. At six feet and nearly two hundred pounds, he was larger than the world's greatest gymnasts, and yet he slipped from roof to roof lithely, his weight a feather touch, each footfall noiseless. Three steps led into a graceful, arcing dive. Hands braced, biceps bunched, he sailed across 48th Street. The vault fell short, as he'd known it would, yet he sliced through the air unafraid. When his feet touched down as he squatted briefly on the edge of a fire escape, he sprang to the roof, and continued on.

He was the man without fear, and without fear he was free.

Battlin' Jack Murdock got his life's wish. After his death, his son Matt did leave Hell's Kitchen, going on to become one of the most celebrated defense attorneys in Manhattan. And, to aid in the cause of justice, Matt also became Daredevil—taking on the name that he'd been taunted with as a boy—a costumed hero who was as celebrated in his own way as Murdock. Though Matt never forgot the lessons he had learned there, he had left Hell's Kitchen behind. Or so he thought.

A man named Wilson Fisk, the Kingpin of New York's crime syndicate, took Matt's new life away. Slowly but surely, he had destroyed all that Matt had worked to create, manufacturing a scandal to get him disbarred so that he could no longer practice law. He had even demolished the building that was Matt's home.

But the Kingpin could not take Daredevil away. In the end, Matt retreated to Hell's Kitchen, and began to build himself a new life. Ultimately, he exposed Wilson Fisk for what he was. No hard evidence, of course, so the Kingpin remained on top, but he was forever tainted by the truth that Daredevil had unearthed.

And Matt had come home to Hell's Kitchen, where he'd played as a boy. The gym where his father had sparred, where Matt had worked out. The rooftops he'd scrambled across before his skills had been honed.

He had come home.

Though he was a hero, and as such, would involve himself whenever his assistance was needed, Hell's Kitchen was different. Hell's Kitchen was *his*. His turf, his territory, his hunting ground. Its people were his family, and he was its ever-vigilant protector.

Someone was screaming—a terrible keening wail, not of physical pain, but of anguished grief. A part of him wanted to tune it out, but Daredevil would not, and could not do that.

Eleventh Avenue and 52nd Street, Daredevil sprinted across the last building, nearly gliding, and took to the air in a soaring swandive. In his mind he was the center of a vibrant ball of shapes and mental images. With his very soul he touched every car, every door and window, the on-ramp to the West

Side Highway, the ridges etched into a sewer hole cover. It was almost as if each scene forced its own unique pressure on his subconscious mind, painting a constantly changing colorless picture, its images processed and acknowledged at a pace that outstripped that of mere human vision.

It swirled around him, yet Daredevil was not distracted by a flash of fishnet-stocking-clad legs from 11th Avenue hookers, nor by the light of a television flickering from a window, nor by the passing traffic on the highway. With barely a conscious thought, in midair already, his legs pulled up and he did a forward roll with a kick-thrust, propelling himself just a tiny bit further than his original leap would have taken him.

Though traffic was moving slowly on 11th Avenue, Daredevil's course of action still would be impossible for anyone else. When he landed in a tuck-and-roll on the roof of a bus heading north at ten miles per hour, he came out of the roll in yet another nearly balletic leap. Contact with the bus had slowed him, but Daredevil's momentum was enough to carry him to the southbound lane. His hands touched the hood of an oncoming car, the smells of oil and gasoline, and the sounds of country music all struck him even as his feet hit the car's roof, launching him into a double somersault. That leap brought him close to the huge blaze that even now heated his face to a level most others would find painful. But he had to get closer still.

"Daredevil, over here!" a firefighter called to him.

"What's the story, Chief?" he asked, the title thrown off as if perhaps a figure of speech. The fire-fighter would not guess that Daredevil could not see the trappings of his rank. "I heard screaming."

"Lieutenant, actually," the man said. "It's a Fisk Industries warehouse, believe it or not. We're just trying to contain it now, keep it from spreading while it burns itself out."

Daredevil did not question the lieutenant, for the heat of the blaze alone was enough to tell him the building was beyond rescue. He felt for the people who had now lost their jobs, their livelihood. Dare-devil was angry. At the same time, he marveled that any criminal in New York City would be so stupid as to do harm to Wilson Fisk's business. The thought stopped him: he hadn't thought to check on who had owned the other burned-out properties this ar-sonist had hit. He made a mental note to do so.

"Any idea who might have set it?" he asked the Lieutenant.

"How did you . . . ?" the fireman began, surprised, and then shook his head. He understood. Hell's Kitchen was under Daredevil's protection. Of course he would know it had been arson.

"We're at wit's end, here," the Lieutenant said, and shrugged. "If you find anything that might help, please let me know."

Daredevil nodded. He had to assume a search of the grounds would be as fruitless as all the others. Luckily, there were other ways to get information in New York City.

Daredevil dropped down onto the sidewalk in front of Josie's Bar, a lowlife dive of a pool hall/barroom in midtown.

The bar was filled with white noise, voices and laughter, music from the juke; it all joined together into an almost melodic hum that would have put a baby to sleep. But then, Josie's was no place for a baby. You could tell that by the smells. Alcohol, certainly, but worse, the smell of alcohol being oxidized through the pores of workers and drunks. Musty, dank, stale smells of beer-stained floors and chair cushions joined the brimstone stench of tobacco and nicotine, a cloud of which filled the place.

And there were other smells, male and female, perfume and body odor, hairspray and cherry lip gloss, cologne and aftershave. The metallic scent of blood and an almost indiscernible chemical reek. Sulfur—a recently fired gun, but not his business at the moment.

This was a bad place, Josie's. Bad clientele. Rapists, killers, thieves and people who just liked to hurt other people. He was certain that, should he attempt to focus, to identify the crowd by their individual heartbeats, he would recognize almost all of them.

But tonight he sought only one man. As he made his way into the place, letting the door shut behind him, Daredevil listened for one particular voice in a room of more than sixty people. And he found it.

As he stepped away from the door, people began to notice him. Someone moved toward him from the bar, standing tall, heart racing, apparently intending to intercept him.

"Obviously you're not a regular here," Josie, a big, unnaturally blond-haired woman, said as she grabbed the man by the shoulder. "Save yourself the hospital bills."

Silence swept across the bar like a wave rolling into shore, all the way into the billiards area in the back. But one voice did not stop, so oblivious to his surroundings was its owner. One voice rose through the silence, the voice of a braggart and a coward by the name of Turk.

"So I says, Mr. Castle, you know what you need?" Turk smiled, flashing his gold tooth, amused by his own cleverness and ambition. "You need vision, I tell 'im. And vision is exactly what ol' Turk's got in spades!"

Turk knocked back the rest of the watery whiskey in his chipped tumbler, then slammed it down on the table.

"I think he's thinkin' about it, Grotto. I think he's considerin' it. He needs me, I got vision!"

Turk was about to go on—he prided himself on an infinite capacity for conversation—when he noticed the silence.

"Grotto?" Turk asked, annoyed.

Then he realized that Grotto wasn't just spacing, that his buddy's eyes had fixed on something specific over Turk's head. Then Turk felt someone grip his shoulder and half-turned to see a red-gloved hand resting there.

Turk leaned forward, resting his head on the wooden table, eyes slitted and lips pulled into a tight grimace. *Not again*, he thought. He banged his head twice, the report echoing in the silent bar, sighed and stood up. Without even looking at Daredevil, he walked toward the door. He'd had enough whuppin's from Daredevil, even if you only counted right there in Josie's, to know better than to try to fight or run away. Nobody in that place was stupid enough to help him out if he tried to go toe to toe with the hero.

"Hey Turk, DD, thanks for not busting up my place again," Josie's face said she was sincerely grateful, and Turk gave her a mean smile. She better give him one on the house when he and the hero finished their business, he thought.

Once outside, Turk leaned up against the wooden doorframe, trying to avoid being humiliated in plain sight of Josie's plate glass window. What had happened in the bar was bad enough, him not even putting up a fight. But let those guys talk, huh? Not one of them would have even *thought* about making a move.

"Turk, are you ignoring me?" Daredevil asked, and Turk only shook his head. The man was a hero, on the side of the angels, no doubt about it. But sometimes Turk thought the red-man got a kick out of playing him for a stooge, forcing him to play snitch. Yeah, there was this tone in his voice that

Turk didn't like one bit. No respect.

"Whatchoo foolin' with me for, Daredevil? I'm Sergeant Schultz, man. I know nothing! I see nothing, okay? Whyn't you just step off, now, and leave a man to his life?"

"Shut up, Turk," the hero said, his words clipped, making it clear he was not playing here. "I want you to tell me about our friendly neighborhood arsonist."

Turk raised his eyebrows. Daredevil seemed to loom over him, though Turk figured he probably had an inch or two on the guy. Daredevil had an electric, disturbing presence, made all the worse by the costume. Fabric covered his eyes, and you had to wonder about that. Was there something under that mask that gave him some kind of enhanced sight? Why else, how else, could his eyes be covered? The costume itself was a deep, dark red, dark as blood, the color, perhaps, of a human heart pulled still beating from its sticky nest.

The double billy club was strapped to his thigh without ornamentation. The letters DD sprawled on his chest, almost as if they'd been carved there and healed up into ugly, intimate scars. A pair of small horns, not much larger than thimbles, protruded from his forehead, and more than one guy Turk knew thought that maybe those horns were really there, under the costume.

All the boys said the costume didn't bother them, that it was the man's track record that made them nervous, but Turk knew that was crap. The man's moves made him dangerous, the costume made him a myth.

A myth. Nobody was that fast, that good, almost psychic in a fight, like he knew where every blow was going to come from. The guy had eyes in the back of his head! And the things he did . . . insane things. They called him the man without fear because of the risks he'd take, but Turk had heard talk that claimed he had no fear because he knew he couldn't be hurt, he wasn't human.

But Turk knew better. He'd seen Daredevil hurt, seen him bleed. He might be afraid of getting his ass whupped again, but he knew the man in front of him *was* just a man.

"Tell me what you know about the firebug, Turk," Daredevil started again, grabbing Turk by the collar and pushing him against the doorframe.

"I got no idea 'bout none of that stuff," Turk said, pushing Daredevil's hands from his throat. "So don't mess with me."

Daredevil stood back and crossed his arms. Turk exhaled, and realized he'd been holding his breath.

"Turk. I'll say this once. Counting today, fifteen people have died because of this guy. Whatever you know, give it up now."

"All I'm gonna say is, I don't know anybody damn fool enough to stick 'is head in the lion's mouth but you. That means I got nothin'll do you any good," Turk answered.

And then all hell broke loose.

* * *

A flurry of movement from all sides, and Daredevil was reacting, arms and legs flashing in a whirlwind of blocks and parries. Then he was on the offensive. Two heartbeats behind him, two in front, and one . . . one above!

Daredevil dove forward in a move that any casual observer would have called suicidal, as it was about to put him on the ground in range of two attackers' weapons. Where he'd been standing, the fifth warrior landed, sword clanging against the sidewalk, even as Daredevil's hands planted on the cement, vaulting him feetfirst into the air and over the two men who'd been in front of him.

Even as they turned, he eliminated them from the fight. The killer on the left held a pike, its staff tipped on either end with deadly sharp blades. He moved in as his partner threw a sai, and suddenly Daredevil knew what the attackers were, and what they were not. Bobbing his head to one side to avoid the sai, he grabbed it in midair even as he kicked up his right foot to block the pike's thrust. Then he brought the sai down to parry a slash from the pike.

They were ninja, more precisely, the Hand, the deadliest sect within that order of assassins. And yet, they were not. They had approached as silent as the Hand, and now that he had touched one of them, heard the rustle of their clothing, he recognized the ritual robes of the sect. But they were not good enough to be Hand.

Over the years, Daredevil had studied every form of martial art, from the most common to the most obscure, and drawn from each exactly what he needed to develop his own unique style of fighting. A style that required one thing of its sole practitioner, one thing more difficult than any move, offensive or defensive: restraint. He would not kill, nor would he injure beyond necessity.

The Hand, however, had a unique trait of their own: upon defeat, their bodies would simply disintegrate as if they had never been. Thus the secrets of the order were protected.

No, these men were not Hand. Still, he had to find out who sent them. The timing of this attack raised his suspicions. If someone was willing to go to these lengths to keep him off the trail, this was no mere petty arsonist at work. There was more going on than he had imagined.

The ninja with the pike lurched clumsily toward him, apparently disconcerted by how easily the hero had batted him away. Now, though, Daredevil was on the offensive. The pike jabbed toward him again, Daredevil let his body turn slightly so that its razor blade whirred past him, then he grabbed the shaft and simply continued it along its path, using the pseudoninja's momentum against him. Daredevil dragged the killer toward him and snapped a kick to the man's jaw as he did so. A blow that might have snapped a neck merely rendered the attacker unconscious.

The others, all three, had been slowly attempting to reconstruct the killing net that he had so easily eluded at first, circling him slowly. Now, as he moved in on the sai-wielder, Daredevil could sense that circle of death contracting around him. When he reached for the ninja with the one remaining sai, the man actually winced in fear, something none of the Hand would ever do. Instead of attacking him, however, Daredevil merely hauled him up and threw him at the swordsman before following with his own weight.

The swordsman retreated toward the front door of Josie's, and Daredevil bowled him over, his fists flashing red. In seconds, the ninja was disarmed and knocked unconscious with a dislocated shoulder.

Daredevil whirled to face his remaining attackers, and finally the words did come:

"Who sent you?" he demanded. The two advanced, step-by-confident-step, spreading out to either side as they planned their attack. Daredevil made sure to steer clear of the three fallen ninja in his retreat. He'd pretty much known they were not Hand, but this confirmed it. In defeat, their living bodies remained undissolved. He had a moment to think how many Hand had died simply because he would not allow them to defeat him.

And then Turk leaped on his back, arms wrapped around his neck, screeching like a madman.

"Kill him!" Turk shouted. "This is my offering to your boss. He needs a man like me!"

Turk! Daredevil had sensed him, all along, of course. Had smelled the beer on his breath, heard his wildly pumping heart, sensed the outline of his form lurking just beyond the fight . . . but he'd subconsciously erased the man from the scene so that he could better concentrate on the ebb and flow of aggression and energy that surrounded him.

"Turk, you fool!" Daredevil reached behind and grabbed the back of Turk's collar with one hand, twisted toward Josie's and tossed the two-bit criminal through the bar's plate glass window. It shattered deafeningly, the glass raining down in a cascade of noise that nearly prevented Daredevil from hearing the *shuk-klik* as someone slammed an ammunition cartridge into an automatic pistol. He couldn't have missed the smell of oil in the gun's barrel however.

Even before he turned his radar had analyzed the situation, both standing swordsmen had dropped their weapons and drawn pistols, the final proof that they were not Hand, not even really ninja. The use of these weapons was an insult to all they stood for.

Police sirens grew louder in the background. Someone must have called the cops when the fight began—not a given in this neighborhood.

Daredevil spun into motion. The gun barrels were being raised as his left hand released the sai he still held. His right side lurched forward and down, fingers outstretched to retrieve a fallen sword. The sai flew straight and true and found its mark, its blade swallowed by the barrel of the weapon even as the warrior pulled the trigger. The barrel exploded, taking the man's hand, even as his comrade fired.

Daredevil was in it, then, that flow of sound and form and energy all around him, the hero a scalpel with mechanical precision, but feral grace. He lunged to one side as the sword in his right hand flew up to deflect two bullets that got near enough to him. And then he was staying ahead of the gunfire, dancing too fast for the gunman's aim to catch up, what appeared to be a dive turning into a slide toward the *faux*-ninja's legs. The flat of his blade cracked the man's wrist and sent the gun flying.

Two squad cars slammed to a halt in front of Josie's even as Daredevil held his last opponent up in front of him, his face mere inches from the other man's.

"Who sent you?" he asked, hearing the anger in his own voice, unable to hide it. "*Who's behind . . .*"

And then the crack of gunfire rang out, sending the cops diving for cover the moment they stepped from their cars, and the man in Daredevil's hands went limp, stopped breathing, started bleeding.

"Stay down!" Daredevil said, diving for cover himself through the shattered front window of Josie's. Inside, everyone had taken cover. He listened to the night, to the world outside, trying to shut out the sound of chattering police radios, swearing patrons inside the bar, screaming voices on the street as late-night passersby, several of whom had been watching his fight with the ninja, ran for safety. He listened for the crack of the rifle again.

And it came, the report resounding among the buildings like an echo down a canyon. But it wasn't just an echo: the sound repeated five times. When it stopped, Daredevil knew it had come from the roof of the apartment building over the laundromat three doors down across the street. He stood to rush into the night, knowing the ninja were all dead, knowing that though they weren't Hand, they still had their own punishment for failure, and then Josie was standing there in front of him.

"Now you listen here, DD!" she said loudly, scolding. "This is the third time in six months you smashed that window, and this time, hero, you're gonna pay to replace it! And I do mean cash!"

"It's a deal, Josie, but just . . ." he began, but the rifle cracked one more time, Josie grunted and crumpled toward him. Daredevil caught her large form and lifted her, a feat impossible for most men twice his size, to the bar so she would not fall in shattered glass.

"Josie?" he asked, listening for her heartbeat. He smiled when he found it.

"What the hell are you doing?" she croaked. "Go get that SOB."

He started to move away, to fulfill her request, when she grabbed his arm.

"What is it?" he asked quietly.

"Don't come 'round here for a while."

Daredevil nodded, understanding, not blaming her as he headed unprotected out the door.

"Get down!" the cops shouted, but he kept going as a SWAT truck screeched to a stop at the curb, its back doors slammed open and elite police corps stormed out. He didn't look at them as he sprinted across the street, aware that the gunman was no longer at his perch, but hoping to catch his trail from there.

In an alley between the laundromat and Chang's Schezuan, he jumped onto a dumpster, then to a window ledge, and then across to the next building's fire escape. At the top, he leaped across to the spot he was sure the killer had stood.

There was no sign of the sniper now, though. He had taken the time to pick up his shell casings. Except for a trace whiff of cologne, a scent Daredevil didn't recognize, it was as if he'd never been there. Daredevil tried to use his enhanced senses to find the man's heartbeat, since he knew it had to be beating incredibly fast, but didn't turn up anything. The guy had gotten away with it.

Daredevil decided to let the cops clean up. Turk had obviously been clueless, though they'd have to talk soon about the way he'd tried to help the killers. This hadn't been the first time he'd turned on Daredevil, and likely far from the last.

Daredevil considered his next move.

Nothing tonight, he realized sadly. He'd had five hours of sleep in two nights, and he still didn't have any names. This wasn't going to be an easy case, he knew now. It wasn't just one guy he had to stop, but a larger conspiracy. And he didn't have a clue what it was.

"Round up the usual suspects," Claude Rains had said, dripping with sarcasm, in *Casablanca*. In Manhattan, few crimes of this nature happened without the Kingpin's okay. There was only one usual suspect and his name was Wilson Fisk. Tomorrow morning, he'd go see the Kingpin, see if the Big Apple's rotten core knew why someone had torched his warehouse, and if Turk's comment about sticking his head in the lion's mouth meant what Daredevil thought it did.

That was first on the agenda tomorrow. A visit to the king.

Chapter 2

"**D**O YOU *EVER* WANT CHILDREN?" BETSY POTTER asked hopefully.

Melvin Potter looked down at the chicken parmesan and ziti he'd cobbled together for dinner and stroked his moustache, unsure how to respond. The moment had finally come: the heart-to-heart, the conversation that he had dreaded for months, ever since the day his wife had first broached the subject of becoming parents.

But he really wasn't sure of the answer. He loved children, their presence alone reaffirmed his belief in the fundamental goodness of humanity. He had lost that faith far too young, and had barely even realized it was gone all through the years of his criminal career as the Gladiator. It was hard to imagine being responsible for the creation of another human being, for the guidance of that new life. There were so many mistakes that could be made, and as a child, Melvin had experienced them all.

And yet . . .

"Yes," he said, looking at Betsy. "Yeah, I really do. But I'm afraid."

"Of what?" Betsy asked, her psychotherapist's directness overwhelming her spousal tenderness, a habit she battled against.

"That my children will turn out like me," Melvin said.

Betsy smiled. "Melvin, if our children turn out to

have half of your honesty and nobility, I'll be a very happy woman."

Melvin speared a freshly cut piece of chicken, but didn't eat it. He twirled it thoughtfully on the end of his fork, forgetting for the moment that it was even there. His childhood had been such a nightmare, and most of his adult life even worse. He found it hard to imagine the pure spirituality he knew parenthood should be.

"Listen, honey," Betsy began, "I know you're concerned about your past as the Gladiator, and even before that. But I was your psychotherapist remember? If anyone would know what kind of parent you would make, it's me. And I think you'll be a hell of a Dad when the time comes."

She smiled as Melvin reached across the dinner table and put a huge hand on the back of her neck.

"I hope you're right, angel," he said in surrender. "And I wish I had your faith in me."

Back when she was just plain Betsy Beatty, she'd been among the hordes of New Yorkers who had followed the exploits of Daredevil, including his battles with a merciless criminal, a costumed thief and sometimes mercenary killer known as the Gladiator. But when the Gladiator was finally apprehended, Betsy had gotten a lot closer than she ever would have imagined. She was appointed by the court to analyze his mental status, to determine whether or not he was fit for trial.

Up close and personal, with the aid of Melvin's

attorney, a blind man named Matt Murdock, she had realized that there was more to Melvin Potter than was broadcast on TV. The poor soul had a terrifying background. She found that he also had a chemical imbalance of the brain that rendered him incapable of judging right from wrong.

Drugs were prescribed to adjust the imbalance and counseling to help Melvin deal with his actions when his sense of morality returned. Betsy had been with him through it all. It had been her testimony, according to Murdock, that had convinced the judge to set Melvin free, on the condition that he continue with his counseling and appear before the court twice a year.

Betsy Potter knew her husband better than most wives ever could. She knew what he was feeling, and she hurt for him.

"Just because your adoptive parents screwed up, doesn't mean you will," she said. "It's not like you could inherit anything from them."

"Biologically, no," Melvin said, looking at her intensely, searching for reassurance. "But environmentally. What about that?"

When Betsy didn't answer right away, Melvin stood and began pacing the small kitchen, running a hand over his bald scalp. He never knew his real parents, but she knew he had a massive internal conflict about his love for the couple who had adopted him.

"My Dad used to say that when the adoption agency called, they felt like they'd won the lottery," Melvin said and smiled sadly. "I remember my Mom giving me a big hug and telling me I'd been the answer to all their prayers."

Betsy nodded. It was a familiar tale. The Potters had been a troubled couple from the outset, and had looked to the five-year-old Melvin to bring them together, to wipe their problems away. They never realized that at that age, a child is desperately looking to his parents to solve his own problems. Yet from all reports, they loved him intensely, and his young life was happy.

Until it all came tumbling down. And Betsy could only wait patiently as her husband relived it all, once again, and be there to hold him when he finished.

Nothing Melvin said to Betsy could ever communicate the pain of that day. And with all his heart, he was glad of it. He loved his wife more than life itself and hoped she would never have to experience such a devastating loss.

He had been eight years old, sitting at the breakfast table eating French toast on a bright Sunday morning. His father was reading the newspaper, and Mom was getting herself a cup of tea when someone began to pound on the apartment door. "Who is it?" his father had called angrily from the kitchen. And the one word answer, "Police!" barked from behind the door seemed to paralyze both of his parents. Melvin knew in that moment, watching their faces, that no matter what he knew of them, no matter how they had loved him, they had done something bad.

And indeed they had. Several nights earlier, his father's boss had been killed in a hit-and-run accident, which was, apparently, no accident. Melvin screamed as the social workers dragged him from the only home he'd ever known and the only people who had ever loved him. His flailing hands latched onto the doorframe, and his eyes fell on the black marks his father made on the molding every two months to gauge his height. All the strength went out of him as he let go of his home, and he had wondered if he would keep growing without his father there to measure him.

He became a ward of the state, was put up for adoption again, and suffered his way through a series of foster families, each more oppressive and hurtful than the last. He got into trouble. Small stuff at first, but getting progressively worse. And even without Dad's marks on the door frame, he grew . . . huge.

"But you'll be there," Betsy said, embracing her husband in their little kitchen. She smiled as she wiped away tears. "You'll be there for our children, you'll mark their growth as the birthdays fly by. I know you want that, Melvin. Don't let what's gone before stop you, stop us from living our lives."

"You're right," he said softly. "With you, I know I can do it."

After they finished the dinner dishes, they moved to the living room to catch *Casablanca* on American Movie Classics. Melvin didn't like most TV, and he wouldn't watch the news. There was too much in it to remind him of the bad old days and his life as the Gladiator. His conversation with Betsy had gotten him thinking again about those dark times, and he silently vowed that their children would never follow that path.

The things he'd done as Melvin Potter, small time criminal, had been bad enough. But when he'd added the blue and yellow costume, the helmet, the deadly sawblades that buzzed on the metal gauntlets at his wrists—when he became the Gladiator— everything had changed. The Gladiator ran with the worst criminals the world had to offer, the real Melvin shoved so far down inside his psyche that he almost always felt like little more than a captive audience to the Gladiator's sins. Never completely stable, the use of the Gladiator identity almost drove Melvin irrevocably over the edge.

And that's where Betsy came in. The DA had never expected his star psychotherapist to testify in Melvin's favor, to testify, in fact, for the defense. Melvin still remembered her words that day in court, when the defense was trying to get a trial delay so Melvin could be further evaluated:

"Melvin Potter is simple," Betsy had said. "Not stupid, mind you, but innocent. He sees life in very clear terms. Good and bad. The things he's done, they're bad. He is aware of that. But Melvin Potter, psychologically, had no choice. His birth mother rejected him. The parents he thought of as perfect were convicted of murder. And everyone else in his young life, police officers, social workers, foster families, and fellow gang members, let him know they believed he'd never amount to anything good. He believed them. Melvin Potter has a great capacity for good. In fact, he has the potential to become an upstanding citizen. But nobody has ever told him that.''

Somehow, Betsy had glimpsed the real Melvin hiding deep inside. She'd believed in him. A long stream of counselors, doctors, and psychologists helped to free the gentle, peaceful man inside Melvin Potter. It was a hard road to travel, with temptations blazing like neon billboards along the way, but Melvin was determined. Betsy often said that determination was what made her realize that she loved him. They'd been married nearly three years.

It was her spirit, her passion and courage, and her faith in him that convinced Melvin they could have a family together. Those wonderful things about her and the love they shared had gotten them this far. If Betsy said they could do it, Melvin believed her. And he knew that, in a way, it was a self-fulfilling prophecy. He would die before letting her down. He would never go back to violence. The mere thought nauseated him.

Amidst peace and quiet, Melvin sat in his favorite chair, reading by the light of a single lamp, darkness gathering in the far corners of the room. The quiet was the city variety, the melody of engines, slamming doors, squeaking brakes, occasional sirens and voices on the street no more bothersome than the deafening roar of crickets would be to people living in the country. A breeze crept in through the open window with a mischievous feline stealth, its October chill bearing the promise of winter.

His peace was to be found in the pages of the book he read, *Frankenstein* by Mary Shelley. The tale overwhelmed him, though this was his fifth reading of it. A creature capable of horrible acts, crafted by cruelty and ignorance, and yearning only for the understanding, the love, that will allow his true nobility to be set free.

"If I have no ties and no affections, hatred and vice must be my portion," Melvin read the creature's words aloud in a low voice. *"The love of another will destroy the cause of my crimes . . . my virtues will necessarily arise when I live in communion with an equal."*

Melvin Potter closed the book. The monster never got that second chance, but Melvin had, and he thanked God for it every day.

It was just past three in the morning. Betsy had long since gone to sleep, but he felt good, strong, despite the lateness of the hour. She liked it that he stayed up late reading, complained if he dared go to sleep before her. With Melvin watching over her, Betsy often said, she felt safe.

He felt the vague urge to relieve himself, put aside his book, and stood. He stretched his six foot eight frame, flexing nearly three hundred pounds of muscle, and went into the bathroom to answer the call of nature.

Melvin looked at himself in the mirror. He was not legitimately ugly, he knew that much. But he would never be called handsome. His blue eyes were like angelic rays of light beaming through haphazard gaps in a huge and terrible thundercloud. He had the face of a fighter, heavy brow and twisted nose, with a thick black moustache. Above it all, his bald head gleamed in the harsh bathroom light, and he rubbed a hand over it with a shake of the head, trying to remember what it felt like to have hair.

He hoped whatever children God gave them would have their mother's hair genes.

Before trudging upstairs to bed, Melvin checked the locks on the door leading down to the shop. In the event anyone broke in down there to rifle the cash register, he wanted to be sure they never got upstairs. He was proud of the Spotlight Costume Shop, which he owned and operated, proud to say that he made all the costumes himself. But only his wife and their home mattered in the end.

The shop took up the first story of their brownstone, with a workroom and storage area in the basement, but the upper two floors were their home. The second story had their living room, half-bathroom and tiny kitchen, while the upstairs had a full bathroom and two bedrooms, one of which Betsy had turned into a small office.

Melvin came out of the narrow half-bath and stumbled upstairs, half asleep. From the top of the stairs, he could see through the open bedroom door. In the diffuse light of the city, Melvin saw the lump that was his sleeping wife, and smiled. He thought he could barely make out Betsy's dark hair in the shadows, but their spread was pulled up high against the chill.

And it was chilly, Melvin realized. He wondered if he should turn on the heat, but decided against it, it being so early in the season. Two steps from the bedroom door, though, he nearly changed his mind. A shiver danced up his spine, and he realized there was an unusually strong draft in the hall, greater than would have been caused by the couple of inches the bedroom window was open. He knew he'd shut everything downstairs, so it had to be the office. He opened the paneled wooden door and flicked on the light, but the one window in there was closed as well.

Old buildings were notoriously drafty, but this was definitely something more blatant than loose-fitting window frames. Maybe Betsy had opened the bedroom window further, he reasoned, though he couldn't imagine why, since she always complained about being cold.

He went back across the hall. Several steps into the room, he could see that both windows were closed tight and locked . . . and his head snapped back, eyes riveted to their bed.

It was empty.

Melvin darted back into the hallway, calling his wife's name. He felt the draft again, and realized immediately where it had come from. The door to the roof must be open! Perhaps she had been unable to sleep, had gone up to watch the lights of the city, and look at the stars above. It wouldn't be the first time. But why hadn't she come down to get him, as she had in the past?

Melvin was worried and confused as he walked up

the steps to the roof, but not terribly. The doors and windows were all locked. If Betsy wanted some time alone, he could understand that. He just needed to make sure she was okay, for his own peace of mind.

As he expected, the door to the roof was slightly ajar. Melvin opened his mouth to get his wife's attention . . . but Betsy Potter wasn't there.

With mounting fear, alarm bells exploding in his head, Melvin ran for the stairs. He nearly tore the door from its hinges in an unconscious burst of strength as he plunged down into the apartment. He raced through the three rooms on the third floor quickly, then realized he had only one hope . . . the kitchen. Maybe he had somehow missed her, and Betsy was getting a snack? He'd been in the bathroom! That might have been when she . . .

All the lights were off, and Melvin knew even before he began turning them on that Betsy was not there. Quickly, he checked the door down to the shop on the first floor, but it was still deadbolted from the inside.

There was only one answer. Someone had taken his wife.

Melvin Potter howled in rage, fear, and despair.

By the time the police had come and gone, with an admonition to Melvin to let them do their jobs and not get involved, it was past six o'clock in the morning. But they were still working on the theory that Betsy had likely met someone else or simply become tired of life with a "reformed" felon and run off. And Melvin wasn't distraught enough to miss the suspicious looks the cops gave him. He knew that it had to have crossed their minds that he was responsible for Betsy's disappearance.

God, couldn't they see what this was doing to him?

Idiots. Betsy would be dead before they could find her. Or worse. And Melvin knew from his days on the streets that there were, indeed, things that were worse than death. The police couldn't do anything, and Melvin wouldn't cross the line, couldn't hit the streets again. He had promised Betsy. All their work together, everything they had accomplished would be worthless if he lost control again. But Melvin did know one man who could help them.

Another hour had passed as Melvin called half a dozen therapists that had worked with him in the past, getting their numbers from Betsy's book in the office. They seemed surprised to hear from him, especially at home and so early, but when he told them what had happened, they understood. The problem was, they all kept him on the phone, wanting him to convince them he would not do anything rash, as if they had no faith in the work they had done for him, the peace they had given him.

The sixth, and last, call he made was to Dr. Francesca Jessup, who didn't have the number he wanted, but got him one step closer. When Betsy was fighting to prove that Melvin was not guilty of his crimes due to mental instability and that he could be cured, she was not alone. After all, every defendant must have a lawyer, and though Melvin couldn't afford it, he had the best. With Betsy's testimony, Matt Murdock had done the impossible, had convinced the courts that Melvin should go free.

Dr. Jessup gave Melvin the new office number of Franklin "Foggy" Nelson, Murdock's law partner. Luckily, Nelson was no slacker and when Melvin called at nine, he was already in the office.

"Mr. Nelson, Melvin Potter. I need help," he said as soon as he heard Nelson's voice.

"Melvin . . ." Nelson began, and he could hear the lawyer's surprise. "Um, well, I'd love to help you, of course, but I've given up private practice."

"No, no, I'm sorry," Melvin interrupted, "I've got to talk to Mr. Murdock."

Silence, then. "Oh, well I thought you knew, Melvin. I mean, Matt isn't a lawyer anymore, you must have seen it on the . . ."

"I know that!" Melvin snapped, irritated. "My wife's been taken. I need to find Daredevil, and I mean right now!"

"Oh God, Melvin, I'm sorry . . ."

"You didn't know, Mr. Nelson," Melvin said and felt sorry for having shouted at the man. "But I really need your help here."

"Well," Foggy Nelson said confidently, "if anyone can get a message to Daredevil, it would be Matt. I'll give you his home number, but I've got to warn you, he's not there much."

Nelson rattled off the number and Melvin scribbled it down. The lawyer wished him luck, offered further assistance, and Melvin thanked him without listening and hung up the phone. He took a deep breath, said a silent prayer and lifted the receiver again. He dialed Matt Murdock's number.

On the third ring, the machine picked up. Melvin bit his lip, near tears.

"Hi, you've reached Matt and Karen's," a woman's voice said. "We're not home, but you know the drill."

After the beep, Melvin paused, at a loss for the right words, such an intimate message to leave with a terribly impersonal messenger.

"Mr. Murdock," he said finally, and found he'd been holding his breath. "Mr. Murdock it's Melvin Potter. I know we haven't spoken in a while, and I'm sorry about all the things you've been going through lately, but I . . . I need your help. My wife, Betsy . . . someone took her Mr. Murdock. And I know only Daredevil can find her. Please . . . help me."

Melvin left his number and hung up, put his face in his hands and let the tears come. For just a moment he remembered the years he spent as the Gladiator, and all the times he tried to kill Daredevil during that time. He never imagined he would need the hero so desperately, but he thanked God that Daredevil had always been that much faster, that much better than he.

Melvin knew Daredevil would come if he was able. He knew it in his soul. All those years that he had believed himself to be bad, Melvin had hated Daredevil with a savage passion because to him the hero represented everything that was pure and good and noble, all those things he had never been allowed to be.

In a sense, Daredevil had always been Melvin Potter's hero.

Chapter 3

SEVERAL WEEKS HAD PASSED SINCE KAREN PAGE first volunteered to work at St. Bridget's Shelter, but she still felt uneasy every time she walked through its doors. Karen had been raised Catholic, even spent a few years in Catholic school, but as an adult, things had happened in her life that just didn't happen to good little Catholic girls.

"Karen, you're just in time," Sister Maggie said as she wound her way through the gathered homeless. "Please see what you can do to help in the kitchen, they're very far behind!"

And with that, Sister Maggie had gone on her way. Karen marveled at the woman. Unlike many of the younger nuns, Sister Maggie was still decked out in the classic "penguin" uniform. Karen sensed the older woman would be uncomfortable in anything else, that the black habit loaned her strength and a purity of purpose that helped push her through her day, much the same way the red costume helped to hone Matt's mission to razor precision.

Matt. He'd been the one to get her this job in the first place, knowing how important it was for her to start helping people again. Though they'd both picked up rather lackluster day jobs to pay the rent, Karen knew that she'd be alone a lot at night with Matt out patrolling the streets as Daredevil. St. Bridget's had helped.

She pushed open the kitchen door and saw that

the place was, indeed, a mess. Lasagna was the mass-produced meal of the evening, which was no problem, but Karen realized right away what had gone wrong. After all, how could she miss the blackened, smoking mass of burned cheese and pasta that sat atop the ancient stove?

"Didn't I tell you to watch the oven?" Sister Ellen was nearly shrieking at Manuela Martinez, another volunteer. "What were you thinking to let it burn like this?"

"Excuse me, sister," Manuela snapped, "but there are two other ovens and four other lasagnas, I can't watch them all every second. I thought that was why there were two of us in here."

"Young woman," Sister Ellen said snidely, though Manuela was probably only five years her junior, "if you think for one moment that I'm going to . . ."

"How's it going, ladies?" Karen asked cheerfully, and both women turned to look at her with surprise, then exasperation on their faces, as if each wanted to say, "Here, look what I'm forced to deal with."

Karen waited patiently as, constantly interrupting one another, they explained what had happened. Then they both stopped, looking to her for judgment, though she was the low woman on the ladder. Karen sighed. The nun, of course, had seniority over Manuela, though she was not one of the more formidable sisters running the shelter. She was a once-attractive, shrewish little woman whose nose nearly always wrinkled with distaste when dealing with other human beings, or human problems. Manuela, on the other hand, had been a volunteer at St. Bridget's since before Sister Ellen was assigned there. She was the exact opposite of Ellen, short, chubby, temperamental, but very loving and open. Karen wondered at times why God had called the one rather than the other.

And who was Karen, that they should be asking her advice? Besides being the newest member of the team, she had lived hard, on the wrong side of the law. But Sister Maggie had pulled Karen under her wing, and Karen did seem to have a pacifying effect on some of the tumultuous relationships at St. B's.

But now they had people to feed, older folks, families, and kids who wouldn't eat elsewhere unless they decided to do something illegal or dangerous or ugly for fast money.

"Manuela," Karen said. "Serve the lasagnas that are ready now, the other folks will have to be patient. Let Sister Maggie explain it to them. Meantime, I'll throw together a gargantuan salad while Sister Ellen puts together another lasagna from the leftover ingredients. That'll have to do. Just tell them to be patient."

St. Bridget's was smack-dab in the middle of Hell's Kitchen. Like the eye of the storm, it was a place of calm where the homeless could come to feel safe. It was warm, with food and plenty of people to talk to, people who'd give advice or just listen. During the day, it was a Catholic school, but after dark, its basement meeting hall/cafeteria became the shelter. It stood next to the church of the same name. Both were classic red brick, now tinged a sickly brown by decades of pollution.

Stained glass that gleamed triumphantly in sunlight was transformed into a shadowy stage upon which ghostly images loomed. The church doors were locked up tight against thieves, unlike the days long ago when such an intrusion would have been inconceivable. But in the basement of the school, lights burned all night long.

The street people of Hell's Kitchen knew that they had a place to go those nights when they just couldn't take it anymore, or when it was too cold or inclement to sleep outside.

From the youngest, a girl just barely six, to the oldest, a seventy-something corner preacher named Abe, they all came together under the flowing robe of Sister Maggie. It was she who had set up the shelter. She showed them at every opportunity that she believed in them, and they tried to believe in her too.

Tables stretched throughout the basement, coffee and sodas spread across them, forgotten for the moment as Sister Maggie, Manuela, Sister Anna, and two other volunteers served the lasagna. Ten minutes passed before Karen rushed out with the first of the big bowls of salad that would complete their meal, and the evening's guests greeted her warmly.

Often, before dinner, the shelter's guests would be in scattered groups, or alone, sitting in shadowy corners. But once the food appeared, they came together, talking and laughing, much as Karen imagined the children who attended school here during the day must at lunch time.

Of course, not all of the guests smiled. The specters of their lives lingered. Many were newly homeless because of the havoc wreaked upon the city by the super soldier, Nuke, only weeks earlier. Others had been driven in over the past few days due to the string of arson fires flaring up in the neighborhood. Karen had never seen war, but she imagined its survivors would look something like these people: shellshocked. Many had lost loved ones, but the worst part of it all was that they were at St. Bridget's in the first place. That meant there was nobody who loved them enough to offer them a bed and a hot meal. Except for Sister Maggie.

"You're a dead man, Monroe!" a voice rang out suddenly, as Karen was placing the last salad bowl on the last table, those folks digging in fast because they hadn't yet received their lasagna.

A terrible blackboard-fingernail screech announced the backing up of a chair on the tile floor, and a tall, gaunt man who looked forty, but was likely a decade younger, shot to his feet. His manner and the hard look on his sharp-featured face were an obvious challenge. Then the knife came out.

"Get up!" the man shouted, motioning with the knife to Timothy Monroe, a younger man Karen had seen in the shelter before. Tim was twenty-three, and heavyset, obviously not a born fighter.

"Roberto, you put down that knife!" Manuela said sharply, striding toward the man before Karen had even thought to move. She'd seen the work of too many knives in her life, and moving closer to one would not be her first choice.

"Not until his blood is on it!" Roberto said coldly, and even from across the room, Karen could see the hatred and fear in his eyes, the apathy regarding his own life and survival. That made him truly dangerous.

Then Sister Maggie came between him and Timothy Monroe.

"Roberto, give me that knife," Sister Maggie said softly, but in the hushed room each syllable was crystal clear. "Now."

"He stole from me, Sister. I ain't lost enough, I have to put up with this punk thief taking my sweatshirt? That's the only warm clothes I got now. He's a dead man," Roberto said the last as though it were a question, or a plea, then started to slide around Sister Maggie.

Crack! the man's head rocked back with the force of Sister Maggie's slap, and he spun his head around to stare at her with wide, disbelieving eyes.

"If that sweatshirt is yours, I will get it back," she said firmly. "But don't you dare ever threaten anyone, don't you dare raise your hand, with or without a weapon, in St. Bridget's again. You should be ashamed of yourself, Roberto."

Roberto's attention was fully on Sister Maggie now, and Karen had a moment of nervousness when she thought the man might actually attack the old nun. Seconds ticked by, and then Roberto crumbled, his shoulders falling in synch with his chin, which slumped to his chest. He handed the knife gingerly over to Sister Maggie, who turned, eyes narrowing, and addressed Tim Monroe.

"Young man, does that sweatshirt on your lap belong to you?" she asked.

"I don't know what he's talkin' about Sister," Monroe answered, but his smirk belied his gestures of innocence.

"You don't? Did you have that sweatshirt when you came in here? I don't recall seeing you wearing it," Sister Maggie said, giving the man a hard look.

Monroe smiled and said nothing.

"Give it back, finish your dinner, and go, Mr. Monroe," Sister Maggie said coldly, then turned and walked from the room.

Monroe stood, dropped the sweatshirt on his plate of lasagna and salad, and headed for the door. "This ain't over," he snarled through his grin as he passed Roberto.

Karen felt a chill run through her. It was that grin. She could see it all in that smile, knew without doubt that stealing sweatshirts was by far the least of Tim Monroe's crimes. His smile was gleeful, not forced. People driven by life's circumstances into crime, they had a tight-lipped grimace about them that was disturbing and sad. This was different, a look she had seen rarely but still all too many times in her life. It was the look of anticipation, of sadism. Karen had known men who'd led dangerous lives and so had become dangerous. They were a grim bunch. But true predators, who don't just survive but thrive on pain and death, they were different.

Predators smile.

The moment Monroe was gone, conversation resumed and there was even some laughter near the back. Roberto picked up the sweatshirt and began to swab tomato sauce and cheese from it with paper napkins.

Karen realized dinner would be over soon, and it would be time to clean up and then get the overnighters prepped for bed. She had meant to clean the ladies room, but she would have to do it right away.

She pushed through the door and was surprised at how dark it was. One of the two bare bulbs in the room had burnt out, and the fluorescents didn't help much. In fact, with the dull white tiles throughout the room, the place looked almost like a morgue Karen had once visited. She'd been there to identify a body, supposedly the body of her lover Matt Murdock. She could still remember the disgust and relief that filled her at the sight of a mutilated corpse that was not his.

"Dear God," a woman's whispered voice came from one of the bathroom stalls, "please help me. Help me."

It was a prayer, but the woman's tone revealed that she prayed not to one definable God, but to fate, the universe, and humanity. At the worst time in her life, Karen had rarely heard such despair. She walked quietly to the stall, and put her hand against the cool metal of the door.

"Hello," she said softly. "I'll help you."

As simple as that. And here, an offer of help could not be rescinded, not when each of the dispossessed guests of St. Bridget's shelter was searching for little more than someone to trust. Once you opened your arms and heart, there would be nothing more destructive than closing them again.

"Go away," came the voice.

"You asked for help," Karen said, "and I said I'd help."

"Even God can't help me now," the woman sniffed, obviously trying to stem the flow of tears. "What can you do?"

Karen was tempted to agree. What could she do? She had no money, no political connections, no perfect role model to present. But that was just her old, broken spirit talking. The new Karen Page was better than that. She had strength, pride, hard-won knowledge of life's ugly shadows, and she had a guardian angel called Daredevil.

"I've seen the worst this world has to offer and come back," she said in a voice almost as much a whisper as the woman's initial prayer had been. "I can listen, and maybe even give you some guidance. Not to mention that I'm the only one I hear offering."

There was a click as the woman slid back the bolt on the stall door, and then it opened. Karen Page had shoulder-length blond hair and crystal blue eyes.

The woman who stepped from the bathroom stall was her polar opposite, early twenties, long auburn hair and eyes the color of milk chocolate. In sunlight and smiling, she would have been beautiful, but Karen thought it had been quite a while since the woman's face had experienced either.

"What's your name?" Karen asked.

"Diana Perkins," she answered, not meeting Karen's gaze.

"So tell me Diana," Karen said as she pushed herself up to sit on the counter between two sinks, "what kind of help do you need?"

"A place to sleep, a place to rest," the woman said, her eyes on the floor. "Revenge."

Karen slipped down from the counter and took two steps to the woman, who winced as she reached out to take her chin in one hand. She lifted Diana's face so that their eyes met for the first time.

"I will help you," she said. "Tell me."

Diana nodded silently. "Thanks," she said. "You're the first person in a week who's looked me in the eye. Most people, even the ones trying to help, just kind of stare off into space, past you. I guess they're numb from seeing so many of us, so many lost souls."

"What happened?" Karen prodded gently.

"I grew up here, in Hell's Kitchen," Diana began. "I lived with my father in a one bedroom above a restaurant on 52nd. I slept on a pullout couch in a tiny living room with a stove and fridge in one corner until I was seventeen. We got by, you know? It's Hell's Kitchen.

"I was a smart-ass teenager, though. I met a guy, moved out, but it all went wrong. Big surprise? I'd been a real bitch to my father, but last year, when I wanted to move home with him—just for a little while, you know—he said he wished I'd never left. Just that. No 'I told you so,' none of that garbage. He was the sweetest man I ever knew."

"Was?" Karen asked, realizing where Diana's story was headed.

"We'd become great friends. Something I never thought would happen. He was my best friend, in a lot of ways. I'll always thank God that I got to know him as an adult, before the fire. He's not dead, if that's what you're thinking. But in some ways, I wish he was."

Karen had indeed thought the woman's father was dead, but her candor now was startling.

"I'm sorry," Karen said. "I don't think I . . ."

"No, I mean, I wish I had him back. More than anything," Diana clarified. "A week ago, our building was burned down. Arson, they said. I wasn't home, and Dad was caught in the blaze because . . ."

Diana's tears came hard then, and she held up a hand as if to ward them off, to hold back the inevitable.

"He was trying to carry a box down the stairs, stuff I had kept from when I was a little girl, a teddy bear, some letters, a little hand mirror. But they were just things," she cried as she wiped the back of her hand across her eyes. "He should have known the only thing I needed for him to save was himself."

"He was badly burned?" Karen asked.

"He's in a coma," Diana answered, her voice small as a child's.

Karen just held her then, close and tight. It was the only thing she could do, and that helplessness infuriated her. As Daredevil, Matt had been searching the city for days for clues to the mystery behind these arson fires, and had come up empty. At that moment, she knew exactly how he must have felt.

"God," Karen said disgustedly, "if I could lay my hands on the guy setting these fires, I know just what . . ."

"That's just it," Diana said, breaking away from her and wiping a sleeve across her eyes. "I was sleeping in my car the first few days, and one night some loud sirens woke me up. Well, there was another fire, of course, that old office building on 49th? I was only a few blocks away, and the commotion, even that late at night, was wild.

"I got out of the car, and there were two men standing in front of me. They were rough types, and I was a little nervous about being out there on the street with them, even though there were cops and firemen running all over the place. I figured I would get back in the car and take a ride, because while they were talking, one of them kept looking at me. You know the look I mean."

"I don't understand where all this is going," Karen interrupted.

"Just before I got back in the car," Diana continued, "one of the guys said something that has really stuck with me. I can hear it in my head, even now. He said, 'If Wiezak is behind all these blazes, the Kingpin'll have his hide.' I don't know anything else, but these guys seemed to think this Wiezak character was setting the fires, so at least I have a name in mind when I need someone to hate."

Karen was speechless. Maybe it was nothing, just a couple of gangsters or wise guys doing their macho-thing. But maybe, just maybe, it was really the name Daredevil needed to bring this string of horrible tragedies to an end.

"Did you tell this to the police?" Karen asked.

Diana scowled. "I'm a homeless person now. I'm invisible to most everybody these days. No, I didn't tell the police."

Her words stung, because as much as Karen would like to have denied it, there had been a long time in her life when she had also treated the homeless as invisible. To see them, to acknowledge their presence would have meant recognizing that the world was not benevolent, or fair, or safe. She had not been prepared to admit that then. Later, that reality had been forced on her.

"I know some people who might be able to make good use of that information," Karen said. "Don't worry, Diana. Whoever this torch is, they'll get him."

"Not for me," Diana said, the tears starting again. "For my Dad."

Karen laid a comforting hand on Diana's shoulder

and fought back tears of her own: for Diana and her father, for all the lives destroyed by the madman who was likely out setting another fire, even as she tried to soothe one of his victims. She couldn't wait to get home to talk to Matt.

"It's going to be okay," she said finally. "It really is, Diana. I know someone who will be very interested in tracking down this Wiezak character, a certain horn-headed hero." Karen smiled as Diana's eyebrows went up.

"Daredevil? You know Daredevil?"

"You stay here, and I'll do what I can to track him down. He'll help," she said confidently.

Diana looked doubtful, but finally said, "If Daredevil's looking for him, the guy won't be able to hide anywhere."

Karen nodded and smiled again at Diana's words: she had no idea how right she was. Matt Murdock was blind, but nobody could hide when Daredevil came looking for them. And if this Wiezak guy was the firebug, Daredevil would make him pay for his sins.

The apartment was tiny: doll-house kitchen, bedroom, and a bathroom for really skinny people. People who heard the words "loft" and "studio," or even better, "studio loft," in reference to Manhattan living space and thought they sounded glamorous had obviously never been to New York. This particular place was saved from being called a studio only because the kitchen—basically a broom closet with a sink, stove, and refrigerator—was not part of the apartment's one room.

So the spacious-sounding "one bedroom apartment" ended up being barely enough room for two people to stretch out in front of the TV. Of course, Matt couldn't watch television, but he could still listen. On Sunday mornings, they put the futon up into its sofa mode and spread the *Times* out on the floor. Matt's fingertips were sensitive enough to touch-read the print because the ink was a hairsbreadth higher than the paper.

The place was spartan. Matt couldn't appreciate adornment, and Karen had no need for it. The fact that they had no money also contributed to the lack of decoration.

Still, it was their place. Together. They were putting their lives back together, making a life with each other. Years ago, Karen had been Matt's secretary. They'd fallen in love, and eventually he'd told her he was Daredevil. Then it all fell apart. She left to make it in the movies, and he moved on. But she couldn't help wondering what their lives would be like if she'd never left. She never would have fallen into the black hole her life had become, never would have sold Matt's identity out from under him just to save herself, and the Kingpin would never have gone after him. Matt would still have a home, his law practice, and his stature in the community.

It was her fault, but he never never mentioned it. He didn't blame her at all. Maybe he blamed himself. Maybe he thought he'd driven her away? *It didn't matter*, he'd tell her. *It happened, we're here now, let's move on*.

Karen sat down in one of the two chairs at the small wooden table in one corner of the bedroom, their "kitchen table." She blew away the steam rising from her Celestial Seasonings mint tea, one of her few brand-name expenditures. She was wearing one of Matt's oxford shirts, a blue one that hadn't been starched in the many weeks since he'd been disbarred. Even though it was clean, it smelled of him, and slightly of her, and it made her feel even warmer than the tea as she waited for him to come home.

She flicked on the TV and David Letterman was just finishing up. She tried to find some kind of syndicated reruns.

A rattling from across the room, and a split second of nervousness turned into relief as she realized that Matt was home. Karen was glad. If the single name that the poor woman had overheard could be of any help in stopping the arsonist, Karen wanted to tell Matt right away.

"Well, good evening, Matthew," Karen said as Daredevil came in through the window and smiled. He and Karen had had about ten seconds together that morning, and he was hoping for at least a few minutes with her before going to sleep.

"Hey, sweetheart," he laughed easily and thought, not for the first time, that he only did that around Karen these days. "Miss me?"

"I thought the day would never end," she said, returning his smile. "And I suspected I'd be spending another night wondering what time you'd sneak in the window. Of course I missed you!"

Even without the radar that his accident had given him, Matt Murdock wouldn't need eyes to see Karen Page. Once upon a time she'd meant everything to him. The lilt of her laugh had been enough to erase the worst of moods, the smell of her hair as she pressed close to him more exotic than a thousand purposeful manipulations, and the beat of her heart when he entered the room had always been enough to betray her love for him, to speed his own heartbeat. In that way, he supposed, he had always had the upper hand in their relationship, even after she knew he was Daredevil.

Then she was gone, and he satisfied himself with his work as a lawyer, his mission as Daredevil, and a succession of women he loved intensely, but not with the abandon that he loved Karen Page. He followed her career as she made a couple of bad action films with some joker called the Stunt Master. But he lost track of her, lost track of a lot of things that mattered to him.

And then it had all been taken away from him, and the regrets poured in, the moments he'd let pass him by, the words he'd left unsaid, the callings that his heart had neglected to answer. In the desperate ruin of his life, the warm arms of a bedraggled ex-girlfriend felt just like home to Matt, a home he'd been missing for a long time. Despite Karen's misguided betrayal of his secret identity, Matt didn't blame her for what happened to him. How could he? In some ways, he felt responsible for setting her on the path that led inexorably back to his own destruction.

Well he wasn't about to let life slip past him anymore. There was no way Karen Page was going to get away from him again. The outline of her face was not entirely distinct, no face was, regardless of how tightly he focused his radar. Matt let his fingers drift lightly across the smoothness of her cheek, and infinite messages sprang to his brain, attempting to give him a mental picture of her. Perhaps a wrinkle or two more about her eyes, a much more serious set to her mouth, but other than that, she was the same woman.

Wounded. Healing. They had that in common.

But there was something else bothering her tonight, a reservation in her tone, even in her laugh. Her face was too quick to lapse back into the concerned frown she wore most always of late, the expression under his fingers now as he caressed her face.

"What is it?" he asked, removing his mask, and did not need to say more.

"I met a woman tonight..." she began, and paused. The climate in the room had changed almost imperceptibly. Though his enhanced senses unfortunately did not extend to such intricacies as human emotion, this was something too obvious to miss. The warmth and the love were still there, but obscured by whatever thundercloud hung over his lover's head.

"Go on," Matt urged when she seemed at a loss.

Karen shared Diana's story with Matt, and he could hear in her voice how deeply the encounter had disturbed her. He understood. There had been far too many stories just like Diana's in the past couple of weeks.

Then she told him the name Diana had overheard: Wiezak.

"Rings a bell," Matt said, nodding. "Small-time hood, as far as I knew. Maybe he's trying to move up in the world. But I don't . . ."

He stopped as a thought struck him. The warehouse that had been burned earlier that night belonged to Wilson Fisk, the Kingpin. But a man with Fisk's wealth had to own property all over the city. He would have to begin looking into that. If a pretender to the Kingpin's throne wanted to hurt Fisk, hitting his wallet was a good way to start. On the other hand, it was Matt's expert opinion that you had to be a little crazy to stick your head in the lion's mouth.

And what did that say about Matt himself?

"Well," he sighed, "I'm afraid that's the good news tonight."

Karen sighed, and Matt heard the sadness in it.

"You've got to go out," she said flatly. It was not a question.

"I got a message from Melvin Potter off the machine about an hour ago. His wife has disappeared.

He believes she's been kidnapped.''

"Oh my God!" Karen gasped. "The poor man. Is he all right? He hasn't done anything . . ."

"No, he seems okay," Matt answered. He knew what Karen was getting at. Melvin had been a solid citizen ever since he'd gone into therapy, but he had to wonder, as Karen had implied, if something like this wouldn't send him over the deep end. There was no way he wanted to face the Gladiator again.

"Still, I told him I'd come by around one. I've just got time to grab a quick shower and then head to the costume shop. This Wiezak guy will have to wait until tomorrow, even if he is the arsonist."

"Tell Melvin my thoughts are with him, would you?" Karen asked.

"Daredevil will carry a message of support from both of us," Matt answered, but as always, he couldn't help but note the irony of referring to himself, Daredevil, in the third person. The day he stopped thinking it was odd, he often thought, was the day he ought to retire.

Matt gave Karen a kiss, and then removed the rest of his costume and headed for the bathroom.

One shower later, he was back in the costume, and it wasn't Matt Murdock who slid up the window and stuck his head out, it was Daredevil. The city stretched before him. Its sounds and smells, its shapes and forms leaped at him in an overwhelming horde. Something inside him had created the hero, but in many ways it was the city that defined him.

And yet, it was that same city that had swallowed

children whole, that now hid them in its stinking acid belly and that might spit them up again, broken, twisted, perhaps rotten. The evils in the city were vast and unfathomable at times, but every once in a while, Daredevil was gifted with a target. And during those glorious moments, the hero never waited to strike.

Chapter 4

EVEN AT THE BEGINNING OF OCTOBER, CAIRO, Egypt, baked in the sun, the heat rising to the mid-eighties most days. At night, temperatures dropped to around sixty or so, but it could get much colder in the desert.

The desert! Out by the great pyramids of Giza, that's where Bullseye had imagined this hunt to take place. He had pictured it in his mind as soon as he got the assignment. One of his targets was very wealthy and known for his love of horses and riding . . . owned his own stables. In Bullseye's mind, the hunt unfolded, following Target A, Kalem Aziz, out of the city in a stolen taxi. Aziz would have bodyguards, of course, perhaps his mistress along. They would rent horses from the stable by the pyramids, and ride off across the desert.

And Bullseye would follow.

He would approach them as a fellow rider, lost now in the desert and grateful to see them. The bodyguards would be falling bloody to the desert sand before they knew they had been betrayed, and the mistress would go moments later, mouth gaping wide with shock. And then Aziz would run, and Bullseye would let him. He'd ride the target down like a rodeo star taking down a prize bull.

That's how he saw it in his mind, the whole thing flickering through his brain like a bloody B movie. Unfortunately, it wasn't going down that way. His romantic image of hunting Kalem Aziz was shot to hell by Target B, which had been added to his contract just before he had departed for Egypt.

In the end, Bullseye didn't care. It was all a means to an end. Do a pair of terminations for his new employer, and that would bring him back to New York. Once there, he could begin his two-sided campaign. He would use his new employer's aspirations as a stepping stone toward returning to his old job as the Kingpin's enforcer, and at the same time begin a slow, painful vendetta against Daredevil.

But first, Target A and Target B. Kalem Aziz and Graham Cullen.

Cullen was an American diplomat representing the secretary of state of the United States. He had come out to stay at Kalem Aziz's palatial family home in Cairo. Both of them, in one way or another, worked for the Kingpin. Despite his honored place as a speaker at the peace conference, Aziz was involved with covert armaments smuggling. Cullen, on the other hand, was just one of dozens of politicians in the Kingpin's pocket. He enjoyed politics, Wilson Fisk did.

The pair had been holed up in the well-guarded home of Target A for days, and Bullseye had begun to think he would have to risk infiltrating the palatial estate. Finally, and to Bullseye's great relief, hospitality forced Aziz to take Cullen out to explore Cairo for a day.

And the heart of Cairo, not just the tourist city but the city of the Egyptian people, was the Mouski.

Mouski was the name of a street, but it was not the

same as *the* Mouski. The Mouski was an enormous marketplace made up of small *souqs*, or bazaars. Along the length of the street were tiny shops whose entrances were shaded from the sun by wooden awnings propped up by thin wooden poles. Its standing-room-only crowd of shoppers was more reminiscent of the running of the bulls in Pamplona, Spain than any marketplace, and yet dollars, pounds, and piasters flew, merchants sold, and shoppers purchased.

Gold, silver, brass, and copper; pearls, glass, and alabaster; silk, leather, and carpets. And most importantly, perfumes and spices. While the tension of being surrounded by so many people, swept into whirlpools and along tidal patterns, crammed into the sweltering heat of a hundred, a thousand, bodies pressed against your own with the sun baking the entire herd, while all of that might be enough to cause the average person to faint, it was nothing next to the smell.

It should come as no surprise then, that in the midst of such crushing madness, in the confusing whirlpool of hot flesh that was the Mouski, it was exceptionally easy to commit murder. A common thief might slip up behind you on the street, relieve you of your wallet, and leave you to slump to the dirty street with a rusted dagger in your back. You would fall in the midst of that mob, bleeding to death as the flow of bodies passed around you, some trampling your arms and legs, accidentally kicking your head, perhaps falling themselves. Eventually, some kind soul would stop to help.

But it would be too late.

Yes, it was extraordinarily easy to kill someone in the Mouski, and yet it did not happen very often. Far less often, in fact, than Western culture would have us believe. Such crimes were far less common in Egypt than in the United States.

Nevertheless, they did happen.

Therefore, despite the demands of hospitality that led Kalem Aziz to bring Graham Cullen to the Mouski, Aziz was not fool enough to simply delve into the Mouski like a typical local man or a common tourist. In fact, with his own men, Egyptian government agents and American operatives protecting Cullen, Aziz himself probably did not have an accurate count of exactly how many people were in the crowd and on the roofs of surrounding buildings, weapons at the ready, prepared to take a bullet if need be to protect his and Cullen's lives.

But Bullseye did. Twenty-seven. There were twenty-seven men and women in the Mouski whose sole purpose was to protect Kalem Aziz and Graham Cullen, not counting the two who followed immediately after the diplomats as they went from shop to shop, haggling over the price of any little thing that happened to catch Cullen's eye.

It was a hot afternoon and he could have taken his time, could have let the ebb and flow of humanity take him on a leisurely journey of deception and eradication . . . Bullseye could have killed them all, and laughed in the faces of his targets before ending their lives.

But that would have been too easy.

No, the challenge here, the only way he could make this assignment even remotely interesting, was not to kill *any* of their guards. It was insanity, but Bullseye was plainly insane, and well aware of it.

As he weaved his way through the crowd within the copper bazaar, the dull sound of dozens of hammers on metal chipping away at the air like hail pounding aluminum siding, Bullseye was ecstatic just thinking of what he was about to do, the chances he was taking. Killing Aziz and Cullen was really not the problem, but getting out of the Mouski alive afterward without killing anyone else, that was not a simple thing.

"This is gonna be fun," he whispered to himself.

In fact, the only thing that Bullseye was not happy about was that he was not wearing his costume. He was no less skilled, no less confident without it, but it had become traditional, especially during his time in New York. It declared his identity, it told people who it was that had killed them, discouraged people who might want to interfere with his enjoyment of a given day, of life in general. It just didn't feel right, not wearing the costume; but he *was* a professional after all.

A block ahead, he saw Aziz and Cullen, their two grim-faced personal guards close at hand. He stopped to feel the softness of a yard of blue silk, which lay on a rickety wooden table behind which stood a nearly toothless old man whose skin was wrinkled almost as badly as those super-expensive puppies . . . what the hell were they called? The man tried to pitch his wares in English, unaware that Bullseye spoke Arabic . . . a fact that Bullseye himself had been unaware of, or forgotten, until the previous day. But he didn't want silk. Though he looked at many tables, he didn't want anything.

He allowed two of Aziz's men to pass by him, then slid into step behind them, the ocean of people carrying him toward his target. He brushed by the two rudely, actually elbowing one of them sharply in the chest in a feigned effort to cross toward another shop, this one with rolled-up carpets stacked in front. The man cursed quietly, but didn't pay any attention to Bullseye. After all, he was a typical tourist, blond hair and blue eyes, tall but not conspicuously so . . . and arrogantly unaware of those around him. Apparently.

Bullseye had no real plan. He meant to get up close to Aziz and Cullen, kill them, and then, well, escape. It would be fun, as far as he was concerned. But then there was a jostling behind him, high-pitched words muttered in Arabic, and a young Egyptian boy in a loose cotton shirt and black market Levi's ran by, barefoot and obviously going about some very important task. Sent on an errand by his father, perhaps. But no matter, he was the perfect tool.

"Stop," Bullseye shouted hysterically, a panicked American. "Stop! Thief! Stop that boy!"

Hand on his back pocket, as though feeling for a wallet that was suddenly missing, he set off in a crazed pursuit of the boy. The crowd was so thick he slammed into people at random, even as they tried to get out of his way. Some of the local merchants, though, seemed almost purposely to bar his passage. Whether or not the boy had stolen, they were determined that he should not be caught by a foolish American tourist.

"He took my wallet! Stop him!" Bullseye shouted.

The boy finally turned around to see what the commotion was. He was no more than thirteen years old, probably younger, and his eyes went wide at the sight of the tall, blond American man chasing him and shrieking. He had not stolen from Bullseye, but he ran faster nevertheless. Either he was a thief after all, or simply too smart to believe the police would take his word over a rich American's.

He took off, and Bullseye ran even faster.

"Somebody please help me!" he screeched. "Stop that boy!"

Up ahead, just slightly to the right of his present path, Aziz and Cullen, flanked by their two bodyguards, were standing shoulder to shoulder and grinning widely at the spectacle before them. Bullseye was playing the role of fool to perfection, and they were entirely convinced.

"Stop hi-ooofff . . ." he stumbled purposely and flew directly at the point where his Targets' shoulders met. Both men reached up to stop his fall as a reflex. All three of them crumpled to the dusty street, grunting as they hit the ground.

"Sorry, I'm really sorry," he mumbled to the two

new corpses. "Got to get that damn kid!"

And then he was up and running, shaking off the hands that reached out to stop him, ignoring the shouts of the bodyguards behind him, who threatened to shoot if he didn't stop. They were reacting as they were supposed to, but they as yet had no idea what had happened, and it wouldn't do to shoot an American tourist in the back over a simple misunderstanding.

Up ahead, the fleeing boy ducked down a side street, moving quickly away from the Mouski. Bullseye followed, even as shouts went up in the crowd to find him, to stop him, that Kalem Aziz and the American diplomat had been murdered.

"God," he said to himself, barely breathing heavy as he ran, "took them long enough to turn the damn bodies over!"

"Not another inch, Poindexter!" somebody shouted, and he dove for the open back door of a shop, the only safety he could find in the alley, even as bullets punctured the street sending up little plumes of dust.

On the roof across the street, one of the American snipers assigned to Cullen had successfully followed him. The idiot, though, called him Poindexter. His name was Bullseye, as if they didn't know. And he hadn't used the Benjamin Poindexter identity in over a year. On the other hand, the guy had recognized him right off, which gave him a warm sensation inside. When all was said and done, fame was a total high.

Bullseye took a glance up at the sniper and ducked back as bullets plunked into the wood frame by his face. Just one out of twenty-seven agents, not bad at all. But it wouldn't be long before a bunch of his buddies came along, and then it was going to get quite crowded in that alley. If that happened, he might have to kill one or two of them, and that would ruin the game.

He reached out his right hand for a weapon . . . and anything was a weapon once it was in his hands. He saw that he'd ducked into a brass-merchant's shop, and he wrapped his fingers around a brass candlestick. In one continuous movement he dove across the doorway, targeted the sniper at a distance of about twenty-five feet and hurled the heavy metal at him. Bullseye was out of sight on the other side of the door when the sniper's firing abruptly stopped, and then he heard a large thump. He hadn't seen it, but he knew that the candlestick had struck a glancing blow across the man's left temple, just hard enough to knock him out, and that he'd tumbled to the street below.

Bullseye was out the door in a flash, checking to be sure the man was alive—which he was, despite several broken bones—and then the assassin happily set off again at a trot, ecstatic over having fulfilled his mission within his personal parameters. He loved to kill, but sometimes it was harder not to, and he couldn't resist a challenge.

Glancing up, he saw a flash of blue disappearing around a corner, and he sped up in pursuit. He turned down into an even narrower alley, and up ahead, as he suspected, was the barefoot boy he'd used so brilliantly. The kid had obviously hung back and spied on his run-in with that sniper, and Bullseye had to admire his temerity.

"Boy!" he shouted. "Boy, wait! I know you didn't steal from me. I just want to talk to you!"

The boy ran a few more steps, but stopped when he looked over his shoulder to see that Bullseye was no longer running after him. Bullseye approached slowly, walking nonchalantly so as not to spook the child again. This was a child of the streets, the same around the world. He must know already that he had been used as some kind of diversion, and that the man coming toward him now was dangerous. And yet, though he stayed alert and his body was tense, ready to take off in a second, he did not move.

"I just wanted to thank you for your assistance," he said, wondering for the first time how much English the boy would understand. Educated Egyptians spoke English and French; Bullseye suddenly didn't feel like speaking Arabic.

"Do you understand?" he asked. "Do you speak English?"

No response.

"Parlez-vous française?"

"I understand," the boy said finally, in heavily accented English. "Thank me why?"

"You helped me," Bullseye said, smiling. "Whether you know it or not."

He reached into his pants pocket and pulled out

a small package of tissues, then slipped two fingers inside the package and came up with a crisp, fresh American one hundred dollar bill. The boy's eyes lit up in amazement as Bullseye offered the money to him, grinning widely. The boy looked up, as if asking whether the offer was for real.

"What, you'd rather have piasters?" he asked with a laugh, and the boy shook his head emphatically.

The boy took the bill from him and held it up, stretched taut in his hands, in front of his eyes. He stared at it for a moment, then looked up at Bullseye with an open, sincere smile of gratitude.

They heard the pounding of several sets of hurrying feet back out in the main alley, and looked back up that way, and then at one another.

"Taxi, mister?" the boy asked, and Bullseye smiled warmly. The kid was all right.

Bullseye was happy. He had completed his mission. The deaths of Cullen and Aziz would hurt the Kingpin badly. Everything was going according to Gary Wiezak's plans. And Bullseye was content to help Wiezak put his plans into action until the moment they stopped coinciding with his own.

Though it was thinning, Gary Wiezak's hair had yet to recede. With a widow's peak and the tightly trimmed beard he wore, he had an almost demonic aspect. It gave him no end of pleasure to look in the mirror. A scar ran across his face from a knife fight he dimly remembered from his youth, but he barely noticed it. Unless he caught someone staring.

It wasn't healthy to be caught staring at Wiezak's scar. He was a wiry man in fair shape, but he tried to do as little of the dirty work as possible. What was the point in being boss if you had to take the risks yourself? No, he paid others to take risks. They took his money, but he didn't trust anyone except Shane.

Shane Cairns had been his best friend and right-hand man for years. The big guy followed Wiezak around like a lost puppy, and Wiezak found that ingratiating. Shane watched out for him, and he'd try to do the same. He trusted Shane with all the important jobs, all his plans and secrets. Shane wasn't stupid, but neither was he extraordinarly bright. He knew his wagon was hitched to a horse named Gary Wiezak. And Wiezak reminded him from time to time, just to make sure.

He'd sent Shane out to pick up Bullseye at the airport. The assassin was reputed to be totally unpredictable, which wasn't good for business. But Shane could usually handle unpredictable, and Bullseye would be invaluable in Wiezak's war on the Kingpin, and later, when Daredevil sat up and took notice of the new crimelord of New York.

Wiezak smiled. He could imagine what it would be like to be supreme, but he couldn't feel it. Not yet.

He sat in an office in his warehouse on the East River. Shane was to bring Bullseye here because Wiezak didn't want him to know the whereabouts of the penthouse until they had met. Only then would Wiezak know if Bullseye really wanted this job. And even then, he wouldn't trust the man. After all, Bullseye was a maniac.

Gary Wiezak's warehouse was just another block of ugly gray sheet metal, indistinguishable from dozens of others in the area. At least from the outside. Inside, it was filled to capacity with arms shipments, stolen technology, and all manner of illegal imports and exports. If there was money in it, that was the business for Gary Wiezak.

Pitts, a burly man who worked in shipping for him, popped into the office door.

"Mr. Wiezak, a call for you on Line Four."

"Got it," he answered, and Pitts walked away.

Wiezak picked up the phone and pressed a button next to the blinking red light.

"Yeah?"

"Plane was right on time, Gary," Shane said. "We'll be there in a couple of minutes."

"Looking forward to it," he confirmed, and hung up. Shane had not sounded pleased. Wiezak knew him too well not to pick up his tone, his mood. He could only assume that Shane was not getting along too well with Bullseye. That was fine with Wiezak, though. He didn't want Shane to like the assassin. Not when he might have to kill him in the end.

Scant seconds after he'd placed the phone in its cradle, it began to ring again. He ignored it, as he always did. If it was something important, Pitts or one of the other guys would come get him. But it kept ringing, and after several moments he had to look down at the red light blinking next to Line Seven.

Seven?

Nobody called on Line Seven, ever. That was Gary's emergency line and was only ever used for . . .

"Christ, no!" he swore, and picked up the phone. "Hello?" he asked, cautiously.

"You know who this is," a female voice said, and it wasn't a question.

"When?" he asked.

"Any time now. They're already gone," the voice answered.

Wiezak slammed the phone down, grabbed his jacket, and ran from the office. The call was a tip-off from one of several people he had inside the NYPD.

"Pitts!" he yelled. "Wreck it all! We're gonna be raided!"

He rounded a corner, and Pitts was there, eyes wild.

"What do we do, boss?" the big man asked, his hands nearly flapping at his sides.

"Set the timer, and get out of here," Wiezak said, trying to calm himself.

Pitts's jaw hit his chest.

"You're just gonna blow the whole thing? Boss, that's like millions of dollars in product alone, never mind the building and equipment, how can you . . ."

Wiezak had been pushing past Pitts, but he spun on the man now and whapped him on the forehead with an open palm.

"Don't be an idiot," he snarled. "I'm worth a hell

of a lot more than what's in this warehouse. I'd rather take five years to make my losses back than have the cops find all this and spend the rest of my life in jail!''

Pitts only nodded, the muscles in his face slack with his fear at their situation. Then he followed his employer out into the immense openness of the main warehouse, and both of them began to yell.

Wiezak ran to the back of the warehouse, where a huge bay door opened to the dock there on the East River. Sliding the door open half a foot, he didn't see any cops. Not yet.

When Shane pulled up in a nondescript black sedan, Wiezak yanked the warehouse door open and waved urgently for Shane to drive in.

"What's going on?" Shane asked, slightly panicked by Wiezak's quivering energy.

"Raid," he said. "Cops'll be here any minute."

"Damn!" the burly man shouted, shaking his head. Then he took a breath to calm himself. "What's the plan?"

"We're outta here. We have to blow the place," he responded, nearly laughing with the insane freedom of such a decision.

Then another man emerged from the passenger side of the sedan, and Wiezak stopped thinking about the cops. If he hadn't seen pictures, he would never have believed that this blond, average-looking citizen was one of the world's deadliest assassins. He just looked too normal. At least, until you saw his eyes. They ruined the whole picture.

Bullseye had crazy eyes.

"What's going on here?" the killer asked.

Shane Cairns and Gary Wiezak exchanged glances. Then Wiezak said: "A slight change of plans, my friend."

"I'm not your friend," Bullseye said coldly. "I'm your employee. Don't make that mistake."

Wiezak saw the anger on Shane's face, saw him tense to launch himself at Bullseye. He appreciated his bodyguard's loyalty, but valued his life too much to let him throw it away.

"Shane, forget it!" he said quickly, then turned to stare hard at Bullseye, wondering if he had made the wrong decision in hiring him. But no, he realized. Whatever trouble he might be was balanced by what an asset he would prove against the Kingpin. He'd better be, for the money Wiezak was paying.

Pitts ran up and handed the remote detonator to Wiezak, who looked at it and cringed at the thought of the losses he was about to take. Then he realized something. His warehouse going up might help turn both the Kingpin and the cops away from him as a suspect in the arson fires. In the end, that alone could make up for his losses.

"All right, everybody out!" he screamed, then turned to Bullseye. "And you, in the car."

With Shane behind the wheel, and a half dozen of his men in a van behind them, they tore out of the parking lot mere moments before the first police car rolled up in front of the warehouse behind them. Wiezak saw several others in its wake. There were likely a couple of his men still in the warehouse, but he couldn't let that stop him. Without a second thought, he thumbed the button on the remote detonator, and the warehouse went up in an explosion that turned over two police cars and blew out the back window of the sedan they were in.

Bullseye was disgusted. What kind of penny-ante operation had he hired on for? Wiezak seemed to have the cash flow, but obviously his organization left something to be desired. The cops were all over him and he'd just taken a major hit to his arms trade, and then some.

"You're awfully quiet, Mr. Poindexter," Wiezak said. "Something wrong?"

"Other than glass all over my lap, not a thing," Bullseye said with a smile. "And my name isn't Poindexter."

"Oh? Well, what shall I call you then?" Wiezak said condescendingly.

"You know what to call me," he answered with a sneer.

"I guess I do, Bullseye," Wiezak admitted. "When are you prepared to start your latest assignment?"

"I just need a day to get settled," he answered. "Look up an old friend."

"Fine, fine," Wiezak waved a hand. "Just don't let it interfere with business."

"I'm a professional, Mr. Wiezak," he said coldly. "To me, everything is business."

Wiezak obviously didn't know how to respond to

that. Bullseye could see they weren't going to get along. Even worse, the bodyguard Cairns had clearly somehow developed the opinion that he and Bullseye were in the same league. He had to fight the urge to kill them both right there in the car.

No, this wouldn't do at all. He'd go along with Wiezak's campaign against the Kingpin for a while, but it couldn't last. Eventually, he'd go to Fisk and offer to erase Wiezak, for a price. And in the meantime, he could take his time tearing Daredevil's life apart. In the end, the agony of the hero was the only thing that mattered.

Chapter 5

NEW YORK IS OFTEN CALLED THE CITY THAT NEVER
sleeps. While most of America simply shut down
in the wee hours from midnight till dawn, Manhattan Island rocked on with late night restaurants
and clubs, all night diners, and the milling of street
people. Neon blazed a twenty-four-hour false daylight, with a soundtrack of distant shouting, and sirens much too close.

New York was a city of action and interaction, but
it could be the loneliest city in the world.

Above the neon haze, stars twinkled in the crisp,
clear night. Clad in a t-shirt and jeans, Melvin Potter
shivered in the early fall chill and stared up into the
endless night, tears streaking his face. The night's
minutes ticked by, but dawn seemed farther off than
ever. He'd been waiting for more than an hour. He
knew Daredevil would come, and that nothing he
did could get the hero there faster, but that was cold
comfort. Betsy was out there, somewhere, alive.

She had to be. Or Melvin didn't know what would
happen to him. What he might do.

"Sorry I'm late," a familiar voice said behind him.

Melvin sighed and lowered his head in relief, not
bothering, not ready, to turn and face Daredevil. A
moment later, a gloved hand lay on his shoulder,
and now Melvin did look up. There was strength in
Daredevil's face, in his posture, in his mere presence.
Melvin stood, but did not wipe the tears from his

face. He was not ashamed of them, had none of the foolish pride of his youth. His wife, his love, his very soul was gone, and this man could get her back. Nothing else mattered.

"What am I going to do?" Melvin asked.

"I'll find her, Melvin," Daredevil said confidently. "You've got to be here in case whoever took her calls. Maybe they want something from you. Maybe . . ."

"I don't have anything, DD. Never have," Melvin spread his hands in exasperation, then slapped them on his thighs. "I just don't get it. Betsy never hurt anyone, I don't hurt people anymore. Why would someone do this?"

Daredevil didn't have an answer.

"Why don't you let me check out the apartment, see what I find?" he asked finally, and Melvin nodded, then led the way. In the darkened apartment, the deep crimson of Daredevil's costume was nearly black.

It was odd, actually, having Daredevil walking around inside his apartment. Betsy had friends who came over sometimes. But while Melvin had plenty of customers, he didn't really have any friends except for his wife, and maybe Matt Murdock, the lawyer who'd helped to get him acquitted. And Daredevil. Yes, he'd have to count Daredevil as his friend. In some ways, besides Betsy, Daredevil was his closest friend. He could always count on DD to be there, despite all the wrongs Melvin had done him in the past. It was amazing, in a way.

Melvin didn't even know who Daredevil was. Didn't know anything about him beyond his honor and his dedication to justice. But that was enough. Though Daredevil had visited him countless times in his shop, though Melvin had made him several costumes over the years, the hero had never been inside the Potters' apartment. His presence now was a comfort to Melvin not merely because he wanted to help find Betsy, but because he was a friend.

"Find anything?" Melvin asked, after Daredevil had gone quickly from room to room, searching for some trace of foul play.

"Nothing," Daredevil said grimly. "If someone actually came in here and took Betsy, rather than from the shop or the roof, it had to be a professional."

"What now, then?" Melvin asked, his hope melting slowly. "What's the next . . ."

"Melvin," Daredevil interrupted, his head tilted back as he sniffed the air. "Do you wear cologne?"

"What?" Melvin asked, puzzled. "Never."

"They were in here, at least one man," Daredevil said, and Melvin's hope returned. Nothing escaped Daredevil's notice.

"I've smelled this scent before," Daredevil added, his head cocked to one side, "but I can't recall where. I'll promise you this, though, Melvin. If I smell it again, I'll have found the man who took your wife.

"What's the name of the policeman you spoke to?" he asked.

"Bryce," Melvin answered. "Lieutenant Bryce, I think."

Garth's eyes fluttered open, but he waited a moment to see if he would fall back to sleep. It didn't happen immediately, and that gave his bladder time to remind him he'd had too much to drink. With an annoyed sidelong glance at the ghostly green glow of the alarm clock, he realized with disgust that it was going on two in the morning.

Garth Bryce sat up in bed and ran his hands through his close-cropped curly black hair, scratched his goatee, and then froze. He'd completely forgotten . . . what was her name again. He looked at the woman in bed beside him. She'd tugged the sheets up under her chin, but he didn't need to see her body to remember it. Her skin was the color of chocolate mousse, and against the stark contrast of the white sheet, her face looked even more beautiful than it had earlier in the evening.

Kenya. That was her name. She'd approached him at the smoky little, cluttered bar in Live Bait. He'd been there with Scott Shapiro, a detective newly assigned to his squad. But when Shapiro left, Lieutenant Bryce became plain ol' Garth, and it wasn't long before Kenya brought him over a Blackened Voodoo. She was a little forward, a pleasure to talk to, and an ever greater pleasure to look at. A dangerous woman.

And that's why Garth sighed now as he looked at her sleeping peacefully beside him. If he hadn't

112

been halfway to Inebriation City, he wouldn't have brought her home, and if he hadn't been so wiped out after, he would have asked her to leave. It would have caused a scene, but he'd rather have dealt with it then instead of having to be sweet to her in the morning.

Garth Bryce was a good man, really he was. It was just that the last woman he'd been involved with, Shari, hadn't survived her relationship with a cop. Garth didn't think he was ready to care about anybody else. Not yet.

Shaking his head, and then chuckling to himself because he just wasn't the kind of guy who stayed upset very long, he rose from the bed. Seemed like every time he did that it got harder, and he was only thirty-nine years old. In the bathroom, he relieved himself, then washed his hands and splashed water on his face. He looked at himself in the mirror, skeptical. Why would a woman as gorgeous as Kenya want to be with him? Hell, he wasn't bad looking. Garth's parents were Jamaican, but his skin had a light, almost Hispanic hue that only contributed to the overall impression he gave strangers . . . one tough SOB.

He was a relatively big man, five eleven, two hundred pounds, broad shoulders and large hands that curled into enormous fists when needed. His hair and goatee framed a ruggedly handsome face. Women seemed to gravitate toward him. They always told him it was his attitude that got them, his humor. Garth was imperturbably pleasant to most people, but crack that outer veneer, and watch out. Still, with

Kenya sleeping in his bed, he couldn't really complain.

Too awake to climb back into bed, he retreated to the living room in search of more room to move. He hit "start" on the CD player, volume turned down real low, and the Neville Brothers slithered from the speakers. He knocked a filtered Camel from Kenya's pack. As he flick-flared her lighter, he wondered for the first time how old she was, or more precisely how young. He took a long drag on the Camel.

"Damn," he said as he breathed the smoke back out into the room. Maybe she wouldn't want to stay, maybe she'd be embarrassed in the morning and want to slip out quietly. Garth was thinking of Shari again, and that was unhealthy any time of the day, but most especially in the wee hours of the morning with only moonlight and the burning tip of his cigarette to keep the ghosts at bay.

And then a shadow crossed the moon, blocking out most of its light, and Garth rolled off the couch and onto the floor, instinctively reaching for a gun that wasn't there. He wore only boxer shorts, and the gun was in the drawer of his bedside table. Quickly, he put out his cigarette.

His mind raced. He had to get his head together. Maybe he could somehow distract the guy and make a break for the hallway, for the gun in his bedroom?

Tap, tap, tap.

The guy was tapping at his window! Tapping to be let in! What the hell was . . . he couldn't help thinking of Poe, then. *The Raven*. "Suddenly there came a tapping at my chamber door."

Tap, tap, tap.

He decided he had to risk a look. It was pitch-black in the room now, and it was unlikely the intruder would notice one quick look, especially if Garth peeked around the side of the couch instead of over the top. Sliding his body on the carpet, he worked his way around to the side of the sofa, and looked up.

Tap, tap, tap.

"Jesus Christ!" he yelled, then hushed himself, remembering Kenya was still sleeping in the other room. Still, he was pissed.

Standing on the ledge outside his living room was Daredevil. Garth stormed over to the window, unlatched it, and let the hero in.

"You idiot," Bryce said, pulling no punches. "You scared me half to death!"

Incredibly, Daredevil actually looked embarrassed.

"Uh," the vigilante grunted. "Sorry."

"Sorry?" Garth sputtered. "What the hell are you doing here at two in the morning in the first place?"

"I wouldn't have bothered you if you hadn't been awake, Lieutenant, and not if it weren't extremely important."

"Important, huh?" Garth said sarcastically. "This couldn't have waited until tomorrow?"

Any discomfort Daredevil had felt was obviously gone by now. He stood to his full height as he looked at Garth, jaw set and face visibly stern, even under the tight fabric of the mask.

"No," he said firmly. "No, it couldn't wait. I'm looking for Betsy Beatty Potter. Melvin told me he'd spoken to you, but he had no idea we knew each other."

"Do we?" Bryce asked. "I'd never thought of it that way."

Daredevil had lent him a hand from time to time, delivered certain perps nearly gift-wrapped a year before, and Bryce had always been forthcoming with information when the vigilante needed it. But he couldn't honestly say that he and Daredevil *knew* each other. How well could anyone know a man like Daredevil?

"I just wanted to ask you to take Melvin seriously," Daredevil said. "I've known him and Betsy for quite some time. He's harmless now, violence is anathema to him. And nothing in the world could cause her to leave him. Something bad has happened here."

Bryce nodded. He had been less than willing to take Potter at his word, at least not until his wife had been missing for a few days. Daredevil's presence in his apartment at two in the morning did a lot to change his mind.

"I'm assuming you want us to share information on this one?" he asked.

"Thanks, Lieutenant," Daredevil said, and smiled with relief. "Between this and trying to hunt down some leads on the arsonist, I'm pretty much at my wit's end these days. Any headway on the fires, by the way?"

Bryce didn't answer right away. He wasn't sure

what to say. Sometimes the police had to be very delicate in putting together a case, and the flying fists of a red-garbed super hero were not what he would call delicate.

"Some," he answered. "But I can't really go into it right now. Do you have any new leads?"

"A name on the street, a new crime family being built by a guy called Gary Wiezak. Some folks say he's behind the fires. What do you say?" Daredevil asked.

Garth tried to hide his surprise. Wiezak had been a small-time hood, and in the past few weeks, had begun to make some serious moves in an effort to take away some of the Kingpin's action. They were going to be moving on him slowly, were trying to find a way to link him to the fires, and Garth didn't want Daredevil to get in the way.

"If that's the way you want to play it, Lieutenant, it's okay with me," Daredevil said coldly. "But I wish you'd just tell me instead of trying to pretend."

Bryce was astonished. He was certain that his face had remained impassive at Daredevil's question. How had the vigilante known he was hiding something? It was unnerving, like he had some kind of sixth sense.

. "I just don't want to lose this guy, DD," Bryce answered. "You understand. He's on the way up, and we want to take him down before he gets there. Or before he steps too hard on the Kingpin's toes and gets himself and a lotta innocent people perforated for his trouble."

Immediately, Bryce regretted the remark about

the Kingpin, but Daredevil said nothing. Still, he knew his words had not gone unnoticed.

"Just please, do me a favor and check in with me before you do anything?" Garth asked.

"Don't worry, I've got Betsy Potter to worry about, too," Daredevil answered.

Daredevil stood silhouetted against the moonlight, looking every inch the hero that the street myths made him out to be. For a moment, Garth envied him the freedom of working outside the law. He didn't like the feeling.

"I never liked you much, Daredevil," Garth surprised himself by admitting. "I've worked with you to get the job done, but I'm not real comfortable with anyone working outside the law. I don't want you to think we're not going to look for Betsy Potter, but this time around, I have a feeling we're really going to need you."

"I'll check in," Daredevil said, then turned and dove out the window. Garth ran to the sill, but didn't see the vigilante anywhere. He finally spotted him, swinging from some sort of cable attached to a fire escape on the next apartment house, his momentum carrying him to the roof of a four-story brick building down the block.

Lieutenant Garth Bryce's eyes were wide.

"Guy's friggin' nuts," he muttered to himself.

How many nights had he abandoned Doris like this? It was a rhetorical question, impossible to answer. Ben Urich never left the office before eight P.M.

Rarely by nine. Several times a week he was there until after midnight. Sure, he didn't get in most days until noon, but that didn't make it fair to his poor wife, home watching television all by herself. Staying up through David Letterman's monologue at least, hoping, then giving up on him.

Ben didn't deserve Doris, even more so because she never said it. What guilt he felt was there because he rarely said it either.

During the day, the frenetic insanity of the *Daily Bugle*, its denizens like lab mice in a maze, distracted him to no end. Who could think with the publisher, Jameson, stomping around the City Room, screaming his lungs out? Not Ben. Nope. He might come up with good ideas during the day, might hit the pavement and research them. But when it came to writing, and writing well, it had to be dark outside, it had to be quiet all around him, and it had to be in the office.

Sitting at home, he found it impossible to say anything of consequence. After all, who was he? But at work, behind his desk, with the bulky specter of the *Bugle* sleeping all around him, the power humming quietly within its walls, that was a different story entirely. He was more than just your average Joe then. He was the word of the people.

There was one reason he couldn't work during the day that overwhelmed all of the others, however. Reality. It burrowed into his belly, darkening the circles under his eyes and leeching the energy of his calling.

Ben Urich sat in the dim light of a green-glassed,

brass banker's lamp, his new PC boring him with muted gray tones. He'd asked for a color monitor, but they were lucky Jameson didn't have them all pounding away on old Royal typewriters. Ben hadn't stayed this late in the office for more than two months, and he knew Doris would be worried if she woke up and saw the time, so he promised himself he'd go soon. Just another half hour.

It was already two-thirty in the morning.

Ben almost spilled his coffee when the knock came at the window of the City Room. Such knocks had become familiar and welcome. In fact, one of the reasons he stayed late so often was the occasional visit from Daredevil. They'd been few and far between recently, after that whole thing with the Kingpin, and Ben was happy to see him tonight.

"Ben," the hero said as he slid through the window, his feet almost gliding to the floor. "What were your parents like?"

The newsman's eyebrows went up in a question that didn't spread to the rest of his face.

"Matt, what is it?" Ben said, concern knotting his brow. Ben Urich was one of only a handful of people who knew that Matt Murdock and Daredevil were one and the same. It could have been the story that made him, that sent his career into the stratosphere, and at one time, that's what he had intended to do. The look on Matt's face now, even under the mask, the horror and sadness that Ben saw there, the pure goodness of the hero, was what had stopped him. His conscience would not allow him to deal such a blow to one of the few genuinely good things that New York City still had going for it.

"What *were* they like, Ben?" he asked again. "Your parents?"

Ben shrugged. "I guess they were like most parents that stay together. They loved me and each other. I got spanked, but I was treated pretty well. They fought a lot, but I guess that's only natural. They weren't the Cleavers, but then, who is? Why do you ask?"

"My father loved me," Daredevil said, ignoring Ben's question. "Sure we had our disagreements, and he did some things that I like to think he regretted. But he was a good Dad, a good man, over all."

"What's going on, Matt?" Ben asked.

"It's the fires," Daredevil answered finally. "They're starting to get to me now. I mean, how does somebody grow up thinking it's okay to set fire to a building with people inside, some with whole families in them, homes and lives? How does that happen?"

Ben chewed his lip, all trace of his smile gone. "I wish I knew," he said sadly.

"Now Betsy Potter's been kidnapped," Daredevil said. "And I don't even know where to begin looking for her."

"Betsy . . ." Ben began, searching his memory. "Oh, you mean the Gladiator's wife?"

"I try not to call him that anymore."

"Sorry," Ben said. "Habit, I guess. Anything I can do?"

Ben Urich had more respect for Daredevil, for Matt Murdock, than he had for any other living being. He felt that respect returned in large part, but he tried to ignore any feelings of pride at the friendship, relationship, association, or whatever that he and Matt had developed. Instead, he did everything he could to assist the man with his mission, and by doing so, move further along with his own.

In his own way, Ben Urich was a hero, and Matt Murdock's was the example to which he aspired.

"Just let me know if you hear anything," Daredevil said, then added: "About the fires, though, I'm looking into a guy named Gary Wiezak. Seems to aspire to the throne, possibly taking potshots at Fisk. See what you can find out about the burned properties, their owners, and any background on this Wiezak guy. If he's doing the arson, he'd better hope the cops find him first. One way or the other, though, Ben, when you go to do the story . . ."

"No worries, Matt," Ben said firmly. "I'll crucify the bastard."

Chapter 6

"I TOLD YOU I'D NEED A DAY OR SO TO MYSELF, WIE-zak," Bullseye snarled. "Did you not hear me correctly?"

"I heard you fine, Bullseye. Do you want this job or not?"

Bullseye's nostrils flared and his eyes narrowed. God, it would be so easy to simply launch himself across the desk and throttle the man. Or better yet, to bend a paper clip straight and fling it at him, piercing his left eye. In his mind, he could see himself doing exactly that. But using Wiezak was going to be the best way to get to the Kingpin. After their last unpleasant parting, Wilson Fisk wouldn't take Bullseye back unless he had to, and Bullseye intended to make sure Fisk had to.

"Yes, I want the job," he relented. "Just don't push me. It isn't healthy for either of us."

Bullseye knew Wiezak was afraid of him, but the man was also too proud to back down.

"Is that a threat, Poindexter?" Wiezak snarled with false bravado, and Bullseye had to stifle a giggle. He was like a school boy standing up to the neighborhood bully, knowing he was going to get a whuppin' but knowing just as certainly that he could never face his friends again if he backed off.

Bullseye's amusement saved Gary Wiezak's life.

"I've asked you not to call me that," he said softly. "I won't ask again. Now, what's the big rush job you

125

need me for? I hope you're not going to waste me on these silly fires and explosions your little errand boys have been taking care of."

"Nothing so mundane," Wiezak agreed. "I've figured out which of the cops I had in my pocket gave up the address of my warehouse. A detective named Tyson. Do him."

"You got it boss," Bullseye said, his entire mood changing. "I love New York! Fun city!"

Morning came much too soon for Matt Murdock. He'd slept barely three hours, and awoke to the sound of Karen turning on the water for her shower. Sun streamed in through the double window in their one little room, the slight curtains little more than gauze against its warmth. He lay basking in it, allowing it to cheer him despite his exhaustion. It cheered him the way a beautiful sunny morning might also affect someone with the gift of sight.

He sat up in bed, threw his legs over the side, and stretched, bones and muscles popping, a sharp pain in his lower back reminding him of his mortality. He wasn't a teenager anymore. Matt ran his fingers through his dark red, almost auburn hair, and over the stubble of beard that had snuck up on him as he slept.

"Ugh," he groaned, working the kinks from his neck. "Got to get moving."

When Karen came out of the bathroom, he showered quickly, then joined her for a breakfast of bagels with cream cheese and fresh melon. They chatted happily, the kind of morning talk they had always shared as a couple, even when it had just been Matt the lawyer and Karen the secretary during coffee breaks at the office. The specter of Betsy Potter's kidnapping and the constant threat of the arsonist were there with them in the room, though. They taunted Matt, pulling him inexorably into his uniform and back down onto the street.

But not yet. He just wanted to carve out a few minutes for himself and Karen. They deserved that much, at least.

Then he smelled the smoke.

Daredevil was late.

He'd known it from blocks away, as the sound of automatic weapons and pistol shots reached his ears as perfectly clear and as distant as a canyon echo. There was a virtual tidal wave of sound coming from the burning building, which joined with the stink of the blaze to attack his senses. Beneath the smoke, he smelled the sulfur of weapons discharge, the noxious fumes from the exhaust of late arriving police vehicles left running, the rusty-metal scent of blood.

Two policemen had already been wounded. Three blocks away, Daredevil's acute hearing monitored their hearts, and he bit his lip softly as he realized that one of them seemed to be dying.

Daredevil was late.

He knew Karen would be trailing him several blocks back. This was the first time she had been near when the arsonist struck, and she would want to be there to offer whatever assistance she might. He wished he could have talked her out of it, but he hadn't had the time, and he knew any such effort would have been useless.

Daredevil glided across the roof of a warehouse adjacent to the burning building, launching himself into the air as he reached its edge. Even as he fell, twisting in the air, he was reminded of another building, the night before, another fire. This was vastly different, the stakes were much higher. There were people in there, and they were armed. The cops and the firemen just wanted them to get out alive, but whoever was holed up in the building wanted nothing to do with the cops and was shooting at them from shattered windows.

His radar sense picked up several figures escaping through a side window, and he was glad to see that at least some of them had sense. Then three front windows blew out, nearly incinerating a gunman, and the front exit was completely blocked by burning debris.

Daredevil landed with a bang like a cymbal crash on top of the thin metal roof of a SWAT truck and leaped to the ground. Instantly, two rifles and half a dozen pistols were pointed at him, and he held his hands up in response.

"Daredevil!" an officer said, then turned to yell across to another group of cops, pinned down by automatic fire that had scarred their vehicles.

"Bryce!" the officer called. "Bryce! Over here!"

A head peeked around the bumper of one of the

unmarked cruisers, and Lieutenant Garth Bryce's eyes lit up as he saw Daredevil. He turned to mumble something to a comrade, then set off toward them at a run. He made it to where Daredevil crouched unscathed.

"I never thought I'd say this, but I'm glad to see you!" Bryce said. "We're waiting for backup, but we've got a real situation here. We figure they've still got about a dozen guys in there, heavily armed. They must be on something to stay in there with the place coming down around them."

"Either that or there's something in there they don't want you to get, something their boss might kill them for leaving unguarded," Daredevil suggested.

"They're going to die anyway if they don't get out of there! The Kingpin can't reach them if they're dead!" Bryce growled.

"How many of the fires have been Fisk buildings?" Daredevil said as he scanned the blaze with his radar for a safe point of entry.

"All of them," Bryce grudgingly admitted.

Daredevil wasn't surprised. "I'm going in," he said.

Bryce didn't argue.

Daredevil turned back toward the adjacent warehouse, and ran. His radar reached out, feeling with his mind for the a shape or combination of shapes that would give him immediate access to the roof of the building. The pattern appeared before him as though highlighted, his radar showing him the way.

He sped up, building momentum. Right foot on a car fender, left on the trunk, right on the roof and then flying through the air, stretching as far as he could to grasp the aluminum sill of an open second-level window. From there he tossed the curved end of his billy club, cable hanging down, to the edge of the roof like a grappling hook. It snagged on a furnace pipe, and he scrambled the last fifteen feet to the roof in seconds.

Daredevil hurled the club across the gulf between the two buildings, and gave it a slight tug when it looked as if it might overshoot his target. It landed perfectly, and he pulled it snug against a protruding metal vent until it caught, hoping it would hold.

It was very possible that he could have gotten up to and inside the building without being burned or shot. But he and the foolish thugs inside needed every moment of surprise and confusion possible if no more of them were to die.

He jumped from the roof, getting a hold as far up the cable as he could. It was like falling, rather than swinging, at first, and then he was being pulled toward the blazing building. He pulled himself up into a tight ball, gaining speed, hurtling toward the blacked-out windows.

Then he slammed into the window, barely missing the sill, and let go of the cable. Glass flew everywhere, and he tucked his knees up to his chest as he slammed, hard, into two large armed men. They went down, the wind knocked out of one, but the other hit his head with a hard crack on the cement floor. No time to listen for a heartbeat; Daredevil only hoped that his desperation, the momentarily unavoidable loosening of the restraints he always put on himself, hadn't caused a man to die.

Guillermo Rodriguez never considered his actions to be good or bad, simply necessary. It had been that way since he was a small boy, despite his parents' insistence on labeling his behavior at every available opportunity. No, Guillermo merely considered himself a practical, logical man. He identified his goals, and did whatever was necessary, without exception, to achieve those goals.

Guillermo stood a block away from the burning building, watching the catastrophe he had created with interest and amusement. Gary Wiezak was the best boss he had ever had, simply because he paid Guillermo extremely well to do things he would have done for free, for fun.

And it wasn't over yet. As ordered, he had waited to see if Daredevil would show, and he hadn't been disappointed. This day was getting better every minute. He was enjoying the show: a righteous blaze, dead Fisk goons, wounded cops, the bullet-ridden police vehicles, and now Daredevil. He'd wait until the last possible moment before starting the thirty second countdown to detonation. He wasn't in any hurry, as long as he caught the red-man in the blast.

Guillermo flipped open the remote, which looked like nothing more sinister than a small cellular telephone, and entered the code to arm the explosives planted throughout Fisk's building. His thumb hovered over the pound sign.

Amid the heavy smoke and flying embers, Daredevil dove for cover behind a long metal desk. Fisk had obviously been using this location as part of his numbers operation, given the computer and television monitors, the many desks, and the vault in one corner.

Fisk's goons shouted their plans loud enough for an ordinary man to hear them, and Daredevil tracked two heartbeats, two pairs of feet slapping concrete as they ran toward his hiding place, then rounded the corner.

Every muscle taut, he kicked his legs out in front of him, bouncing his entire weight on his arms even as he swept his legs around to topple both men in a heap, one on top of the other. They struggled to get their guns free, to shoot him, to kill him, but Daredevil was much faster. A flat-handed chop at the point where neck met shoulders, and each man was out cold. They'd wake up with headaches, but that was better than they'd get if they kept shooting police officers, or stayed inside the burning building.

How much was Fisk paying these guys?

Click!

That was not the sound of a bullet being chambered, or a safety being turned off, not the sound of an ammunition cartridge sliding into place. What was that sound?

Tick . . . tick . . . tick . . .

"Dear God, no," he whispered to himself.

Most of the gunmen were at the far side of the building, firing at the police. Several others were behind him, only a few of them armed. Two large men armed with automatic pistols stepped into the light, their weapons pointed at Daredevil's chest.

He had no idea how much time he had before the bomb, or bombs, went off, or how large the explosion would be. Wiezak's hired guns couldn't hear the ticking, didn't know that their lives were in immediate danger.

Tick . . . tick . . . tick . . .

"Everybody out, now!" he shouted as he threw the weighted fighting baton that was the mate of his curved billy club, painfully disarming one of the guards, then ducked to one side, falling into a somersault to avoid being shot by the other. "There's a bomb! A bomb!"

Tick . . . tick . . . tick . . .

Holding his right hand tight against his body, the larger guard scrambled to pick up his weapon. The other continued to fire, and though saving their lives was his priority, Daredevil was forced to attack directly. With all of his senses, including his radar focused with the deepest concentration he could muster, Daredevil moved in with extraordinary speed. He smelled the oiled barrels of the guns, the sulphur scent of weapons discharge, the sweat of the men themselves; from their breath he could have told you what they'd had for breakfast. He heard their heartbeats hammering away, heard the ratch-

eting of the trigger, could pinpoint the tiny burn of
the bullet exploding from the gun barrel.

Tick . . . tick . . . tick . . .

His radar picked up the bullet slicing through the
air, but by that time, his ears had long since picked
up the sudden jump in the heartbeat of the gunman,
signaling his intention to fire, and the sound of the
trigger. By the time the bullets reached their mark,
their target had moved up into the air in a
somersaulting dive. Daredevil's legs stretched out of
the somersault and he continued to twist as he
slammed into the gunman, his weight bearing the
man down to hit the cement floor hard. When Daredevil rolled away from him, the man lifted his hand
to fire again, then looked down, stunned, to see that
his gun was gone.

Tick . . . tick . . . tick . . .

Daredevil moved in, not a second to waste, and hit
him with a punch Battlin' Jack Murdock would have
been proud of, and the guy was down for the count.
Up ahead, Fisk's men were still firing on the cops,
but he could hear several of them coming up from
behind. He didn't have time for this.

The larger guard, who was still conscious, had re-
covered his gun, though he held it with his left hand
now; the right was obviously still numb, perhaps
sprained. He stood with his back to a row of blacked
out windows, perhaps foolishly thinking the shadows
would give him an advantage.

Tick . . . tick . . . tick . . .

"There's no time for this . . . the bomb," Daredevil began to say.

Click!

The ticking had stopped. And Daredevil knew what that meant.

Instinct took over. It was too late for anything else. His brain was filled with one word. *Out!*

Two steps took him straight into the man in front of him, then he used every ounce of strength in the muscles of his legs to launch himself, thug in his arms the only life close enough to save, into the air toward the darkened windows ahead of him.

They didn't make it.

"YEEEAAAAARRRRRGGGHHHHH!" Daredevil screamed as the noise of the explosion crashed into his ultrasensitive eardrums, the pain like a hammer on his skull. The window had shattered from the force of the explosion a moment before they reached it, and glass shards flew just ahead of them, then around them, as they were shot like a ball from a cannon through that opening. Daredevil felt the heat searing his back, the fireproof synthetic fabric of his costume seemed to shrivel and tighten along with his skin. The pain in his head was sheer agony.

Though he was barely conscious, his radar picked up a police cruiser below them, and he realized a split second before impact that they were going to hit it. Daredevil tried to twist his body to keep himself and the Kingpin's hired gun away from the bar of flashing lights on the roof of the vehicle, but as groggy and shaken as he was, he overcompensated.

While Daredevil slammed into the cruiser's roof longways, the man whose life he had saved crashed through the shatterproof windshield of the car and landed, wrapped in a splintered glass shroud, on the front seat.

Wracked with pain from the fall, he tried to listen for the man's heartbeat, to see if he was still alive, but his ears were filled with a hissing roar like the sound the television made when the cable went out, and a terrible throbbing that pulsed along with his heartbeat. It was like the pressure his ears felt upon takeoff and landing whenever he traveled by plane, but he couldn't get his ears to pop.

And then, suddenly, the world rushed in. The hissing was still there, but in the background, like the ringing after a loud concert. The sounds around him were overwhelming: people shouting, high-pressure hoses spraying water on the building, sirens wailing still, and many pairs of feet running and walking all around. Someone was trying to talk to him as he sorted through the sounds.

"Come on DD, you're still alive," the voice said. "What happened in there?"

"Give him a break, Lieutenant," a female voice chimed in, "the guy can barely move."

Ah, the cop. Bryce. And judging by the shape of her jumpsuit and the official tone of her voice, the woman must be an EMT.

"Keep those people back!" he heard another cop shout. "We don't know if this is over!"

"Feel like I got spiked in the end zone," Daredevil

said, sitting up finally. "The place was wired to blow, but there were a lot of munitions in there to begin with. Fisk just took another big hit. I don't know if . . ."

His words trailed off because his brain had finally recognized that there was something wrong in his surroundings. A sound that simply didn't belong. He scanned the area again, listening intently, ignoring the racing heartbeats of the fire and police officers, ignoring the spray of hoses, the voices, the sirens . . . what else was there? What had alerted him?

The footsteps. Gawkers milled around, and more arrived by the moment, walking briskly, some even running. Firefighters and police officers ran around with purpose. There were even steps receding, walking away from the area. But one person, a man judging from the heavy slap of his feet, was running away. He was two blocks south and, though Daredevil couldn't focus on his heartbeat in the cacaphony, he knew the man wasn't running for his health—sneakers don't have leather soles that slapped pavement.

"I don't know if you're crazy or stupid, going in there like that," Lieutenant Bryce was saying, "but it's got to be one or the other since I don't believe in courage. One way or the other, though, I gotta say you're okay in my book."

"Thanks, Lieutenant. I appreciate that," he said sincerely, still tracking the running man two, now three blocks away. "But I have a little errand to run. I'll be back in five minutes."

"Hey!" the EMT shouted as he got up from the

hood of the car. "You're in no condition to . . ."

She went on, but Daredevil was no longer listening. He left her and the lieutenant gawking as he bounded from police car to fire engine to street lamp, putting him nearly a block away in seconds.

The arsonist, or at least the button-man on the explosions, must have stayed behind to watch his handiwork, to enjoy the show and feel the thrill of the flames. This guy must have waited for the rain of debris to end and then taken off at a run, pumped full of adrenaline from fear and excitement. When he'd still been a lawyer, Matt Murdock had represented several accused arsonists. Two had been innocent, but the third had been psychotic, in desperate need of help. He'd described the thrill of his obsession, of seeing the flames . . . but he'd never laughed about it.

This one was laughing, though. Daredevil could hear him a block and a half away. He was whooping victoriously, and as he slowed down, he began to do a little half-skip dance that made Daredevil furious.

Karen had still been a few blocks away from the burning building when it exploded. Silently, she screamed her lover's name, and cursed him for being so much faster than she. He lived in constant danger, but she couldn't stand to think that she had been there, so close, if he'd died just then.

She began to run. Ahead of her, she noticed a handsome Latino man doing an odd little jig, then leaning out over the edge of the curb as he hailed an approaching taxi.

And behind him, swinging down from a billboard advertising some Broadway show or another, came Daredevil. Karen saw the anger in his every aspect, and despite her relief that he was alive and her love for him, even she was afraid.

The arsonist was waving down a cab, but Daredevil was not about to allow that. He swung down toward the sidewalk, the cable from his billy club taut above him, and brought his body together to gather speed. This man was not getting away. A yellow taxi screeched to a halt in front of the firebug, even as Daredevil landed on the sidewalk twenty feet away.

In midstride, Daredevil snapped the straight half of his billy club, a weighted fighting baton, out of its sheath at his side and launched it toward the man. His throw was perfectly balanced against the cool wind, timed to coincide with the man's ducking to enter the cab, hurled with just enough strength to do the job, and aimed so that the club would barely glance off the back of the man's skull.

The man slumped to the ground next to the waiting taxi, and the cabbie stepped out to see what had happened even as Daredevil landed by the fallen arsonist.

"Oh, DD, it's you!" the cabbie said happily, pushing the cap back on his head. "What'd this guy do?"

"Murder. Arson," Daredevil answered as he lifted the man across his shoulders.

"See," the cabbie nodded, his voice turning serious, "that's why I like working this section of the city. Those super-powered folks, they don't take a personal interest, never notice the little guys. But around here . . . say, you need a ride anywhere?"

"All set, fella," Daredevil said, heartened by the cab driver's words. "But thank you very much."

As the cab pulled away, Daredevil hefted the unconscious arsonist onto his right shoulder and turned to head back to where the police congregated around the devastated building.

"Daredevil!" Karen called behind him, and he turned swiftly, surprised he had not noticed her approach before.

Then the shots rang out, three quick pops, as the storefront window behind them shattered in a glittering rain.

"Get down!" he yelled, and Karen did. Daredevil laid the arsonist's body on the ground, and he and Karen began tearing the man's clothing to staunch his wounds. The man was still breathing, but Daredevil could hear his heart slowing.

"Stay here until the police arrive, and keep your fingers crossed that this guy doesn't die," he asked Karen, and she nodded.

Daredevil headed across the street toward the Janson Hotel. The sniper's shots had come from the hotel roof. This was the second time in as many days that he'd been shot at, and suspects he'd apprehended had been taken down hard. He wanted answers. He bounded to the roof of a concession truck, then launched himself at the flat face of the hotel, tossing out the cable of his billy club while in the air. It hooked on a flagpole that jutted from the hotel's upper floors, and he pulled it taut and put all his weight behind the swing.

Within seconds, Daredevil was standing in the sniper's tracks. Like the fake ninja, the sniper left nothing behind, not even shell casings. If Daredevil hadn't taken the time to try to save the arsonist . . . but he had, and would do it again under the same circumstances. Then again, perhaps it wasn't too late? The sniper might not have made it to the street yet!

Daredevil dove over the side of the building, but as his hands grasped the flagpole, he noted a scent, a fragrance from the rooftop that he'd smelled before. It was the same sniper, it had to be! Same m.o., same cologne, though it was much stronger at this scene than it had been after the shootings at Josie's Place.

More importantly, it was the same fragrance he'd noticed in Melvin Potter's apartment the night before. Whoever was doing these shootings, he was also the man who'd taken Betsy Potter from her home. Daredevil didn't know how the two were connected, but he was certain now that they were.

Unfortunately, when he reached the street, there was no sign of that scent. The sniper was gone.

Lieutenant Bryce and several other officers were standing with Karen as EMTs hustled the wounded arsonist into a waiting ambulance. Bryce and Karen were speaking animatedly. Even without his incredible hearing, Daredevil couldn't have avoided listening to their words.

"Tell me again," Bryce was saying with sarcasm, "exactly why you think this guy was our shooter."

"Don't patronize me, Lieutenant," Karen said angrily. "I just saw a man shot, and I'm trying to keep my cool!"

"Shooter got away, Lieutenant Bryce," Daredevil said as he approached. "Hi, Karen."

"Hello, Daredevil," Karen said, and he tried not to laugh at the forced formality between them. "I've been trying to tell the Lieutenant that I think I saw the shooter leave the building."

"Wait," Bryce interjected, "you two know each other?"

"For years," Daredevil said, as if that was all the explanation necessary, "and if Karen Page says she saw something, then she saw it. She knows criminal law, Lieutenant. She was Nelson & Murdock's legal assistant for years.

"Now," he said, turning to Karen, "what exactly did you see?"

"Tall muscle-bound guy, black case in his hand, scoping the skyline and the roof for any sign of trouble. He scooted out the door, then disappeared down the street. My bet would be the subway station. You want to know why I know it was him? Okay. I'm kneeling next to someone who looks pretty dead, blood is all over the street, in plain sight of the hotel lobby. This guy? He doesn't even glance my way. Got it?"

"If we knew what was in that case, I'd be more convinced," Lieutenant Bryce said, but it was clear he was impressed with Karen and had already begun to believe her. "One way or another, at least we can get a sketch artist working, maybe have you check some mug books. Better yet, show you some surveillance photos of some of Gary Wiezak's crew."

"What about the guy I pulled out of the explosion, the Kingpin's man?" Daredevil asked.

"On his way to the hospital with a couple of broken ribs," Bryce answered. "But he'll be fine. Name's Sean Mallory, former IRA. We'll get him to take a look at our dead arsonist here and see if he can make an ID. If he can, then we need to link this guy to Wiezak as well. It's a start, though. The bad guys are starting to get sloppy. Stupidest thing they did was not make sure Rodriguez was dead."

"Rodriguez?" Daredevil asked, confused.

"The firebug," Lieutenant Bryce sneered in disgust. "Oh, he knows he's going down for a long time, arson and multiple murders makes it tough to plea bargain. But he's pretty pissed off that his boss tried to have him taken out, and he'll get a little help from the DA's office if he testifies. Yeah, my guess is we'll have Wiezak in the bag by week's end."

"I'm glad to hear it," Daredevil said. "Let me know if I can do anything, and Lieutenant?"

"Garth."

"Garth. Please keep me posted on the Potter case."

"How do I do that?" Bryce asked.

"Let Melvin know, or call my attorney, Franklin Nelson. I'd appreciate it. Good seeing you, Karen," Daredevil said, then moved off as she replied.

Across the street he leaped up to grab the hanging ladder of a fire escape twelve feet from the ground. In seconds, he was sprinting across the rooftops once again. Daredevil realized he was still slightly disoriented from the explosion. He remembered the cabbie who'd offered him a ride earlier, and wished he were still around.

His mind raced. Karen would be fine down at the station, and he was sure she'd put a face to the shooter for the police. He had a lot to do and would have to hook up with her later. For now, he had to consider Bryce's many assumptions. The sniper was probably working for Wiezak as a cleanup man, as Bryce had theorized, but it was still possible he was an agent of vengeance for the Kingpin, taking out Rodriguez, the firebug that had been such a thorn in Fisk's side of late.

Which made it all the more important that he follow through with his original plans for this morning.

A visit to the Kingpin.

Chapter 7

AREDEVIL AVOIDED TIMES SQUARE AS HE MADE HIS way across town, running along entire blocks of rooftops when possible. When he needed to cross the avenues, he would swing from one building to the next, the retractable cable from his billy club taut under his weight. Spider-Man did it a lot faster, but Daredevil's method was still a heck of a lot better than walking, or God forbid, taking the subway.

Once in a while, when he was actually on the street, or swinging low enough, some citizen might wave, or call out to him. In his own way, Daredevil was famous. But it was a strange kind of fame, far from the celebrity of so many models, actors, musicians, and other super heroes. Except inside the invisible boundaries of Hell's Kitchen, the number of people who called or waved a friendly greeting was very small. He knew this wasn't the case with all costumed heroes. Captain America, for instance, drew cheers wherever he went.

But then, he had not become a hero for the cheers.

He realized he ought to have called Melvin Potter this morning, but there was nothing he could do about it now. Besides, now that he believed there was a connection between the mob war and Betsy's kidnapping, he hoped to know more after his unannounced, unwelcome meeting with the Kingpin.

The Kingpin! Even the thought of Wilson Fisk was

frustrating to him. They had been adversaries for so long, but had rarely come to physical combat. Instead, they played a deadly game of chess, New York the board and all its people pawns. For years Fisk had passed himself off as a legitimate businessman, while in truth he ran New York's underworld from an office high above Manhattan.

He would make a move, and Daredevil would be forced to counter, thwarting him at all costs, time after time. But even when Matt Murdock still had his license to practice law, he could never find the evidence to take Fisk down. The man was too powerful, too wealthy. He owned half the politicians in the city, and enough lawyers to drown himself in a sea of privacy. He had been one of the most respected citizens in New York.

But he went too far. When he found out that the red-garbed thorn in his side was actually an attorney named Matt Murdock, the Kingpin of Crime let things get too personal. From a distance, he ruined Matt using the government, the IRS, and the police as his weapons. Murdock's legal practice was lost, his money was gone, his credit cards canceled, his life falling apart at the seams. He was living in disgrace, and he had no idea how it had all happened, for there was no sign of Fisk's handiwork in any of his troubles.

And then the Kingpin had blown up Matt's home, tipping his hand. A big mistake. Hatred brought him back from the depths that Fisk had pushed him into, and he fought to expose Fisk as the Kingpin, to link him to one of the city's most heinous criminal empires, at least tangentially. It wasn't enough to put him away, but it was enough to completely ruin his image as a legitimate businessman forever.

It had felt very, very good.

Still, though, the matter of Wilson Fisk was even more complex. Daredevil wanted nothing more than to see the Kingpin stand trial for his crimes, to go behind bars, to spend the rest of his life there. Another man, and Daredevil knew many like this, would have simply tried to murder Wilson Fisk. He could not do that. Murder was not justice, and justice was what he craved. He was no killer.

But life in prison, that sounded good.

The problem was that if the Kingpin were removed, toppled so to speak, that would leave an enormous vacuum in the underworld that dozens of lieutenants would rush to fill. A gang war the likes of which New York had never seen, and which could very well bring the city tumbling down, would be inevitable with Fisk's fall. In comparison, Wiezak's current attempt to overthrow Fisk, if that was indeed what was behind the arson fires, would seem like child's play. Daredevil's ulimate goal, his final victory, whenever that day came, could cause more harm than good. He would have to be extraordinarily careful.

But that day was not today.

Today he was seeking only information. It looked like Wiezak had a relatively large operation going. He couldn't have set that up under the Kingpin's nose, which meant that Fisk must have taken Wiezak under his wing at first. When Wiezak started to reach for the brass ring, he must have gone underground or the Kingpin would have had him killed by now. Which made Daredevil wonder how the cops were going to even find Wiezak, and whether they would let him plea bargain in exchange for help taking down the Kingpin.

Which would be a wasted effort. The Kingpin owned too many cops, too many politicians, to be put away with anything less than concrete evidence . . . in other words, videotape of him actually committing the crime, or computer files from all his illegal businesses. No, if they let Wiezak plea bargain, justice would not be served.

Come to think of it, though, Daredevil found it hard to believe that the Kingpin could not find Gary Wiezak. No, it was more his style to give the upstart enough rope to hang himself and then destroy his operation by example, thereby showing anyone, especially those in the international crime community, who the Kingpin really was.

The biggest question in Daredevil's mind, however, was how Betsy Potter's kidnapping fit in with any of this insanity. The Kingpin might have an answer, but first he had to get in to see him.

Wilson Fisk was an intelligent man. In fact, he was a genius. But being a genius did not mean he was immune to pride. It would have been more practical for his offices and living quarters to be in the center of Fisk Industries' Tower, but Wilson Fisk was the

Kingpin. Therefore he would live and work in the top floors of the tower, and from its penthouse, he could look across his city and feel his prodigious chest swell with the knowledge of his power.

The building was surrounded by structures far smaller, making it impossible for him to get very high on the outside. Half a dozen times or more, Daredevil had fought his way from the lobby up, the Kingpin's goons simply no match for him. During the day, however, the lower floors were populated by thousands of people employed by the Kingpin's legitimate businesses, coming and going all day long. There was only so much security could do in the lobby . . . and the underground garage, well, forget it.

Daredevil arrived at the edge of the roof of a four-story brick office building across from the back entry to the garage, and let his senses expand to take in the entire block. His radar spotted a service truck approaching, and as he focused upon it, he could hear the click-clack of a directional signal, he could smell rye and wheat, pumpernickel and seven-grain, cornbread and cinnamon raisin . . . a bakery truck, delivering breads and bagels to the deli in the lobby.

From the roof to the black cable upon which traffic signals hung, then to the pavement, Daredevil moved. He landed hard, and sprinted for the truck, reaching it, even as it turned down into the garage entry approaching the sentries at the guardbooth there. He used the truck's own bulk to block himself from the sentries' view, and when it stopped, he climbed underneath and held tight to the steel ramp the delivery staff used to unload. It would have been simpler to climb onto the truck's roof, but he had to assume there would be cameras on the ceiling of the garage.

Cleared for entry, the truck waited a moment as a door with steel jaws opened quickly to allow them in. Its upper fangs did not recede all the way into the ceiling, a reminder that it could close as fast as it had opened, trapping you inside the garage, or perhaps, with your vehicle in its grasp. Daredevil heard the heartbeats of the two men within the truck, smelled the sweat and cologne of the four discreetly armed sentries . . . who would likely be out of a job this afternoon.

The truck rolled to a stop and Daredevil dropped to the cement underneath. He crawled toward the front of the truck, then waited. The driver pressed the elevator button, then went to the back with his partner and began to load plastic racks of bread onto their two hand trucks. With a double ping, the elevator arrived, and the bakery driver walked around the front again to press the button that would hold the elevator there for them until they were ready. He paid no mind to the dozens of people who would be inconvenienced by the temporarily disabled elevator.

Then he went back to work.

Daredevil slid from under the truck and in half a dozen steps was inside the elevator, releasing the hold button and smiling to himself at the reaction he imagined the disappearing elevator would elicit from the truck driver. There were forty floors in Fisk Industries' Tower, but the elevator only went to the thirty-sixth. The thirty-seventh floor was nothing more than a huge security web. The thirty-eighth was the Kingpin's office level, and the last two his home.

Daredevil pressed the button for the thirty sixth floor, and pushed open the trapdoor in the elevator ceiling. He had taken a gamble that, having already seen the bakery truck arriving, the camera monitors (for there were most assuredly cameras in the elevator) would not be paying much attention to that one screen. But there was no reason to linger. He pulled himself up through the trap and put back the door. People would get on in the lobby, and other floors as well, but it would be only a matter of minutes before he was close enough to hear the Kingpin's heartbeat.

Wilson Fisk stood alone in a dark office made of glass and marble. It might have seemed a fragile room at first glance, but there was nothing fragile about it. Two walls were a burnished black marble, shot through with cold white veins, while the stones in the floor were a dark gray, glittering richly with crystalline branches. Recessed lights sat in black steel sleeves on the walls, pointed toward the dark ceiling to diffuse their brightness, casting dim shadows throughout the room.

The other two walls were not walls at all, but windows facing south and west. Perhaps one third of the way from the western glass wall, a huge oaken desk with a top the same marble as the floor faced the huge double oak doors of the office, the only way in or out . . . except perhaps the windows. The doors were four inches thick, and took great strength to open. If you could not open those doors, you could not work for the Kingpin.

Behind the huge desk sat an equally large chair made of steel and leather. There was nothing special about this chair beyond its size, for Wilson Fisk decried the mythic image of a "seat of power." The power was in the king, not his throne. And there was, indeed, power in Wilson Fisk.

The Kingpin of Crime stood at the juncture of the western and southern walls of his office. The glass had been tinted to screen out the glare of daylight, but he could still see his kingdom, New York City, perfectly. Though his empire was international, most of his business, all that was important to him, was done right there in the Big Apple.

The big man frowned. The people down there, the ants, didn't think of him as their benefactor any longer. Even the employees in his many companies knew that, though the government had found it impossible to cobble together enough evidence against him, or find anyone alive willing to testify, still he had been revealed as a criminal. He was proud of his work, proud to be the Kingpin, but the public's knowledge of his power made it more difficult to hold, to use, to gain more. It was a major inconvenience, and one day he would take payment for every moment of discomfort in the currency of pain, payment one man would give. Daredevil. Matt Murdock.

At the moment, though, there was a different wrench in the works. Daredevil had spent years chipping away at the Kingpin's empire, but theirs was a seminal rivalry, an eternal hostility. The recent losses he had suffered at the hands of that sniveling pipsqueak, Gary Wiezak, held nothing of the kind of admiration, nobility, or glamor that his relationship with Daredevil had. Wiezak was a particularly bothersome gnat. It gave him great pleasure to know that the gnat was about to be swatted, and that Wiezak's downfall would only serve to solidify Fisk's working relationship with the NYPD and the mayor.

He loved politics.

Calmly, he snipped the end of his cigar and lifted it to his lips, took the gold lighter from the pocket of his pants and lit it. He inhaled deeply, savoring the flavor of the tobacco, and breathed out through his nose. His huge body was like a bellows, and the cigar would not last long.

From the hall outside his office, he heard men, his men, shouting to one another. Through the thickness of the doors, he could not make out their words, but he did not need to. The Kingpin knew everything that happened around him. There was a huge thump against the door, and a sliding sound, but the Kingpin did not turn around. He simply stood by the window and continued smoking his cigar. He heard the loud clatter of something metal on the marble hallway floor, and he knew it was a katana, a Japanese dueling sword, falling to the ground, probably dropped.

The Kingpin turned slowly away from the window and faced the door to his office. Diffuse sunlight from the tinted windows created a sort of silhouette around his huge form, a dull gleam shone on his bald pate.

Like his office, at first glance, Wilson Fisk was not at all what he seemed. He stood six foot seven and weighed four hundred and fifty pounds. He appeared to be an extraordinarily fat man, and the Kingpin worked at the deception. Every ounce of his "fat" was drastically overdeveloped muscle tissue; he continued to work out every day with martial arts and bodybuilding.

There was quiet in the hall for a moment, and then the doors were shoved open, swinging wide to reveal the self-proclaimed hero, the man without fear, Daredevil, standing grimly outlined by the harsh fluorescent hall lights.

But he was not alone. Two of the Kingpin's personal guard rounded the corner in the hallway and went at Daredevil with hand weapons, one had a spiked mace and the other a simple wooden staff. The Kingpin slipped into his chair and puffed contentedly on his cigar as these two attacked together, underestimating their foe as so many of his employees had, as he himself had far too often in the past.

Hector swung his mace at Daredevil's head just as Everett stabbed with his wooden bo-stick. But Daredevil was much too fast. Wilson Fisk knew that Everett and Hector would be incapable of understanding how it happened, would not have seen the move coming, despite the fact that they had studied what little film there was of Daredevil fighting. The Kingpin wondered for a moment if it would be cruel to punish these guards for failing to stop the hero, even though he had fully expected that failure.

Daredevil grabbed Everett's staff in both hands, simultaneously kicking him in the chest and using the stolen staff to block the swing of Hector's mace. The chain wrapped itself around the staff, the spiked ball clacking to a stop as Daredevil yanked the iron weapon from Hector's grasp. Both men had been disarmed with one smooth move.

Daredevil tossed the mace away, back into the hallway, even as Everett and Hector came at him. Now weaponless, however, they had no chance at all. Daredevil's body moved at a seemingly impossible angle, right leg planted as the left kicked up and slammed into Hector's chest, knocking him back half a dozen feet. Then he brought the staff sweeping around toward Everett's ankles. Everett leaped over the swing of the staff, but wasted time being proud of himself even as the other side of the oaken stick slammed into the base of his neck.

What the Kingpin marveled at most was not the hero's moves, not his skill or strength, but his restraint. It would have been so much easier for him to kill, or even to truly incapacitate his opponents. But it was a rarity for them to end up with even a broken limb. It was far more likely, in fact, that they would simply be knocked unconscious, or caused enough pain that they were unwilling to move. Such restraint took far more skill and far more precision than simple brutality. The Kingpin was forced to admire Daredevil's abilities, though he was repulsed by their impractical expression. That was why he did not allow his guards to draw guns of any sort on this particular, and strangely frequent, intruder. He could disarm them just as easily, but hand to hand combat was so much more interesting.

Everett was out cold, but Hector rose now, fuming like a bull in the ring and launched himself back into the office in a blind rush toward the man who had so humiliated him. Daredevil was looking at the Kingpin and did not even turn around to face this renewed threat. His right arm swung back, releasing the staff, which did a half-spin in the air before slamming against Hector's shins. Hector sprawled to the marble floor in pain.

"Well done, Daredevil, as usual," Fisk said in a flat tone, leaning forward slightly in his chair. "But you are running slightly behind. I had expected you sooner than this."

"If you were expecting me, why waste my time with these delays?" Daredevil asked, sweeping his arm back to indicate the two unconscious men in the office and the dozen or so others in the hall, his usually serene face revealing more annoyance than surprise.

The Kingpin ignored his question. This was his place, his world. Though Daredevil had proven difficult to kill in the past, Fisk could most certainly kill him now with his bare hands, there on the marble floor of his office. But that was not for today. Despite the harm that Daredevil had done to his image, his empire, his plans, it was refreshing to have a worthy opponent. And Daredevil could be monitored, manipulated. He could turn out to be very valuable.

And the Kingpin could always kill him later.

He knew that Daredevil was Matt Murdock, had used that information to destroy the hero's life, to ruin him. But here he was, back again. Fisk was surprised, really, that they were having this confrontation so soon after hurting one another so badly. But then, he could have come as Murdock, couldn't he, and not faced any of the guards, simply had the receptionist call up and the Kingpin would have seen him right away.

But Matt Murdock was among the walking wounded. His law practice gone, his home gone, his friends distanced from him. The Kingpin had hurt him, and maybe Matt Murdock was a little afraid of Wilson Fisk. Daredevil, on the other hand, was the man without fear. He was certainly not afraid to face the Kingpin, and nothing would ever change that. Matt Murdock and Daredevil, one in the same man. But the costume, for all the trouble it caused, made a tangible difference.

"I'll make this short and sweet," Daredevil said, and the Kingpin merely raised his eyebrows.

"Tell me where I can find Gary Wiezak, and why he's still alive."

Daredevil's question hung in the air, a tangible object separating the two men. The Kingpin let it linger there, unanswered, for a full minute before leaning back in his chair and tilting his head slightly to the left.

"Mr. Wiezak's more distasteful activities came to my attention some time ago, Daredevil," the Kingpin said thoughtfully. "As soon as I became aware of them, I did my civic duty and passed that information on to the, hm, proper authorities? Of course, with the terrible losses my corporation has suffered due to his criminal actions, I was more than happy to give the police whatever information I had. Yes, I believe I was most helpful."

Daredevil frowned, and as he had so many times before, the Kingpin felt as though the hero were reading his mind. If Murdock had any psychic abilities, however, he had not been able to discover them. Therefore, he assumed that it was merely a feeling, perhaps a tactic Daredevil used to intimidate lesser opponents than Wilson Fisk.

Still, the hero's thoughtful gaze was often unnerving to the Kingpin. So just in case, Fisk did his best to tell as much of the truth as he could afford to whenever Daredevil was around. Just enough of an answer to create more questions.

"I pulled one of your guys, Sean Mallory, out of an explosion this morning," Daredevil said. "He's in police custody now. What I want to know is what you're planning to do about all this?"

"Thank you for your timely assistance. I was aware

of the events this morning, and I'm sure Mr. Mallory owes you a great debt, as do we all. As for your other questions, I'm sure the police have things well in hand.''

"Can we stop playing legit, here, Fisk?" Daredevil snapped in frustration. "It's not fun anymore, not since the press fingered you as the Kingpin."

Fisk's eyes narrowed. "Will that be all?" he asked, indicating that it was indeed all. "I've a busy day ahead."

"No, there's one thing more," Daredevil said, and took a step closer to the big desk. A step the Kingpin did not like.

"Betsy Potter."

"Ah yes," the Kingpin nodded. "The Gladiator's wife, I'd heard about that. A pity."

Daredevil could not disguise his surprise at the Kingpin's response.

"How did you hear about that?" he snapped.

The Kingpin merely smiled.

"You know," he said. "The grapevine. You hear things."

"You're connected to Wiezak, and Wiezak is connected to this woman's disappearance," Daredevil said with certainty, taking another step toward the desk. "What do you know, Fisk?"

The Kingpin moved forward to lean on the desk with his huge hands, his face betraying his calm for the first time as annoyance clearly showed through the facade.

"You presume too much, Daredevil," he said

sharply. "I'm afraid you'll have to ask Mr. Wiezak all of these questions."

"I plan to," Daredevil said, not backing off, but not approaching any further either. "In the meantime, however, what do you know about Betsy Potter's disappearance?"

"Only what I've been told," the Kingpin said drily, not attempting to hide his contempt now, just wanting the hero to leave. "I've no interest in the Gladiator's wife."

"He's not the Gladiator any more," Daredevil said defensively, then turned and walked toward the open oak doors. "He's just Melvin Potter, a harm to no one. You'd do best to remember that."

"A harm to no one?" the Kingpin mused aloud. "I don't know about that. In the face of such trauma as this, who knows what a man might do? Especially a man with Mr. Potter's, hm, colorful past."

Daredevil turned back toward the Kingpin, wishing he could search for the hidden meanings of the man's words in his eyes, but unable to see them or anything else. He was wrong about the Gladiator though, Daredevil was certain. The imbalances in Melvin's brain that had fostered such twisted development had been repaired, his life filled with love and happiness.

But what did Fisk care? Was his comment merely an attempt to divert Daredevil from further questions? It did indeed seem that the Kingpin knew more about Betsy's disappearance than he was letting on. Daredevil asked the last and most important question.

"Do you know who kidnapped Betsy Potter?"

He listened carefully, to the beat of the Kingpin's heart, even as his radar scanned the man's form for uncomfortable or unusual shifts. Fisk seemed reluctant to answer at first, as though he knew that lying was dangerous. That hesitation was enough to let Daredevil know that the Kingpin was involved.

"No," Fisk said flatly. "You may go now."

He went, all right, but he had the real answer. The Kingpin had said no, but his heartbeat had skipped significantly. He was lying. If he wasn't actually involved in Betsy's disappearance, he certainly knew who was.

Daredevil knew he was working on sheer conjecture, but it was entirely possible that before the police started moving in on Wiezak, prompting the Kingpin to cut him off, Fisk might have ordered the lowlife to snatch Betsy Potter. It was possible. It made a sick kind of sense.

But what now? Where was Betsy now?

By the time Matt Murdock arrived back at his apartment, peeled off his Daredevil costume, and flopped onto the bed, he was completely wiped out. And the scary thing was, it was barely three-thirty in the afternoon. He lay exactly as he fell, trying to calm his brain, quiet his thoughts, lull himself to sleep. He didn't need to move, to feel the pain, to see the yellow and black and blue splotches in the mirror to know that he was badly bruised, especially his back. Between the explosion and his collision with the police cruiser, he'd taken quite a beating.

He had nearly a dozen small cuts from flying glass, but he was stunned that there were so few, and none were serious. He'd been lucky, very lucky, yet he found it difficult to think of himself that way when so many had been so terribly unlucky. It had been so strange, flying through the air like that. Like he had some sort of force field around him. Some kind of protection.

He remembered a story Karen had told him once. She'd still been a teenager, so it had to have been late high school or early college, but Matt didn't really recall. Karen and a friend had been driving up to Bear Mountain to ski when it had started to rain. It was very light, so she didn't really pay any attention until she was finally forced to turn on the wipers. The rubber scraped across the windshield, skittering and jumping on the ice that had formed there. It was freezing rain, and the entire highway was covered with a sheet of ice.

They'd been about to crest a hill, so she took her foot off the accelerator and just gave the brake a couple of short, light taps, not enough to cause a skid and just enough, on the hill, to slow them down to about thirty. When they came over the rise, there stretched out across the highway just ahead, was a pileup involving fifteen to twenty cars across four lanes.

When Karen had told Matt the story, he'd been

proud of her cool in such a situation. Most people would have panicked. Karen just kept her feet on the floor, touched nothing, and eased over to the one opening she could see, the breakdown lane. Cruising through demolished vehicles, people still inside in need of help, she said she felt like she'd been in some kind of invulnerable bubble.

Another car came over the hill behind her, the driver braked in panic, went into a spin and was headed right for her rear end. Just before he reached her, Karen tapped the accelerator and jumped forward just a bit. The new arrival missed her by a foot and slammed into the guardrail, but she and her friend just glided through the wreckage and continued on their way, as if they were watching the entire scene unfold from some safe haven.

At the time, Matt thought he understood Karen's story, the phenomenon of that feeling of safety. The same feeling that, in wartime, sometimes overcame the logic of soldiers who had narrowly escaped death, perhaps by standing on a land mine that did not explode. Some came to believe they were invulnerable, unkillable . . . until, of course, they were killed.

Matt had believed he understood. He'd narrowly escaped death thousands of times as Daredevil. But nothing had ever quite equalled today. The entire building had exploded around him, but its force conspired with his own momentum to snatch him from the arms of death, to shoot him through that window. Despite his cuts and bruises, he'd felt somehow as if his life were charmed, as if he was protected by some invisible force.

He'd thought he understood Karen's story back then. But until today, he really hadn't *known* what she was talking about. Now that he did know, however, he did not feel invulnerable, unkillable. Not at all. Instead, he only wondered *why*. Why him and not one of the people inside?

Ah, but then, Sean Mallory had also been saved. He'd been in that protective bubble with Matt. On the other hand, he hadn't landed quite so safely. It was a strange feeling, to say the least. It made Matt thankful for his life, for Karen, for everything he had, despite the hell the Kingpin had put him through. It made him rethink himself, remember the days when being Daredevil had been a little more fun, a lot less grim, than it was now.

Perhaps, though he knew he was not invulnerable, he had been given a gift of sorts. A new beginning, after his life had been torn down. He and Karen had squirreled themselves away in the little apartment, but maybe it was time to reconnect parts of his old life again. Not to leave Hell's Kitchen, or pursue his status as a disbarred attorney, but maybe he owed Foggy Nelson, his friend and law partner for so many years, more than a phone call to say he was alive.

Matt Murdock felt as though he'd been woken up, been reminded that he was a man, alive, and that being Matt Murdock was equally as important as being Daredevil. After all that had happened, it was a difficult thing to admit.

But it felt good.

And now that the cops were going to pick Wiezak up, he could concentrate completely on finding Betsy Potter. Melvin had a real life, with a real family, and he deserved it. Matt was determined to see that he got it back. He owed Melvin a call, but it would have to wait until morning.

It was barely four o'clock in the afternoon when Matt Murdock fell deeply asleep and dreamed of how lucky he was.

Chapter 8

"**Y**OU SEEM TO HAVE ALL THE PIECES, LIEUTENANT, but the puzzle isn't complete," Captain Stanley said in that condescending tone that so often infuriated Bryce. He knew he shouldn't let the captain get under his skin, but the guy had an incredible capacity to burrow in there like a bloodthirsty tick.

"Here's the scenario, Captain," Bryce said, his words clipped and impatient. "Fisk's flunky, Sean Mallory, is willing to testify that Guillermo Rodriguez was hanging around outside the building for a couple days before the place went up. Mallory's turned down police custody, by the way. Big surprise. Now, Daredevil caught Rodriguez, but of course you can't testify with a mask on. Luckily, the criminologists picked enough physical evidence off Rodriguez's clothes and out of his hair that we'll have no trouble sticking him with that one arson job.

"Not that it would matter," Bryce continued, "because Rodriguez copped to the whole lot of 'em and has agreed to testify againt Wiezak, who he says put him up to it, in hopes of leniency, but with no guarantee or plea bargain. We don't have an ID on the shooter yet, but this Karen Page woman got a good look at him, and we hope to be able to pull him in and use him to get to Wiezak as well."

"With all the other information we have, shipping manifests, videotapes and all, we've got plenty to pick up this scumbag today," Captain Stanley declared officiously. "So why isn't he in a cell right now?"

"The address on his motor vehicle registration turns out to be a Chinese restaurant in the Bronx. We've been out to every building he owns directly or under a corporate umbrella. We just can't find the guy, Captain," Bryce said, angry that he had allowed his frustration to show in front of his superior officer.

Captain Stanley's eyes narrowed, and Bryce was momentarily taken aback by the fierceness on his face. The captain, recently promoted after Captain Grobé's retirement, was more politician than cop. He'd gotten where he was by diplomatic means, not by merit. He was respected by his subordinates only because of his rank, and even then only grudgingly. Of all the adjectives, mostly unpleasant, that Bryce might have chosen to describe Stanley, he never would have considered the word "intimidating." Until today.

"Don't move," the Captain said. "I'll be right back."

Lieutenant Bryce sat behind his desk as Captain Stanley left his office in simmering silence. He watched the man stalk through the squad room and into his own office on the other side. Over the heads of the officers in Captain Stanley's command, Bryce saw Stanley pick up the phone and jab a number into its face. When he spoke, his expression betrayed a commanding quality it rarely did on the job. Then he was writing something down, tearing a sheet of paper off a pad on his desk, and storming back across the squad room and into Bryce's office.

"There's your address, Lieutenant," Stanley said calmly as he laid the paper on Bryce's desk.

The words "how did you get this" were on their way to Lieutenant Bryce's lips, but he shut his mouth tight when he realized what a foolish question that was. The captain's political and diplomatic efforts obviously extended beyond the police force itself. He wasn't the kind of cop whose tour of duty gave him the opportunity to establish relationships with street snitches. Therefore, he had to be involved with organized crime in some way, but Bryce didn't want to guess how high up that mob/police relationship went.

Lieutenant Bryce lost what little respect he'd had for Captain Stanley at that moment. He would have to keep an eye on Stanley, see if there was anything he could do to trip the Captain up, to take him down. Men like him didn't deserve to wear the badge. Captain Stanley certainly knew Bryce well enough to know that revealing his true colors would be dangerous, that Bryce would come after him eventually. But he'd done it anyway. Which made Bryce realize that Captain Stanley wanted Wiezak behind bars not because that was his job, but because that was what whoever had bought his integrity had ordered him to do.

Bryce was disgusted. But he picked up the piece of paper and put it in his pocket. He would get Wiezak out of the way first. There would be plenty of time to take Captain Stanley down. In either case, he knew that there would always be someone to step into the void. The thought depressed him.

Karen Page was sitting at a corner desk talking to a sketch artist. It looked like the artist was finishing up, and Lieutenant Bryce walked over to speak to Karen.

"How'd we do, Miss Page?" he asked.

"You tell me," she answered and motioned for the artist to show the picture to Lieutenant Bryce. "I was a little fuzzy in a couple of places, but I really think the sketch looks like the shooter."

"The guy you *think* is the shooter," Bryce corrected, but he really didn't doubt Page's story. She seemed to have her head on straight, despite the things he'd found when he'd checked her record. Still, if Daredevil vouched for her, she had to be okay.

"Pierre," he said to the artist, "get that thing on the wire, but leave a copy for Miss Page to refer to as she scans the mug books. Miss Page, I'm going to have to go out for a while. I think we might have a lead on this Gary Wiezak's whereabouts. Miss Page, if you don't find anything, please feel free to go. An officer can take you home if you like. Just be sure we know where to reach you. Thanks again for your help."

"Anything I can do to end this insanity, Lieutenant," she answered, and Bryce liked the way she smiled.

*　　*　　*

Lieutenant Garth Bryce was sorely tempted to tear the smile off of Gary Wiezak's face. The guy's pompous smirk had been a constant offense since Bryce and three officers had arrived at Wiezak's small SoHo apartment. The place was squeaky clean. So clean, in fact, that Bryce had to wonder if he actually lived there, or simply used it for convenience's sake and as a mask for his real residence.

In any case, that was where they found him . . . and his lawyer too! Obviously someone in the department had tipped Wiezak off that they were coming. So Fisk had people in the department, and so did Wiezak. Bryce imagined every two bit hood in New York City had a couple of cops on the payroll. It was a part of life that truly depressed him.

"Since my client is coming with you of his own volition, I don't think it is really necessary for you to handcuff him, Lieutenant," the attorney, a woman named something-Haupt, argued in a tone that implied an expectation of cooperation.

"Your client is wanted on a dozen counts of arson and twice as many counts of murder. He is under arrest. He gets cuffed," Bryce said calmly, but with a thinly veiled warning against pushing him further.

Wiezak said nothing, which made that smile all the more infuriating.

Most of the people who had sought shelter at St. Bridget's for the night had already turned in. Sister Ellen and Sister Anna would spend the night, but

Sister Maggie had gone back to the convent. She spent her mornings at a local youth center, and she needed her rest to get up so early.

An amazing woman, Karen Page thought. Days offering shelter and safety, sympathy and sustenance to children who had nowhere else to go, nights taking care of homeless men and women, feeding people, nursing them back to health. Karen had no intention of ever joining the convent, couldn't imagine such a life, but it made her happy to help in any way she could. And spending time with someone as special as Sister Maggie was an added blessing.

There was something between Matt and the aging nun, something Karen didn't quite understand. It was as if they shared some secret, a secret they never discussed, even together, but one they treasured nevertheless. The only thing she could think of was that perhaps Maggie knew that Matt was Daredevil, but Karen doubted that was it. If so, Matt would have told her.

No, this was something he hadn't shared with her, perhaps wasn't ready to share yet. She couldn't help wondering what it was, and she hoped to find out one day. But she could wait. She loved Matt and their new beginning together was more than she ever could have hoped for.

''Karen, why don't you go on home, now? You had a tough day, what with the fire and the police and all,'' Sister Ellen said in a tone far less brusque than usual, one that teetered on the verge of sounding kind. Wonders never ceased.

"Just as soon as we're done, Sister," Karen said. "I'm here, I might as well help you finish."

"Whatever you say," Sister Ellen shrugged.

"Besides," Karen said, "Diana didn't come down for dinner, and I want to see her, make sure she's all right."

"Somebody say my name?"

Karen turned to see that Diana had come down after all. She weaved her way through tables, barely acknowledging the few other people still in the room as she headed for the kitchen. Diana looked much better, but Karen could still see the despair in her eyes.

"You look well," Karen said, meaning it but managing to sound worried anyway.

"Even though it won't help my father, I feel much better knowing they caught the arsonist and the guy who hired him to do it," Diana said quietly. "I don't understand it, but I'm glad they're in jail."

They sat down to talk. Karen asked about Diana's father, but before the woman could respond the door by the kitchen burst open startling Sister Anna into dropping the platter she was carrying and scattering leftover pasta across the floor in a messy spray of bolognese sauce.

A hush fell over the room, and even Sister Ellen seemed frozen in place as a tall man stumbled to his knees and fell to the floor, clutching his chest. There was blood everywhere.

"Jesus!" Diana said next to her, and that sent Karen into action.

Then Karen recognized him. Roberto something.

He was the man, who the night before had been willing to kill Timmy Monroe for stealing his sweatshirt.

"Help him!" Diana hissed, right hand covering her mouth in horror as the man's blood seeped into a widening pool.

"I'll call the police," Sister Ellen snapped, then disappeared.

Karen knelt by Roberto, afraid to turn him over. Concerned that he might not be able to breathe, she finally decided she had to get him on his back, and turned him. She wished she hadn't. His hands were splayed over at least half a dozen deep wounds, some lost in the folds of his sweatshirt. His eyes were beginning to roll back in his head, and Karen realized that he would be long dead before the police arrived. She bit her lip to keep from crying, and hoped he was not in terrible pain.

Suddenly, Roberto's eyes seemed to focus on her. She saw recognition there, and he gasped one word as his life expired: "Monroe."

There was a clamor in the doorway, and Karen looked up in alarm thinking Monroe might have followed to finish the job. She was surprised and relieved to see the blue uniform of a police officer emerge from the shadows. The officer, a tall woman with a hard face, knelt by Roberto's side.

"You know this guy, ma'am?" the officer asked.

"His name is . . . was, Roberto. I'm afraid I don't know his last name," Karen answered. "I think he's dead."

The officer felt Roberto's neck and wrist for a pulse, listened to his chest for breathing, looked at his eyes, but finally she confirmed Karen's opinion.

"He got into a fight in an alley with another guy," the officer said.

"Timmy Monroe," Karen said, nodding.

"Yeah, that's the guy," the officer said, looking up in surprise. "He's dead too. Coupla other homeless guys saw the whole thing. Your buddy here had a gun, shot this Monroe, but didn't kill him right away."

Karen was stunned. It was too much, too much all to be happening at once. Two lives destroyed in one night, the danger, the insanity of the street. Death could come at any moment. She saw Diana out the corner of her eye and turned to see that she too was stunned into reflective silence by the tragedy that now unfolded before their eyes. Sister Ellen came in and began talking to the police woman, and Karen stood up and backed away. She just wanted to be home now, safe in Matt's arms.

Karen grabbed her jacket and headed for home. Her mind was racing with thoughts of the death she'd seen that night and the violence she'd experienced earlier in the day. By day, at least, she was unafraid. Even at night, for the most part, she didn't worry much. Everyone knew that Manhattan was dangerous at night. Of late, the streets of Hell's Kitchen had been just a tiny bit safer, the thieves and killers thinking twice now that Daredevil was on the prowl, making them pay for their sins. But Daredevil couldn't be everywhere at once.

Karen Page was a fairly muscular woman, now that she was in shape again, and Matt had taught her enough self-defense techniques that she felt confident in her ability to take care of herself. Even so, she usually took a taxi the short distance home when it was particularly late at night, unless Matt came to meet her, and then they'd walk home together.

Tonight, though, she was reacting against the fear that threatened to overwhelm her. She would not be cowed by the city, would not become a frightened animal huddling inside, away from the big bad world. Karen figured that Hell's Kitchen had seen its share of death and misery that night, that it was somehow sated for the day, its quota of blood fulfilled.

She really needed the walk, the chill fresh air, the time to think. It was coming up on eleven o'clock, and it was already fairly quiet. For all its delis, restaurants and offices, Hell's Kitchen was a residential area. The average person was already in bed.

It wasn't the average person she had to worry about.

But she forced herself not to worry, not to be afraid. The neighborhood was packed with cops trying to figure out exactly what had happened to leave two men dead. It would be an hour or so before the vermin crept back onto the streets, after the flashing blue lights had receded. She'd be home by then, for sure.

Karen turned left, walking north up Ninth Avenue.

There was a deli she knew would still be open, and she wanted to pick up some orange juice for breakfast. She decided to see if they had any fresh bagels left, and crossed her fingers superstitiously, hoping for cinnamon raisin, her favorite. An elderly couple passed her, walking a tiny dog, and she was pleased to be on the avenue now where "average" people were going about their business. Just couldn't sleep, she figured.

There was safety in numbers, though, so that was good. A man in a dapper-looking business suit came toward her on the sidewalk, then crossed over to the other side, smiling as he went. She smiled back. Poor guy, she thought, still in his work clothes at this time of night.

Light streamed out of the deli just ahead, and she picked up her pace. She hadn't spoken to Matt since just after the arsonist had been shot, and she was looking forward to seeing him.

"Ouch!" Karen snapped, and knelt down to massage her ankle. The granite slabs that made up the sidewalk were uneven and pitted in many places, and she'd turned her ankle. It wasn't sprained, she realized happily, but it would definitely be sore in the morning.

There was a tap on her shoulder, startling her to her feet. She stumbled back a step when her eyes reached the face of the man standing before her: the sniper! Her stomach turned in fear; bile surged in her throat. Wiezak was in jail. So was the arsonist who had worked for him, but nobody had been able to identify this guy. But obviously he hadn't had any trouble identifying her!

It was almost surreal. People passed by as if nothing was happening. Karen didn't know what she expected, maybe for them to at least shy away from the beast standing there, to keep far away as they went around him. But no, they brushed right past. As if nothing were wrong, as if she weren't in mortal danger, standing there only three blocks from her house.

She was in danger. That was without dispute, despite the smile on the sniper's face. The smile was real, and that was what upset her the most. It was not insincere, not in the least. But neither was it a friendly greeting. Rather, it was a smile not unlike the one Monroe had on his face the night before as he scanned a room full of potential victims.

It was the smile of a predator.

"Kaaa-rennn?" the sniper cupped a hand to his mouth, as if he were calling her from a long distance. "Earth to Karen?"

"I'm sorry, do I know you?" she asked, though he couldn't possibly have missed her initial reaction to him. Karen mentally noted that the deli lay only a few yards away, behind her, that even with her sore ankle she would be able to make it there if she could get in one good blow, fist or foot, it made no difference.

"Just so we understand each other, Miss Page, my employer has asked me to let you know that you were a fool to cooperate with the police. A woman with your background should know better,'' the sniper hissed, coming up close, entering her personal space. Karen felt nauseous.

"Wasn't today trash day?" she asked, a hard look transforming her face.

The sniper's smile never disappeared, but it no longer reached his eyes. They narrowed now, the predator sighting its prey, and he moved just a tiny bit closer, but Karen would not back off.

"Come on, Karen," he said, nearly snarling, not even attempting to hide the cruelty within him. "You don't have to be so mean. My assignment is to deliver a message to you. Whether I do it nice or nasty is completely up to you. You seem like a smart girl, and you're definitely not hard on the eyes. I know from your record you're a good-time lady. We could have some fun together, and I wouldn't even have to hurt you. How's that sound to you?"

Karen turned slowly, deliberately, without another word, and began walking toward the deli. The lights were like a beacon, calling her to safety, but she knew the risk she was taking, turning her back on this savage. Still, it was the only way. She would not speak to him, would not face him, would not show him fear. All of those things would give him power, and she refused to give him a single ounce of hers.

"Karen, my employer has a team of lawyers on his side, millions of dollars to pay them. They'll tear you apart. Hell, your background is a matter of record. My boss is already back on the street. His bail was more than you'll ever make in your life, and he didn't shed a tear when he paid up."

Karen kept walking.

"You're forcing my hand, lady. I coulda been nice to you, but you just keep pushing my buttons. You make me hurt you, I can't promise you'll live through the experience."

Karen kept walking.

"Don't you turn your back on me you bitch!" he shouted, and Karen felt the danger, felt every inch of her back as one large target. The deli was right in front of her.

The sniper grabbed her by the shoulder, squeezing hard. He'd underestimated her, obviously didn't expect her to be able to put up much of a fight. Idiot.

Karen elbowed him in the stomach, knocking the wind out of him. He lost his grip on her shoulder and went onto his knees, hard, on the sidewalk. He scrabbled at her, trying to get a grip, ready to fight back, ready, more than likely, to kill her if he could figure out how to get her off the street.

She kicked him in the groin, which stopped the scrabbling. Though she wanted to do more, though he deserved so much more, she turned and ran. The deli was warm inside, and the white-haired Asian man who owned the place looked at her with kindness and obvious concern. He knew something was wrong.

"Please," she said, thinking only of hearing Matt's voice. "I need your phone."

There was a double knock on the glass door of the

deli, and she looked up to see the sniper standing at the door. He pointed his finger at her, thumb in the air, like children did playing cops and robbers. His thumb fell, firing at her. Before he disappeared into the night, he waved goodbye and smiled that terrible smile.

A predator's smile.

Chapter 9

ORNING CAME TOO SOON FOR MELVIN POTTER, but he dragged himself out of bed regardless. He had to go on, had to force himself to perform the duties of his life, day by day. The past couple of nights he'd been up late, on the street, going from corner to corner, store to store, bar to bar, with a photo of Betsy.

A lot of people recognized him, many more, in fact, than he would have imagined. It seemed that the Gladiator had made much more of an impression than he'd known, and he was not happy with that small celebrity. It repulsed him, in fact. His efforts met with shrugs and pitying glances, both responses equally upsetting.

He pulled on his robe and rubbed a hand over his bristly chin, then ducked to avoid banging his head on the doorframe as he went out into the hall, then down the stairs and into the kitchen. He wiped sleep from his eyes and headed to the fridge for some orange juice.

Ever since Betsy had disappeared, Melvin had felt short of breath, his heart pressed against the inside of his chest. It felt the way he imagined the beginning of a coronary might feel. He had expected to hear from Daredevil the day before, but had not. It only made him feel more alone. Alone. The apartment was barren of any pleasure for him without Betsy there to smile at him, to say she loved him.

Melvin went into the bathroom, but avoided looking at the mirror. He didn't want to see his face, or the awful knowledge that could be read in his eyes, the knowledge that Betsy might well be dead already. He fought the little voice in his head that told him those things, that urged him to give up hope, to give in to despair and eventually, of course, retribution. He didn't want to see his face, his eyes, didn't want to know what they knew.

When he came out of the bathroom, Melvin chugged his juice, downed a bowl of Cheerios, and whipped through a shower and shave. Twenty minutes later he was dressed and walking downstairs to the door that opened into the back of his shop, Spotlight Costumes. The shop had been closed for two days, but he couldn't put it off anymore. He had orders to fill that were already late, and it was closing in on Halloween. Betsy would want him to keep the business going. There were probably a trillion messages waiting for him. It didn't seem right to him that the world didn't stop the moment Betsy disappeared. But then, it didn't stop for anyone, did it?

Not until you got off.

He opened the door and stepped into the shop shivering a little and vowing to go back up for a sweater after dealing with the messages and the mail. He walked through the back room and out to the front to unlock the door and turn around the "open" sign . . . and stopped short. On the counter, next to the cash register, were a box of donuts and two steaming cups of coffee.

"Good morning, Melvin."

Melvin spun around, immediately on guard, though he knew who his visitor was, who it had to be. Daredevil, standing in front of a row of costumed mannequins: Spider-Man, Freddy Krueger, Thor, and one of Daredevil himself.

"I'm sorry I couldn't get here yesterday," the red-man said, "it was a crazy day."

"You probably wouldn't have found me in anyway," he answered. "I've been out looking for Betsy."

Melvin Potter looked at his former nemesis, his friend and confidante, and then looked away, anywhere but at Daredevil.

"No luck," he said.

"I'll be straight with you, Melvin, because I know you don't have the patience for anything less," Daredevil said, walking up to the counter, picking up a coffee and handing it to Melvin, who sipped at it without looking. "I've got nothing solid, but I have a lot of suspicions. I've been working on this other situation . . ."

Melvin looked up, surprised and slightly annoyed. Betsy was out there, dead or dying, and Daredevil was running around town doing errands?

". . . which I have reason to believe ties in to Betsy's disappearance."

Melvin felt guilty then, for questioning Daredevil's actions. There was more going on in the world, as he'd been forced to acknowledge that morning, than a woman gone missing. The mission Daredevil had set out for himself was a significant one, but he was concentrating his efforts to find the wife of a man who'd done nothing but try to kill him for years. How could he expect any more? And yet, as a husband, how could he not expect more?

"So tell me about it," he said, and sipped his coffee, even as Daredevil picked up the other cup.

"Yesterday, the cops picked up the guy who's been setting all these fires lately, and the guy they believe hired him, a man named Gary Wiezak. Wiezak is after the Kingpin's crown. I've been shot at twice the last few days by a guy who may be working for Wiezak, or for Fisk. And I'm pretty sure he's the guy who took Betsy."

"So even though the cops have this Wiezak guy, he still might have Betsy. Or it could be Fisk, right? I mean, I've never even heard of this Wiezak character," Melvin said, feeling both sick and angry now, the thought of his wife in the hands of someone like the Kingpin making him tremble with an urge to strike out at something, a profound hostility he had thought all but gone from his mind, his soul.

"It could be either, but I'm betting on Wiezak right now," Daredevil answered. "Whoever hired that sniper."

Melvin was puzzled.

"What would this Wiezak, or even the Kingpin want with Betsy and me?" he asked.

"I wish I knew," Daredevil answered. "Though if they've gone to all this trouble to take Betsy, it had to be to get to you. The good news is, that means she's probably still alive. The bad news is, we have no idea what they want with you."

"Betsy's my life," Melvin said quietly. "If they hurt her, I don't know what I'll do."

Melvin knew that, though he couldn't see Daredevil's eyes, the hero was watching him closely. He wanted to reassure Daredevil that he was only referring to the shambles his life would be without Betsy, not to any retribution he might take. But he wasn't sure himself.

"What I still don't understand is why we haven't heard from anyone, if they took Betsy to get to me?" Melvin asked in frustration.

Silence. Then, finally, "I don't know. Maybe they've been otherwise occupied?"

Melvin sipped his coffee, flipped open the box of donuts and then shut it again. "What now?" he asked, at a loss for a next move.

"I may have to see the Kingpin again. He's happy to get Wiezak in deeper, and I'm hoping I can use that to find Betsy. If not, Wiezak's already out on bail, so I can tail him to see if he'll be stupid enough to lead me to Betsy."

"And what in God's name do I do in the meantime?" Melvin asked, on the verge of tears, his hands steadied only by the coffee cup between them.

"You wait for them to contact you, and whatever goes down, you work with me on this. You're not alone, Melvin."

"No, DD, I'm not alone. I've got you on my side." Melvin turned away. "But Betsy's my whole life, and she's totally, completely alone.''

Melvin heard an intake of breath, as though Daredevil were about to say something. Moments later he heard the tinkling of the bell that hung over the shop's door, and when he turned, Daredevil was gone.

Daredevil swung uptown, slicing through the cool fall morning with a grace that belied his inner turmoil. He was boiling inside. The judge had let Wiezak walk on bail despite the significant arguments ADA Marcia Martinez had made that he was a flight risk. Daredevil didn't think the guy would run, not with all that money and power hanging in the balance of the Big Apple's criminal hierarchy, but that wasn't the point. Give him time on the street, and he'd only continue what he'd been doing, and have plenty of opportunity to try to get to the witnesses or the jury.

Wiezak would go to trial, all right. But that didn't mean he'd get convicted.

Meanwhile, Karen was the only one who had gotten a good look at the sniper, and the cops hadn't been able to identify the guy. Daredevil railed against the thought of Karen facing the killer on her own in the middle of Hell's Kitchen, their own neighborhood. He should have been there for her. Luckily, Karen could take care of herself in most circumstances, but this was too much. The police wanted to put her in protective custody, but Daredevil had his own ideas about protective custody. He'd meet her at work later and escort her home, then sit with her and hope the sniper would come after them. He had a few questions he wanted to ask the guy . . . hard questions.

The worst thing of all, though, was the guilt and anger that he felt at not having found any more leads in Betsy Potter's disappearance. He had to just pursue the Wiezak matter and hope they could find the sniper who could then lead him to Betsy. There were too many questions burning in his brain. Why didn't Betsy's captors contact Melvin? What did they want? Daredevil knew he had done all he could thus far, but he couldn't avoid feeling somewhat helpless. Melvin was counting on him. Somewhere, Betsy was counting on him. He was supposed to be a hero, but he already felt like he was letting them down.

The morning had held nothing but bad news. Though he felt guilty about giving up the time, Daredevil was headed for a breakfast date with his former law partner and best friend, Franklin "Foggy" Nelson. He needed to take his mind off the case, just for an hour or so, and it would be good to see Foggy again.

He stopped atop a building on 53rd Street to change his clothes. Lately, the only time he'd spent as just plain Matt Murdock had been at home with Karen. It felt good.

Franklin Nelson walked up Broadway, wishing he'd worn a t-shirt. He had on a cotton shirt and a fall suit, but he always overestimated the power of the sun this time of year. Maybe outside the city, or even outside midtown, it wouldn't be quite so cold. But as he crossed 50th Street, all he could think of was how Manhattan was nothing more than a cross-hatched series of wind tunnels. Of course, it didn't help that the sky was hung with heavy, dark clouds, promising to dump a lot of water on New York at any moment. And Foggy without an umbrella!

Still, he shook off the shivers and concentrated on his destination, half a block ahead: Ellen's Stardust Diner. The place was cozy, with the best breakfast around. Even better, though, was the decor. It was fifties all the way, stools at the counter, red leather booths, those silly paper caps on the heads of waiters . . . it was the kind of place where Hollywood actresses had been discovered once upon a time, but now it was just quaint, or a gimmick, depending on how cynical you were.

But Foggy Nelson wasn't cynical at all. He hadn't even been born in the fifties, but he loved Ellen's. A cheeseburger, fries and a chocolate shake had become a typical lunch for him, and the place was his second home. Third, if he had to count the office. Which he didn't want to do. He'd always been prone to tension headaches, undue stress and anxiety, but ever since he'd taken his current position at Barron, Gardner & Shaw, Foggy had been even more on edge. He'd gained weight, partially because of his many visits—escapes was more like it—to Ellen's, but he felt he'd been driven there by pressures at the office.

It wasn't that he wasn't completely capable of the job. The firm had placed their confidence in him because they knew his track record and his abilities. He was great in preparation and research, a great performer in court, taken seriously by judges, but he just wasn't that good with clients on a one-on-one basis. That was a definite weak spot. Despite his record, and his brief stint as DA, he often had a hard time getting clients to believe in him.

That had always been Matt's job. Matt Murdock had been Foggy Nelson's best friend since college. They'd opened their law practice together, and as far as Foggy had been concerned, they would have closed it together as well if fate had not gotten in the way. Matt had been the point man, the one who dealt with the police, with the press at times, and the one who won over the clients when necessary. So sometimes Foggy got stuck with more of the grunt work. So what? It was worth it for them to have what they always wanted.

But then Matt had been wrongly accused of a myriad of crimes and unethical activities. He had been disbarred, and Nelson & Murdock had gone under. Foggy took the job with Barron, Gardner & Shaw in order to save his career. But he didn't like it. He missed Matt, their dynamic together, their ability to choose the people they would represent, to fight for justice without ever worrying about compromising their beliefs.

And nobody at the firm called him Foggy. It was Franklin, or Mr. Nelson, but never Foggy. It just didn't feel right, there. Nothing did. To Matt, though, he would always be Foggy.

While his life was going sour, Matt had gotten paranoid, pushed all his friends away. He'd even suspected for a while that Foggy had something to do with his troubles. That had hurt. Badly. But Foggy forgave him, of course. He had no idea what he would have done in the same situation.

It had been weeks since he had seen his former partner. He hadn't even been there when Matt had come by to take his stuff out of their old office. Foggy had been there for Karen while she was going through some rough times. He'd taken care of her when she'd come back to town with an abusive boyfriend in tow. But once Karen and Matt got together again, they seemed to disappear from his life. Not that he had romantic feelings for Karen, oh no. But he loved her just the same. They'd shared too much in the old days when she'd been Nelson & Murdock's secretary, then Matt's girlfriend, for Foggy not to care.

For days, he had no idea what had happened to the two of them. And then he'd gotten a phone call late one night. Matt wanted Foggy to know that everything was all right, that he and Karen were getting by, and that he knew Foggy was a loyal friend. But Foggy was still worried. He tried to convince Matt to let him go to bat again, to try to get him reinstated to the bar so he could practice law again, so they could be a team again. Matt didn't want to talk about it, and Foggy's only hope was that maybe his old friend just wasn't prepared for that kind of battle yet.

Foggy shivered, wishing again that he'd worn a t-shirt as he pulled open the door of Ellen's Stardust Diner. There was a small line, but he moved to the front and told the hostess he was meeting someone, a Mr. Murdock. The woman knew right away who he was talking about . . . they always did, people didn't forget a young, handsome blind man too quickly. A waiter led the way into the main dining room and Foggy saw Matt there, in a corner booth. He was going to wave and then felt foolish. How many times had he forgotten Matt was blind? Thousands. But the guy was so comfortable with his blindness, so adept at maneuvering through his surroundings, that he made it very easy to forget he couldn't see at all.

Foggy was excited and dismayed. Excited because he hadn't seen Matt in person for a while and was happy to see his friend looking well. Dismayed because he had some very bad news to share.

"Hey, Matt," he said, taking the seat opposite his friend, "it's great to see you. You look good."

"Thanks, Foggy," Matt said with a warm, genuine smile. "You seem like you're doing pretty well yourself."

"Yeah, well, I'm doing okay I guess. How's Karen?" Foggy asked, and Matt smiled even wider.

"She's great. Her work at St. Bridget's really has her going, and her day job is a drag but brings in a couple of bucks," Matt said.

"Hey, now, Matt," Foggy said quickly, "you know if you ever need . . ."

"No, Foggy, but thanks. We're doing fine. I'm doing a little work at home, and between us we're getting by very nicely. I do appreciate it, though. I can always count on you."

The waitress came then, and Foggy ordered his usual. Matt listened carefully and just asked for the same. The poor guy, Foggy thought. He couldn't even see the way the waitress beamed at him with obvious attraction, a blind guy in jeans and a sweater. Now that was quite a disadvantage. Foggy was pleased that Matt had ordered just what he'd gotten. That was another thing he could always count on Matt for, no jokes, comments or otherwise unwelcome remarks about his weight. So he was carrying an extra forty or so, it wasn't like he was obese!

"How's the new job?" Matt asked, and Foggy snapped to attention. This was, after all, what he'd come to talk about, but he had wanted to ease into it.

"Something the matter?" Matt asked, when he'd been silent too long. "Foggy?"

"Yeah," he finally answered. "Yes, Matt, there is definitely something the matter."

Matt cocked his head, listening. Prepared to help, as usual. At that moment, Foggy knew with perfect clarity that never in his life would he have another friend like Matt Murdock, and once again he was grateful their friendship had survived the recent turmoil. It hadn't helped that Foggy had started dating Matt's shrugged aside girlfriend, Glorianna O'Breen. The guilt from that had been extraordinary. But it didn't seem to matter to Matt. There was too much between them, and besides, he had Karen back now. Glori was another life, one that almost seemed to belong to a completely different person.

"I'm making a ton of money, Matt, money I could never have even dreamed of when we were partners," Foggy said sadly.

"This is a bad thing?" Matt asked, with a half smile.

"Not the money, no," Foggy admitted. "But it isn't what I wanted for me, for Nelson & Murdock. It's not what I ever wanted, to be in some high-priced firm making money hand over fist working for celebrities and keeping guilty people out of jail."

"Ah," Matt nodded, understanding now. Foggy knew his old friend shared his feelings about the law, and justice, and the ethics of the legal profession. That's why he'd wanted to talk to Matt about his current situation, and also why he feared their discussion.

"So they've got you defending criminals and you feel like one yourself, like you're doing something crooked for money?"

"Sort of," Foggy mumbled. "But it's more than that."

"Foggy, listen," Matt said, searching across the table for his friend's hand and grasping it tightly for a moment before letting it go again. "Our constitution guarantees everybody a right to fair trial and, essentially, to an objective defense. Even the guilty. If that makes you uncomfortable enough that you can't enjoy the money, then quit. If you can reconcile it as just doing your duty as an attorney, you shouldn't have any problem."

"But, Matt, some of them I *know* are guilty," Foggy pleaded. "What would you do?"

"Me?" Matt asked. "Well, Fog, I'm not a lawyer anymore, so I don't know what I'd do. I suppose I'd follow my heart."

Foggy heaved a sigh.

"That's okay, Matt," he said. "I know what you'd do, I know where your heart would lead you. And you're right. But I still think I've got to deal with this on a case-by-case basis. Maybe this dilemma is why they invented plea bargaining? That way, the defense attorney can feel like he's doing his duty to his client and the client still gets convicted and goes to jail. Maybe it's not enough, but it's something, isn't it?"

"It's something, at least," Matt answered, his face etched with sincerity. "Some time is better than no time . . . but that isn't all that's bothering you, is it Foggy?"

"No," he shook his head. "it isn't. That's just the core of it really. What's really getting to me is something you're not going to want to hear any more than I did, something I'm afraid I can't turn away from, something I need to do something about and I want your input on it."

The food came then, and the two men fell into a natural, comfortable silence. They'd been friends for a long time. Matt didn't push. He simply waited quietly for Foggy to come out with whatever it was he wasn't saying. Finally, he did.

"We've been retained to defend Gary Wiezak, and I'm on the defense team," Foggy said, the shame in his voice audible even to himself. "I don't know if I can do it. I'm really thinking about quitting."

Elbows on the table, Matt steepled his fingers and rested his chin on top, almost as if he were looking right at Foggy, almost as if he could see.

"God, I wish we were back in business, Matt," Foggy said, and felt his eyes begin to fill. "Can't we start working on getting your license back? I need you, Matt."

"No you don't," Matt answered insistently. "You just need to be Foggy Nelson. You're a great man and a great attorney, Fog; you'll know what to do. We learned together to do what was right, within the confines of the law. But I don't serve the law anymore, so my answer may not be appropriate for you. You still serve the law, so you've got to think of that, and then decide whether you stay or go."

"But Matt," Foggy said softly, "the things he's done. The fires are just part of what they've got him for. But that alone is enough. A lot of people died, Matt. How can I . . . ?"

"I wish I could help you, Foggy," Matt said. "And once you decide what to do, I'll back you a hundred percent. But this one you've got to figure out on your own."

"You know," Foggy said, shaking his head. "I always know what you're going to say, and I always know you're going to be right. But I guess I just need to hear you say it."

They ate their meal in a haze of small talk—business, friends, gossip—and when Foggy picked up the bill, Matt let him. Times certainly had changed, Foggy thought, and not for the better. One of these days, Matt Murdock would be back on top, happy again.

Mighty presumptuous of you, Foggy, he admonished himself. *You don't know Matt's unhappy.*

Maybe he was just projecting.

"Thanks for lunch," Matt said as they went out into the overcast gray pall of Broadway, leaving the fifties wonderland of Ellen's Stardust Diner behind. Foggy realized then that Matt couldn't really enjoy the atmosphere in Ellen's, and he wondered how aware Matt was of how much of life he was missing. He hoped not too much.

"Thank *you* for meeting me," Foggy answered. "It was really great to see you, Matt. It's been like getting a divorce, not having you around after being together so long."

"I know what you mean," Matt said with a warm smile. "Y'know, if you're not doing anything tonight, why don't you come over to our place? Nothing fancy, maybe pizza? I'm sure Karen would be very happy to see you. About eight, if you're free?"

"That would be great, Matt," Foggy said effusively. "I really miss you guys."

"We miss you, too, Foggy," Matt said. "And one of these days, maybe I will be ready to fight for myself again, to try to take back what's mine. We'll be the team supreme again. Until then, you know I'm always here if you need anything.''

"Funny," Foggy smiled. "That's what my ex-wife said.''

Chapter 10

FTER THE MORNING HE'D HAD, THERE WERE TWO ways Daredevil's mood could have swung. One option was depression: after talking to Melvin Potter about Betsy's disappearance, and then hearing from Foggy that he was supposed to be defending the monster whose criminal ambitions had left nearly two dozen people dead and many more homeless—part of him hoped Foggy would quit, but Matt could understand why he wouldn't—well, after all that, Daredevil had every right to be depressed.

His other major option was fury. It was really no contest.

Daredevil set off across the rooftops for the Kingpin's headquarters, ignoring the cold wind in his face. He could not see the dark storm clouds that hung, pregnant with freezing rain, in the sky above, but he had felt the diminishing strength of the sun on his skin all morning, and he knew without seeing that those clouds were there. He could smell rain on the way. A storm brewed in his soul quite similar to the one above, but he hoped that its explosion wasn't as inevitable.

He felt the first drops of rain sting his face, and was glad, for just a moment, that the clothes he'd left on a rooftop after his lunch with Foggy were in a waterproof briefcase.

Within another block it was pouring. He kept going, but was far more careful now, going down to the pavement when he had to cross a street or avenue. The rain fell in sheets that disrupted his radar, deflected it, confused him. It took all his concentration to keep his footing as he leaped from one building to the next, over a narrow alley. He was relying more on sound and smell than usual, bolstering his now-limited radar with his enhanced natural senses.

Even through the hiss and harsh patter of the falling rain, he heard someone drop lightly to the roof ahead of him. He heard easy breathing and a calm heartbeat, one he almost recognized. If he could just get a scent . . . but the rain was too heavy. His muscles tensed as he moved into a defensive position, hands slightly raised, legs spread.

But then she spoke. "Hello, Matt. It's been a while."

Daredevil relaxed, releasing a cleansing breath, and walked toward the woman on the roof. They met there in the cold rain and regarded each other for a long moment.

"Hello, Natasha," Daredevil said.

Her name was Natasha Romanova, though she'd been called by many others. Once she had been a Russian spy, and her defection had been very, very messy. With help from Nick Fury, the director of the Strategic Hazard Intervention, Espionage, and Logistics Directorate (SHIELD), and the Avengers she'd made the transition safely and used her skills and experience for America instead. Her code name during all of this was Black Widow.

When the Black Widow met Daredevil, something

clicked between them. For a time, Natasha gave up espionage and dedicated herself to fighting crime at Matt Murdock's side. Partners, lovers, friends. And friends they remained, even when the rest had disappeared. They watched out for one another, offered a sympathetic ear, a word of support or advice, or reliable cover under fire. Few people had ever, or would ever, get as close to Daredevil as the Black Widow had.

Matt and Natasha's friendship was eternal, and he felt all the more guilty for having shut her out along with everyone else during his recent troubles.

"Natasha, I . . ." he began, but she put a finger to his lips.

"Not another word, old friend," she said. "Humility ill becomes you."

These days Natasha was splitting her time between working special gigs for SHIELD, because of her loyalty to Nick Fury, and running around acting like what the newspapers had dubbed a super hero. That label was only semi-accurate since, other than being a superb martial artist, and being armed by SHIELD weapons developers, the Black Widow was a normal human woman.

"How are things going for you now, Matt?" the Widow asked, and Daredevil could hear the genuine concern in her voice. "How is it with Karen?"

"Karen's great, 'Tasha. I've got that, at least, to be thankful for. I don't think she and I have ever been closer. We've both been through so much lately . . . listen to me, comparing what I've been through with her tragedies. She's been through hell, and I'm glad she survived it. We're doing fine.

"On the other hand, I'm still recovering from everything that happened recently. Fisk hurt me bad, Natasha. Worse than I could have imagined. And yet in some ways, in destroying my life as Matt Murdock, he seems to have freed me. As Daredevil, I've never felt more driven, more motivated . . . and less restrained by my 'real' life. I'm working things out."

"That's good news," Natasha said, but added nothing more.

The rain was letting up some, and he could make her out fairly well now, especially this close. Even with his radar he could tell that her short, soft hair was plastered to the side of her face by rainwater. He was cold, and he was sure that Natasha was as well.

"You didn't come out here in the rain just to ask me how I am," he said without doubt.

"No," she agreed. "No I didn't. I had a meeting with Fury this morning, on a mission he has coming up that he'd really like me in on. You know I have a real hard time saying no to Nick. Could be his forceful manner, but I think it's just cause I know he'll keep asking until his voice goes, and I say yes just to get out of the room and away from the cloud of noxious stink from his cigars."

Matt frowned. Natasha Romanova was not a woman to avoid a topic. Generally she came right to the matter at hand. This time, though, there was hesitation in her voice.

"Spit it out, Widow," he finally said, and she sighed with obvious relief.

"Look, Nick has a way of telling people things he thinks they should know, or pass on to someone else. He told me something in passing that he claimed was top secret, that I was not, under any circumstances, to repeat any of what I heard. It had to do with an Egyptian diplomat and a minor cabinet member and it's the basis for the mission he wants me for.

"But more importantly, he told me some things relating to the case that he probably didn't have to. And even though I'm sworn to secrecy, and he would never admit it, well, I believe that he told me these things because he knew I would be compelled to tell you.

"In the past several months there have been a significant number of high-profile assassinations in Europe, Asia, and Africa. SHIELD thinks that the killer is Bullseye."

Before Daredevil could open his mouth, the Black Widow continued.

"All accounts indicate the man is loonier than ever, and that he is now on his way stateside, presumably to New York. SHIELD's mission has to do more with the people who were paying Bullseye than with the assassin himself. But Fury implied, in that way of his, that he assumed Bullseye would be coming after you. I thought you should know."

His mind was racing. Why was Bullseye coming back to New York? Did he have an assignment to murder someone here in the States? Was he simply aching for home, or was he returning specifically to come after Daredevil for the umpteenth time? There was no way to tell. The only thing he did know was that now, on top of Betsy Potter's disappearance and the case against Gary Wiezak, his time would be divided even further to include finding out what the hell Bullseye was up to. He was one of the most dangerous men Daredevil had ever known. Wherever Bullseye went, death followed. Daredevil couldn't just let him walk around the city, his city, loose.

"Thanks, Natasha," he said quietly. "For caring, for taking the trouble to find me, for standing in the rain getting soaked. I appreciate it more than you know. And thank Fury for me, too, in whatever politically correct manner you would deem acceptable."

Natasha only smiled, then walked to the edge of the building where Daredevil guessed there was a fire escape.

"You know, Daredevil," she said, not wanting to say his real name too loud, even as she turned to face him again. "It's been a long time since we were partners, but I'm always there for you. If you need backup, or just someone to talk to, you only have to call."

"I know. Thanks."

"Still going to see the Kingpin alone, though, aren't you?" she asked with light sarcasm in her voice.

At first he was going to ask how she knew where

he was going, but then he thought better of it. She was the Black Widow. She knew, or she had guessed correctly, but either way, she was rarely wrong.

When Natasha disappeared over the side of the building, Daredevil went to the edge and through the still-weakening rainfall, could barely make her out as she hailed a cab. It pulled over—nothing short of a miracle during a rainstorm in Manhattan—and she got in, likely soaking the back seat. But the cabbie had probably stopped because she was Natasha Romanova, the Black Widow. Everyone knew her identity. She was famous.

Daredevil wondered for a moment, and not for the first time, what it would be like to do what he did without the mask, without the mythic persona of Daredevil to hide behind. What if he was just Matt Murdock, the way the Widow was Natasha Romanova? What would his life be like? It was an easy question to answer, given recent events. His life had been torn apart, he had almost been killed, simply because the Kingpin had discovered the secret of his identity. As of yet, Wilson Fisk had not chosen to share that information with the general public, or with other criminals, as far as he knew.

Life without the mask would be even more dangerous than it already was. He didn't know how the Black Widow managed it, but he did not envy her celebrity.

The Kingpin had chosen to stash Sean Mallory forty minutes north of Manhattan in a quaint little

Westchester County town called Dobbs Ferry. He owned countless properties, both business and residential, and many of them legitimate . . . until he needed them for more shady enterprises.

Bullseye knew the Kingpin as well as anyone. It hadn't been difficult for him to figure out where Mallory would be hidden. He'd stayed there himself several times. It was a quiet little place called Richard James' Pub that served one hundred different brands of beer and excellent buffalo wings. The building's middle and top floors were two apartments, only one of which was rented. The other was for guests of Wilson Fisk, the Kingpin.

Bullseye remembered Mallory. He'd been a grunt a couple years back when the assassin had first met him, and he was still a grunt. Some people aren't destined for greatness, Bullseye observed, but where would we be without the grunts of the world? Unfortunately for Mallory, he'd been in the wrong place at the wrong time.

Kind of like today.

It was an ugly, rainy autumn day. It'd be no great loss to stay inside all day long. But the two idiots guarding Mallory had decided that, instead of bringing food upstairs, all three of them would come down into the pub for lunch. On top of that, they were drinking thick, dark beer in pint glasses.

Granted, they didn't expect Bullseye. They figured one of Wiezak's flunkies would come gunning for their buddy Mallory. In a way, Bullseye couldn't blame them for not taking that as a serious threat.

But still, that was no reason to act foolish. If Fisk could see these two now, he'd kill them himself. In a sense, Bullseye was already working for him, doing him a favor by erasing these two muscle-bound losers.

Bullseye stood in the rain across the street from Richard James' Pub and watched as a waitress brought a huge plate of steaming buffalo wings over to the table, along with another round of beers. Then he stepped off the curb toward the pub. He shed his jacket and hat, revealing the costume underneath. He didn't pull his pistol, didn't bother with covert action. Stealth was not required in this situation. Bullseye pushed through the door of the pub, a waitress screamed and dropped a tray of drinks. The bartender's face blanched, and he started to reach under the bar, obviously going for some kind of weapon.

"Not if you want to live," Bullseye snarled, rain dripping from the tip of his nose.

The two goons guarding Mallory were so surprised to see him, they were paralyzed for a moment.

"Well," he said, imitating Clint Eastwood, "you boys going to stand there and whistle Dixie, or are you gonna pull them pistols?"

Though they had to have known getting up and running away would have been their only chance of survival, the two men reached for their guns. Poor Sean Mallory merely sat in his chair, his face crestfallen, tears welling in his eyes. Bullseye grabbed a pair of steak knives from the table in front of him and hurled them with incredible speed. Both of Mallory's guards shrieked as the steak knives impaled them each in the heart. They fell to the hardwood floor, guns clattering nearby.

"Pass the A-1!" the killer cried happily.

Mallory looked up at Bullseye, and pleaded. "Hey, man. I didn't do anything to you. Come on, you remember me, don't'cha? I'm just doing what the big man tells me. Please, Bullseye . . ."

Bullseye frowned. He hated cowards more than anything. After killing a spineless jellyfish like Mallory, he always felt dirty from the contact alone.

"Come on, Sean," he said harshly. "Take it like a man."

"Take it . . ." Mallory gasped, realizing he was, indeed, about to die. He quickly scanned the room, then dove for the guns on the floor.

Bullseye snatched a shot glass off the bar, wound up and pitched it at Mallory. It impacted with the target's nose, shattering the bridge and sending bone shards straight into his brain. Sean Mallory was dead before he hit the floor.

Of the three witnesses whose execution Wiezak had assigned to him, Bullseye had specifically chosen Mallory to be first. If the Kingpin had known Bullseye was involved, he would have taken greater, though still fruitless, precautions. Plus, when he killed the arsonist, he was supposed to nail some detective named Tyson as well. Now, the assassin regretted going after Mallory first. It had been too easy.

Either way, though, he was saving one particular

target for last. Wiezak's plans had been getting in the way of Bullseye's vendetta against Daredevil. But now, the two had begun to coalesce. Daredevil had become a real problem for Wiezak, to the point where a confrontation between Bullseye and the redman was inevitable. Even more exciting, one of Bullseye's current targets was a longtime friend of Daredevil's, a woman named Karen Page.

Bullseye looked around the pub. The few customers that had been eating when he walked in were hiding under their tables or had run to the restroom. Two waiters had gone into the kitchen, and he'd thought one of them looked stupid enough to try to come back with a weapon, but it didn't happen. That left a waitress and the bartender, both of whom stood without moving by the long oak bar.

"Tell Mr. Fisk that it doesn't pay to have me employed elsewhere," he said to the bartender. "I'm still seeking a full-time position."

He walked out laughing, his back to the room in an insulting display of diffidence. Bullseye wanted to get back to Manhattan quickly; there was a lot more killing to be done today. Back on the street, he sang softly in the rain, a tune from a Broadway show he couldn't recall.

Daredevil stood in a familiar spot on the roof of a building which faced the rear of Fisk Industries' Tower. The rain had lightened considerably; it was merely drizzling now. He was trying to decide whether to go straight through the lobby this time, just for variety. On reflection, since Fisk had told him that he would not be welcome should he try to visit again, just walking in might be a bad idea. So it would have to be the garage again.

He was waiting for a convenient decoy vehicle when fortune smiled on him for the first time in at least a week. The garage gate opened, its top and bottom jaws widening to allow a long black limousine to slide from the mouth, slowly moving up to the street. Its left turn signal was on, and Daredevil swung on the line of his billy club down into the street, landing right in front of it. The driver started to beep, but Daredevil didn't move an inch. He stood like that lone student in front of a tank in Tiannanmen Square, one soft human body against the power of dark kings. Or in this case, of one king.

The beeping stopped. A cab came up behind the limo and simply went around. The limo started to move forward, slowly but inexorably closing the distance between its bumper and Daredevil's legs.

He could smell roasting chestnuts, and knew that fall was going to turn to winter very quickly. Exhaust fumes were almost overpowering in the city, but he did his best to shut them out. He could hear all the sounds of New York, sirens and street corner hot dog vendors, the squealing of hydraulic city bus brakes, and the high-volume rantings of a homeless former mental patient.

Then he shut it all out, all the noise, every sound, and focused on the limousine, through its bullet-proof, supposedly soundproof glass, he listened for words from inside, for conversation, and found none. There were only the heartbeats of the Kingpin and of his driver, and the scrunching, crinkling noise of the leather seat as Fisk shifted in his seat.

The limo had moved forward as far as it could without hitting Daredevil, and the hero knew that it would go no further. He had hoped to intrigue the Kingpin enough to make him cooperative instead of belligerent, or at least a combination of both. When the rear passenger window began to slide down, he knew that he had accomplished that feat.

A large, meaty hand stuck out of the window, and a single, upraised finger beckoned him to the door. Daredevil, not caring at this point that it was broad daylight and there was a huge potential for people to see him getting into the car with the Kingpin of Crime, moved quickly to the door. He heard it unlock with a heavy click just before he pulled at the handle, and he slid quickly in, next to the man he hated most in the world.

"I thought we had decided that you weren't going to visit me anymore," the Kingpin said immediately.

Daredevil swiveled his head to "look" at his nemesis, though his radar could have picked the man's features up without turning to face him. He often wished he could see colors, for it had been a subject of great amusement for him at times to wonder what color suit would look best on a four hundred fifty pound bald man.

"*You* decided I wouldn't be back, not me," Daredevil said evenly, not wanting to smile or to seem too angry; either could end the discussion in seconds. "Besides, I'm not visiting. I was hitchhiking, and you picked me up."

"It's dangerous to hitchhike these days, Daredevil," the Kingpin said. "I'm on my way to a very important meeting. I would appreciate it if you would get to the point. Your attempts at levity, if that is what they are, are tiresome as well as time-consuming."

The Kingpin leaned forward and pressed an intercom button.

"What are you waiting for, dolt?" the Kingpin asked angrily. "Drive."

"This is not what I came to ask, but did you know that Bullseye is back in New York?"

The Kingpin raised an eyebrow.

"No, but it doesn't surprise me," he said, and Daredevil knew he was telling the truth.

"Why doesn't it surprise you?"

"Not that it's any of your business, but I have reason to believe that a former, hmm, associate of mine has expressed an interest in a hostile takeover of my holdings. I believe that he might know of Bullseye's skills, though from where I couldn't imagine."

"Nor could I," Daredevil went along with the lie, even as Fisk smiled to show what a farce all this evasion was. They both knew exactly what the other was talking about, but the Kingpin always felt it necessary to cloud the issues. He would not admit he was talking about Gary Wiezak, just as he would never admit that he was responsible for any illegal activity. That would be bad business.

Daredevil's radar sense stretched out to its limit and he recognized the area they were passing through, heading north. He guessed that wherever the Kingpin was going, it was likely in the Bronx or Westchester, and he didn't have time to run home from there, so he had to make this Q&A as fast as he could. He listened for a moment to the hypnotic shush-shush of the windshield wipers, and then they began to screech across the glass until the driver clicked them off. The rain had all but stopped.

"It's no secret you've been looking for a new enforcer-slash-bodyguard-slash-assassin . . ." he began.

"I am shocked and appalled by your allegations and your tone," the Kingpin interrupted. "The man you once were would know that the law . . ."

"I don't care much for the law anymore," he lied, but it shut Wilson Fisk up, at least for the moment. "Now, did you decide to give Bullseye his old job back?"

He knew the answer was no because of what the Kingpin had already said, but he wanted to hear it from the big man's lips, to listen to his heart as the words came out.

"Don't be ridiculous!" the Kingpin said, anger mixing with incredulity. "Just for the sake of argument, and speaking hypothetically of course, let's imagine I'm in the market for such an employee. The man you know as Bullseye is a psychotic, certifiably insane. He may be skilled, but he is totally unstable and completely unreliable. What sane person would hire such a man for any job, let alone one that would bring him so dangerously close, close enough to do serious damage if he went over the edge?''

For just a moment, Daredevil thought that Wilson Fisk, the Kingpin of crime, was the slightest bit afraid of Bullseye. But he pushed that idea away. As far as he knew, Fisk had never been afraid of anything.

"Now I think you should go," the Kingpin said.

Daredevil couldn't have agreed more. They were moving more quickly than he would have imagined in city traffic, but then he remembered his earlier thoughts about the power of the Kingpin and of his vehicle, and he knew that even the cabbies would get out of this limousine's path.

"You said you'd cooperate all you could on the case of Gary Wiezak," Daredevil reminded him.

"I am capable of remembering my words."

"Well, I'm tired of verbally sparring with you, so let me cut to the chase."

"Yes," the Kingpin said with amusement. "Oh, yes. Please do."

"Wiezak was working for you, he got too big for his britches and you cut him loose. Now Wiezak is after your job, and you're funneling information to the DA's office in order to help bring him down and keep him down. I don't know why Bullseye is coming, but I suspect I'll be seeing him shortly one way or another. I suspect that you will see him as well . . . one way or another."

Daredevil paused, waiting for that to sink in, then continued.

"Wiezak's going to face trial, and he's going to go to jail. If I can make sure that happens, then that thorn will be out of your side. And mine as well. However, there is one question, the most important question that remains, and that is what happened to Betsy Potter. I know her kidnapping is tied in with this little war Wiezak is waging against you. So let me ask you straight. Do you have Betsy Potter?"

"No," the Kingpin said, a cold anger burning in his words.

"Do you have any idea as to her whereabouts?"

"None," the crime lord said, and the one word was clipped short by the snapping of his teeth, like the gnashing jaws of a rabid dog.

Daredevil listened closely as the Kingpin answered each question. His heartbeat had increased slightly in agitation, but neither time had it jumped the way it would have if he was lying. Clearly, though, he had overstayed his welcome. But at that point, he figured, why not go for broke.

"Did you order, or have anything to do with organizing the kidnapping of Betsy Potter?" Daredevil asked, and he concentrated on the Kingpin's heartbeat as if it was the only sound he could hear . . . the only sound he had ever heard.

"Now, why would I do that?" the Kingpin asked. It wasn't an answer, and so of course he couldn't determine the truth or falsehood of a question.

"I don't know, but I'd have to guess it would be

to get to her husband for some reason," Daredevil said reasonably.

"Daredevil, you are beginning to bore me," the Kingpin said. "The Gladiator would rather sew than kill anyone."

The Kingpin was good, Daredevil had to give him that. His summation of Melvin Potter was an accurate, if caustic one. And yet, Wilson Fisk had managed yet again to avoid answering a direct question, confirming for Daredevil once and for all that Fisk was involved with Betsy Potter's kidnapping. He was certain, however, that he would get no straight answers on the subject today, or any day, if he wasn't willing to beat them out of the gargantuan human filling two thirds of the rear of the limo.

And that would get him nowhere.

"Let's say, hypothetically, that your organization had some knowledge or connection to Betsy Potter's disappearance," Daredevil began.

"Let's not," the Kingpin said, and it was not a suggestion. Daredevil heard the crunch of leather and the rustle of cotton as the Kingpin tensed, prepared to kill, or at least try to kill, Daredevil right there in the limo if necessary. But the hero went on.

"If, hypothetically, that had happened, would it be fair then to say, hypothetically, that with the severing of all ties between your organization and Gary Wiezak, your involvement with the woman's disappearance would have ended."

The Kingpin didn't speak. Daredevil could hear his heart pounding as it pumped blood through the intricate systems of that enormous body. But he could not hear a single breath. When the Kingpin exhaled, Daredevil could feel the warmth of it, like steam from the nostrils of a dragon.

"You are coming dangerously close to angering me," Wilson Fisk said in a low growl. "I should think, after all that we have been through, that you would have grown wiser. Do not confuse boldness for courage. Boldness is merely stupidity."

"It's a hypothetical situation," Daredevil said, leaning comfortably back against the leather now, in a relaxed and smiling pose that would only make the big man angrier. "And it's a fairly easy question to answer. Would it be fair to say that in that hypothetical situation, the severing of ties with Wiezak would end any involvement you might have with the troubles currently facing the Potter family?"

The Kingpin glared.

"Hypothetically," Daredevil pushed.

The Kingpin opened his window slightly, looking out at the street as he breathed in the damp smell of Manhattan after a rainstorm. Exhaust fumes were most prevalent in the air.

"Yes," he finally said. "Hypothetically, yes."

"Thank you," Daredevil said, the words tasting sour in his mouth. He hated this man more than any other. Fisk had essentially admitted that he had been behind Betsy Potter's kidnapping, or had at least been aware of it.

And yet, he wasn't lying about no longer being involved with the situation. Betsy was just one of many files left open when the Kingpin severed his ties with Wiezak, and of no concern to Fisk himself. For Betsy's sake, at least for the time being, Daredevil had to forget about the Kingpin's involvement. Taking down Wiezak was the only thing that concerned him now. He prayed that he would find Betsy unharmed, but it was not a prayer uttered with a great amount of faith.

The Kingpin thumbed a button on a console built into the car door.

"Pull over," was all he said, and the car began to slow.

He kept his face forward, apparently unwilling to look at his most hated enemy.

"If you are an intelligent man, Daredevil . . . and I believe that once upon a time, you were . . . you will allow a significant amount of time to pass before you pay me another visit. I find your company often disturbs me, and I don't like to be disturbed."

Daredevil had the door opened, but he didn't get out just yet.

"Don't flatter yourself, Fisk," Daredevil said through his teeth, his lip drawn back in an uncharacteristic snarl. "You're a powerful man, in many ways, but you've had your chance at me. You've done your worst. And I'm still here, aren't I? On the other hand, I've never taken a real good crack at you."

"The day I fall, it won't be you who pushes me," the Kingpin said. "But on that day, the war to fill the void left by my departure will tear this city apart. It isn't worth it to you to have to deal with the consequences. You don't have the heart for it."

"Perhaps not," Daredevil admitted. "But every day those consequences seem a little less intimidating."

Chapter 11

"I T FEELS WRONG, PROTECTING THIS GUY, LIEUTEN-
ant," Detective Scott Shapiro said. "He's been
driving this city crazy for weeks with those fires.
A lot of people died. It just doesn't seem right."

Garth Bryce chewed his lip.

"The guy's a demon all right," he said. "But if we
can keep him alive, we might be able to take down
the devil himself. Even if it doesn't seem worth it to
you, Detective, as long as you're on my squad, you'll
do whatever it takes to make sure that happens."

Shapiro seemed stunned.

"Yeah, Lieutenant," he threw up his hands. "I
mean, of course. But that doesn't mean I have to like
it. Take a look around, sir. I don't know about you,
but *I've* never stayed anywhere this nice."

Lieutenant Bryce did look around then, and once
again had to silently agree with Detective Shapiro.
The state had put Rodriguez up in the Warwick Hotel, in a suite large enough to give elbow room to
the witness and the two detectives and two uni-
formed officers who'd become his bodyguards. Bryce
and Shapiro had come along just to make sure the
arsonist was safely ensconced in his room, and now
they were getting ready to leave.

But the place itself . . . hell, no, it wasn't right. It
had two marble-walled bathrooms, two bedrooms,
each with a king-size bed and a huge color TV set.
The main room had another TV set and a stereo,

not to mention the wet bar. There was a stone balcony, about fifteen feet wide, which ran outside of the room, nineteen stories above Manhattan. There were gargoyles out there, for God's sake. Friggin' gargoyles.

It spoke volumes about how seriously District Attorney Tower was taking the Wiezak case that they had sprung for a setup like this, and Garth knew that the case would be a huge leg up for Tower's career and reputation. But that didn't take away the feeling of disgust he had as he watched Rodriguez open the small box of gourmet chocolates that had been left by the hotel staff. The firebug looked up at the Lieutenant as he took a piece of candy and popped it, whole, into his mouth.

"Time to go, Detective," Bryce said. "If we don't leave now, I might have to throw up."

"My sentiments exactly, Lieutenant," Shapiro smiled.

"Tyson, we're out of here," Bryce called across the room, and Detective John Tyson, a lean, muscular black man with a bit of a paunch, raised a hand signaling them to wait a moment. He opened a bedroom door and peeked in before Detective Kara Diemer, a buxom red-headed woman, led Rodriguez into the room.

"Hey, Lieutenant," Tyson said as he trotted over to where they stood by the door. "I know the whole squad is going to get a chance to work this detail, but you've got to give me a break. Tonight is a very special night, you know what I'm saying?"

Bryce couldn't help but laugh. Tyson had more girlfriends than there were days of the week, and Diemer, his partner, had taken to calling him "the doctor," because of how smoothly he operated. The other guys in the squadroom had picked up on it, and it had become John Tyson's permanent nickname.

"Look, doc," Lieutenant Bryce said with a smile, "if you can convince Shapiro here to switch with you, it's fine by me. But remember, he comes on at six A.M., and if you switch, you'd better be here on time and without a hangover."

Diemer and Rodriguez came out of the bedroom then, and the plainclothes officers went back on the alert.

"We're all settled in here, Lieutenant," Diemer said, and Garth nodded.

"Come on, Scott, buddy, pal," Tyson began pleading with Shapiro. "You got nothing going tonight, I know that. You haven't been in town long enough to get any business going. Tell you what, you do this for me, maybe we'll go on a double date next week. I'll set it up for you."

Tyson winked, but Garth thought Shapiro looked less than impressed.

"Just think, Scott," Diemer said from the other side of the room, "you switch with John and you get to spend the night with me!"

A sly smile spread across Shapiro's face.

"Well," he said, "when you put it that way . . ."

In an explosion of jagged glass, the doors leading

onto the balcony shattered. Bryce was in the process of drawing his weapon. His target was a body somersaulting across the floor, moving so fast it was nothing but a streak of black . . . until razor sharp shuriken flashed out from the attacker's hands.

Lieutenant Bryce aimed for the intruder, but held off as Shapiro dove in front of him, a pair of shuriken slicing into his chest. Shapiro screamed as he fell to the floor, and beyond him Bryce could see that the two plainclothes officers and Detective Tyson were also down. Tyson and one of the plainclothes cops were both having some kind of seizure, and none of the four were getting up again. He knew then that they were dead, that there was something on those stars. And then he recognized their killer . . .

"Bullseye!" he shouted as he saw the white target on the assassin's chest, even as he and Diemer each fired at that target. The killer was knocked off his feet, landing a couple of yards across the room in a twist of limbs.

"Get back into that bedroom, you idiot!" Diemer yelled at Rodriguez, but the arsonist was enthralled by the arrival of such a famous criminal, sent here just for him.

Diemer stepped carefully toward Bullseye's still form, pistol aimed directly at his head. She nudged the body with her toe. Once, twice, again. Without turning, she said to Bryce, "I don't see any . . ."

"Blood?" Bullseye asked with a laugh, even as he arched his back and kicked her weapon away, grabbing her and holding her as a shield in front of him. It was an impossible move, and Bryce never got a clear shot. He couldn't risk shooting Diemer, but he ought to have known the killer wouldn't be taken down so easily.

"Kevlar is a *wonderful* thing, isn't it?" Bullseye said with a smile.

Bryce wondered then if Diemer was going to be stupid or courageous enough to attempt to break his hold. He wondered what he would do in the same situation.

"Rodriguez!" he shouted. "Get back in that god-damn bedroom right now. Shut the door."

Bullseye looked at him in surprise, then shook his head as if disappointed.

"Don't flatter yourself."

"You've got the upper hand, Bullseye," Lieutenant Bryce said. "What's your move?"

Bullseye's face flared with anger as he sputtered, "Why, you son of a . . . how dare you take that kind of attitude with me! You think I need this woman to have the upper hand against you?"

"No!" Bryce yelled, thinking he'd made a terrible mistake. "No, I . . ."

And then Diemer screamed. She arched her back, almost as if she'd seen something that frightened her, and then she started to fall forward, almost in slow motion. Bryce could see in her eyes that she was dead, and he was firing before she hit the ground.

Bullseye dove under the bullets, taking refuge, Bryce thought, behind Diemer's sprawled form. The lieutenant barely saw the sai slicing through the air before it entered the flesh of his wrist, slamming through his arm between the radius and ulna. His curse was almost a shriek as he dropped his gun and bent over cradling the arm. Remembering Bullseye, he fell to his knees and scrabbled for his gun with his left hand. His fingers closed around it and hope sprang to life in his heart.

And then a white leather boot fell on his hand, and he ground his teeth together as two fingers snapped. He looked up to see Bullseye there, a second sai in his hand, its point inches from Bryce's forehead.

"Rodriguez!" Bullseye called to the bedroom. "It's okay, we got him."

The bedroom door opened and Rodriguez came out. It happened so fast that Bryce barely had time to scream a warning. Incredibly, Rodriguez had half an ignorant smile on his face as Bullseye's blade buried itself deep in his chest with the sound of an axe striking wood. The smile was still there when his corpse hit the hardwood floor.

"Jesus!" Bryce said.

"Tell me about it!" Bullseye shook his head incredulously. "How stupid can you be?"

Then Bullseye leaned over, nearly whispering in Bryce's ear.

"You're lucky I'm feeling particularly lucid today, buckaroo," he hissed. "Otherwise I might not have remembered to leave someone alive. See, somebody's got to tell the press that I was responsible for this so Daredevil will know and come after me. That someone just happens to be you. But don't worry, it doesn't mean I won't come back and kill you later."

Bullseye hauled back his right arm and slapped Bryce hard across the face.

"That's for shooting at me," he said in a huff.

Then he was at the shattered doors, and he turned to Bryce before he went onto the balcony.

Then he was gone. From nineteen stories up.

By the time Daredevil dropped onto the balcony at the Warwick Hotel, startling several officers, one of whom nearly fired at him, the police had already finished going over the scene. He found Lieutenant Bryce sitting on the edge of a king size bed with an EMT carefully bandaging his wrist, and splinting his two broken fingers.

"You should have gone to the hospital," the EMT was saying, almost angrily, as he taped up the bandage.

"No serious breaks, no spouting blood vessels," Bryce answered. "You fixed me up good, Lamarre. Now back off."

"You should have gone to the hospital," Lamarre repeated, then stood back to leave.

"Garth?" Daredevil said, and the lieutenant looked up, angrily.

"Welcome to hell, 'Devil," Bryce said with a sneer. "Pull up a corpse."

"I'm sorry about your people, here, Lieutenant," Daredevil said honestly, and he had a feeling that right now using Bryce's rank would be much more welcome than the chumminess of first names.

"Me too," Bryce nodded, then looked up at Daredevil, and for once the hero was almost glad he couldn't see, couldn't see the pain and anger in the man's eyes.

"I respect you, Daredevil," Bryce said. "As far as I can tell, I even like you. But right now, I don't really want you here. See, this man came in here and killed a bunch of people I was responsible for."

Bryce stood up and went to the window.

"They were my responsibility!" he yelled. "Sure, they knew the chance they took every day on the street, but you hit it right on the head, man. They were my people. I let them down. And no matter how I feel about your involvement, I've got this little voice screaming in the back of my head says it's your fault."

Daredevil didn't react.

"Didn't you hear what I said?" Bryce asked, rounding on him.

"I'm not deaf."

All the steam went out of the lieutenant then, and he relaxed somewhat.

"The only reason I'm alive right now is because he wanted you to know he was back in New York. The only reason! In a sense, your existence alone saved my life. On the other hand, I wonder if your existence had anything to do with ending some of those others." He nodded toward the door that led to the massacre in the other room.

"Lieutenant, I understand your anger," Daredevil said, "and I don't want to belittle it in any way, but we've got another witness to worry about, and I want to make certain that Bullseye can't find her."

"Listen you can't just . . ." Bryce began. "Tell us where to find Page and we'll put her in protective custody."

Daredevil was silent, not wanting to offend. He needn't have worried; Bryce realized the irony of his words.

"Get out of here," was all the Lieutenant could manage, and Daredevil wasn't about to argue.

As a child, nothing had disturbed Matt Murdock more than finishing his dinner on a summer day and not being allowed to go outside because it was already dark. It just wasn't fair. Summer was the time for children. Now, that he was an adult, his feelings had changed. As Daredevil, and even just as Matt Murdock, blind man, he was more comfortable at night. And he enjoyed the chill of autumn. Perhaps the blindness had something to do with it, but he didn't really believe that. He often thought of summer as the time for children, and autumn as the season for adulthood.

Which made him shiver as he thought of winter. No matter how much you liked to ski, skate, snowboard, or whatever, once you passed a certain age, the thought of the frozen, sterile, dark, slow days of winter that lay ahead was depressing. Sure, spring waited on the other side, but it took faith to make it there.

Now the autumn days were flying by much too fast for Matt, and he was certain they were moving even faster for Melvin Potter. It was all happening too fast, Bullseye's return, the Kingpin's evasions, Wiezak's posting bail, the murder of Guillermo Rodriguez. Somewhere out there Betsy Potter was either dead or in the presence of people who'd just as soon kill her as have pancakes for breakfast, whenever the whim struck them. But no matter what his promises to Melvin, he had to make sure that Karen was safe first. Which meant getting her home.

Matt walked quickly toward St. Bridget's. He was blind, true, but his radar more than made up for that. In keeping up the pretense of true blindness, he had forced himself to walk without confidence, to move as unassertively, as inconspicuously as possible. And one day, probably quite soon, he would have to go back to that. As he reconnected with people who knew him as that blind attorney, he risked quite a bit by pretending to be sighted. But for now, he enjoyed striding through the blackness of Hell's Kitchen with purpose on his face.

Matt opened the door to the basement cafeteria of St. Bridget's. Down the stairs and to the left was the kitchen. There he found a somewhat portly woman rooting through a drawer in the refrigerator.

"Excuse me," Matt said, and the woman jumped,

nearly falling over, then held onto the refrigerator door with one hand while pressing the other tightly to her chest, presumably to calm an agitated heart.

"You scared me half to death!" the woman gasped.

"I'm terribly sorry," Matt said, feeling somewhat guilty.

"I'm Sister Ellen," she said, as if he'd asked. "What can I do for you?"

"I need to speak with Karen," he said. "Hasn't she arrived yet?"

Matt's radar could not pick up the telling expressions on people's faces, but most often he did not need to. The body told a story all its own, sometimes even better than the face or eyes ever could. Sister Ellen's heart sped up, and she stood suddenly straighter, muscles bunched. Almost as quickly, she relaxed again, obviously forcing herself.

"I'm sorry," she said curtly, "what was that name again?"

"Karen Page, Sister," he answered. "She's my girlfriend."

"I'm sorry, sir," the aging nun shrugged, and then lied. "We've nobody by that name here. Maybe you ought to try . . ."

"Matt!" Karen called excitedly from the cafeteria, and he sensed her presence immediately. He understood what Sister Ellen had been trying to do and appreciated it, but he was glad that Karen's arrival had relieved him of the burden of trying to convince the woman he was one of the good guys.

"Oh, Karen," Sister Ellen said, almost embarrassed, "this man was looking for you and I thought . . ."

"Don't be silly, Sister," Karen said. "I appreciate your concern more than you know. Just get a good look at Matt, and if any other person of the male persuasion shows up, send 'em packing!"

Karen laughed, and Sister Ellen did too, her apologies quickly forgotten. After being tempered by the fires of her personal hell, Karen was a formidable woman, but she retained a humor and charm that was contagious when she wished it to be.

"I'd say this was a pleasant surprise," Karen said quietly as she led him to a cafeteria table, "but from the look on your face I'm guessing that's not why you're here."

They sat down.

"What's going on, Matt?" she asked worriedly.

"Karen, have you given anyone but Sister Maggie our address or phone number?" Matt asked, not attempting to disguise the gravity in his voice.

"No. You gave it to Natasha and Foggy, and he gave it to Melvin. I can't think of anyone else."

Matt sighed.

"Good," he said. "That gives us a day or so, I hope."

"A day for what?" she asked, grabbing his hand to punctuate her words. "Matt, you're scaring me."

"Bullseye's back and it looks like he's working for Wiezak," he said. "The arsonist, Rodriguez, is dead. And Mallory, the guy working for Fisk, was murdered up in Westchester. It was Bullseye.''

Matt felt Karen's fingers tighten on his own, and he was at once both glad and sorry that he could not see the realization in her eyes, the stunned surprise.

"So I'm next," she exhaled the words, shaking her head. "Well, you're right about the apartment. After tonight, we've got to find somewhere else! He might have found it already."

"He might have," Matt agreed. "But we'll stay together until the trial. It's only three days away, Karen. If they haven't found the sniper by then, you'll be useless and therefore out of danger. If they have, it'll be too late for Wiezak. We'll be okay."

Karen nodded.

"I've just got to clean up a bit and get my things. Let's go talk to Sister Maggie," she said. They stood, walked out of the cafeteria and up the stairs to the storage closet that had been turned into an office for the shelter. Sister Maggie sat staring at something on her desk, pen in hand, when Karen knocked.

"Come in, come in!" she said with pleasure. "I'm always looking for an excuse to avoid paperwork, and you two are the best I can think of. Matt, it's a pleasant surprise to see you."

He took her warm, outstretched hand in both of his and kissed her cheek as Karen sat in the one spare chair in the cramped office. It reminded him of the chair next to the principal's desk in grade school, and Matt smiled at the thought. It seemed appropriate.

"I wish I could visit more often," Matt said, to

himself as well as to Sister Maggie. "You seem well."

"As well as can be expected at my age," she agreed, with a slight edge of bitterness in the last three words.

"Sister, something important's come up," Karen interrupted. "I've got to go, and I don't know when I'll be in next."

Sister Maggie's head inclined toward Karen, and Matt imagined her eyes narrowing with incisive intelligence. She was a very perceptive woman.

"Not until after this trial, right?" the older woman nodded, answering her own question. "Someone's after you. What about the police?"

"The last witness they tried to help is dead, and so are the police who were supposed to protect him," Matt said.

"Karen," Sister Maggie said, deciding upon that information alone, "gather your things and get going."

Karen got up without a word and left the office. Matt smiled despite the seriousness of the situation. Sister Maggie trusted Karen, and Matt as well, implicitly. If they said there was danger, that the cops could not help, that was good enough for her.

"Karen's an amazing girl," Sister Maggie said. "She keeps to herself far too much, but I suppose that's understandable. We value her strength around here. She's been especially good with the families left homeless by the fire. The youngsters love her."

Matt nodded, biting his lip thoughtfully.

"That's the part that angers me the most about

this whole thing," he began. "The families that have lost their homes, the things they've had to endure. It angers me almost beyond reason to know that the people and their children have nowhere else to go. But when I was walking through the kitchen, I could hear a child laughing. It gave me hope."

Matt almost never spoke so openly about such feelings, but with Sister Maggie, it was hard not to open up.

"I know what you mean," she said, her tone prompting him to continue.

"Once, when I was a kid, before I lost my sight of course, I betrayed the one promise I had always made my father . . . I got into a fight. He hit me for that, the only time he ever hit me. Battlin' Jack Murdock, professional boxer, belted his son. It changed me for life, made me realize that even the best people need rules, need laws to follow. That certain things were just wrong, and that someone had to do something about them.

"If that one terrible moment in my life could have so vastly affected my destiny, what will the trauma these kids have gone through do to each of them? How can we expect them to just move on?"

"We can't, Matthew. You know that. Nobody heals alone," Sister Maggie said. She was right. No matter how many years had passed since the death of his father, it was only his rare closeness to others, Foggy, Elektra, Natasha, and of course, Karen, that had helped him to heal.

"I'm *sure* that your father was haunted by his actions until the day he died," Sister Maggie said, and the certainty of her tone shook Matt from his reverie.

"How can you be so sure?" he asked, but Sister Maggie said nothing. Matt couldn't be certain, but he guessed she was smiling.

Jack Murdock raised his son Matthew alone, his wife Grace having passed on when the boy was too small to remember more than a scent, a sound, a hand, or an object that represented all he would know of his mother.

Except that Matt Murdock no longer believed that his mother was dead. He and Sister Maggie avoided discussing Matt's fervent belief that she had once been a woman named Grace Murdock. He had asked her once, blatantly, if she was his mother, and she had denied it. He'd thought, at the time, that her heart had skipped a beat, been sure she was lying. But in the weeks, months, since then, he'd begun to wonder if he wasn't just hearing what he wanted to hear.

No matter. He believed Sister Maggie was his mother. She knew he believed it. They didn't discuss it. He would have hated to discover that he'd been wrong.

"Your mother's with God, son," he could remember his father telling him many times as a boy.

And perhaps that was the safest thing for him to say. Jack Murdock hadn't liked to lie.

Chapter 12

MATT AND KAREN WENT CAREFULLY UP THE BACK stairs to their apartment. Neither of them thought they had to worry about Bullseye catching up to them so quickly, but it was impossible to be sure.

Matt was first through the door, and he knew immediately that there was nobody in the room. If Bullseye had been there, or if he showed up before they could find somewhere else to go, his best defense would be surprise. Bullseye did not know that Matt Murdock was Daredevil. Matt didn't want to reveal that to the assassin, but he would do whatever was necessary to gain the upper hand. Karen snapped the deadbolt behind them as if it would mean something when Bullseye showed up.

The answering machine emitted a soft beep. For Matt, a blinking light was not sufficient, and they had shopped around a bit before finding this model. Matt crossed the room and pressed the "play" button.

"Uh, Mr. Murdock, it's Melvin again, Melvin Potter," he sounded scared and frustrated and Karen came over to stand by Matt and listen to the message.

"I'm sorry to bother you again, Mr. Murdock, but you know I can't reach Daredevil on my own . . . they called, Mr. Murdock, the men who took my wife. They said they were calling for the Kingpin, that they'll give her back if I become the Gladiator again.

I'd do anything for Betsy, but they want me to kill him, Mr. Murdock. They want me to kill Daredevil.''

Karen squeezed Matt's bicep, but he didn't turn toward her.

"Don't know what Fisk would want with me," Melvin's recorded voice wondered aloud. "Listen, though. They said no cops, okay? They said . . .''

Beep!

"Damn," Karen said, "he got cut off."

Then the second message began.

"Uh, it's Melvin again, Mr. Murdock. I need your help, and Daredevil's help, and no cops. Definitely no cops. I don't know what to do. They want me to meet them in Battery Park at midnight, with Daredevil's corpse. Then they'll give me Betsy back. Mr. Murdock, what can I do? You've got to . . . help me. . . . please?''

Beep!

"He was crying," Matt observed, running a hand through his auburn hair.

"Wouldn't you?" Karen asked, and he nodded.

"The cops never really believed Melvin was reformed," Matt said. "Apparently, neither did the criminals. It isn't Fisk, though. I've never been more sure of that. Nobody working for him would ever admit it, especially not over the phone."

Even so, Matt had finally begun to realize what had driven someone to kidnap Betsy Potter. Melvin had been mentally unstable, but therapy combined with medication that altered the chemical balance of his brain had changed all that. Melvin was nearly incapable of violence beyond the most perfunctory self-defense. But if someone were able to drive him to violence, there was no telling whether his mind would recover. The Gladiator gone berserk would be a terrible weapon.

"You've got to go," Karen said, and he knew she was right.

Matt picked up the phone without another word and dialed. He had never called the number before, but had memorized it in case of an emergency. Like this one.

The phone rang several times, and then a voice said, "Daredevil?" the Widow said, not using his real name because their uplink was through SHIELD, and likely recorded. "What's wrong?"

Matt felt relief just hearing her voice.

"Widow, do you remember Karen Page?" he asked.

"Matt Murdock's girlfriend?"

"The very one. Seems Bullseye's eliminating potential roadblocks for a local fighter with his eyes on the heavyweight belt. Karen's in the way, and I can't be around tonight."

He could hear Natasha weighing his need against her current SHIELD assignment. In the flickering moment of silence, he prayed her conscience came up on his side, without even knowing what mission she might be aborting to come to his aid.

"You need me now?" the Black Widow asked.

"As soon as you can get here," Matt answered.

"On my way," she said, and then the line was dead.

Matt hung up and turned to Karen. "I should wait until she gets here," he said, torn by the need to get to Melvin before something went drastically wrong and by his vow to protect Karen, not to leave until it was over.

Karen hadn't said a word as she listened to his conversation with the Widow, but she couldn't be happy about it. Natasha had been his lover, once. Now he had called her to come protect his current lover. Karen might have wished it were otherwise, but there was nothing he could do. Who else could he call on who might have a chance against Bullseye? It wasn't as if he were particularly chummy with the Avengers or Fantastic Four.

"No," Karen finally said. "You can't. We don't know Bullseye is even coming here, and Betsy Potter could die if you don't go now."

"You're right," Matt said, but he shook his head anxiously as he grabbed a small, prepacked gym bag from under the bed and headed for the door. He stopped there and turned back to Karen, who had followed right behind him. She put a hand on his shoulder and leaned in close to whisper in his ear.

"I love you," she said.

"Watch yourself," Matt touched Karen's face, ran his fingers down her cheek.

"You watch yourself," she answered. "I'll be fine, here. Maybe I'll give Glori O'Breen a call and we'll have a convention of Matt Murdock's girlfriends, compare notes."

Matt knew she was joking to cover up her nervousness, and was tempted to turn around and stay put. But Karen must have seen that temptation on his face because she put a hand on his chest and pushed him back to the door.

"I love you, too, Karen," he said. "Always have."

Six blocks from the Spotlight Costume Shop, Daredevil heard screaming. He stopped short at the edge of a ten-story building, looking down at the cabs weaving around one another on the street below. Betsy Potter's kidnappers had finally contacted the woman's husband, they were that much closer to finding her, perhaps to saving her life. Melvin was probably as close to the edge as he'd been since giving up his life as the Gladiator.

For the past few days, he'd tried to focus on the Potters and Gary Wiezak. Let the other guys—the super-powered heroes who looked down on New York from gleaming towers—worry about the criminal masterminds for a week or so. The rest of the stuff the cops could handle. They'd done it before he became Daredevil, and they'd be there long after he was gone.

But the screaming wouldn't stop, and he couldn't help but focus his attention on it, pinpointing its location. His feet took several steps in that direction without him consciously willing them to move.

"Scream all you want, you bitch!" Daredevil heard. "I'll be long gone before the cops get here, and I've got half a dozen guys willing to give me an alibi after what you done!"

Though he heard the woman's screamed reply loud enough, her hysteria made it nearly impossible to decipher the words. All Daredevil knew was that she was in pain, and that the man was right . . . the police would not get there in time.

With thoughts of Betsy Potter nagging at his brain like the jangling of a fire alarm, Daredevil set off across the roof. The screams originated from an apartment across the street and halfway up the block. So close, but he knew a life could end in seconds. Daredevil hurled the grappling end of his club across the street where it fell unerringly across an upraised flagpole that jutted out of the face of a huge hotel, wrapping itself around the pole twice. Snapping the line taut under his weight, Daredevil launched himself from the roof without even checking to be sure it was securely fastened.

He swung to the top of the building next to the hotel, then ran across the tops of two buildings, nearly floating. He dropped down onto the lower roof of a newly renovated theater. His radar sense was burning in his head so strong and sharp that each facet of the roof stood out for him: the raised structure that housed the door leading from the building onto the roof; the roaring hum of the heating system preparing the building for the arrival of its patrons; pipes to let out the stale air removed by fans; the carbon monoxide created by the furnace; a broken and rusted flagpole, its banner nowhere in sight; dozens of empty paint cans and other similar refuse; beer bottles and empty cigarette packs . . .

And the building was there in front of him rising three floors above where he now stood, and the screaming was coming from the top floor. Four long strides brought him to the side of the building where his fingers found any number of handholds on ledges, stone outcroppings, gargoyle-like faces and window sills. It was an old building, the architecture beautiful but no longer practical, unless, of course, you had to climb one.

When he was just below the window of the apartment, the screaming stopped.

"*No!*" Daredevil shouted as he grabbed hold of the stone frame around the outside of the window and thrust his body, legs first, through the glass, his costume protecting him from cuts, though he did get a scratch on one cheek from the falling glass.

But his own blood did not concern him overmuch. What did concern him was the scene that threatened to overwhelm his radar at that moment. A woman with unusually long hair lay sprawled at the center of a round carpet at the center of a living room. Daredevil could smell her blood mingling with the musty smell of that carpet.

Her heart was beating slowly. She was alive, but unconscious.

Over her stood a man of average height with a pot belly. He was bald and wore glasses. His heart was pounding like a double bass drum and he was staring at Daredevil, right fist still frozen in the air, left clamped around the collar of the woman's nightgown.

Daredevil knew he ought to have said, "Step away from her now," or something of the sort, but he couldn't do it. Instead, he went sailing across the room, kicking the man hard in the chest before he could even move. Not hard enough to break anything, not hard enough to stop his heart, but hard enough, certainly, to take the man's breath away. He went down for the moment, and that was what mattered.

Daredevil went to the woman's side and searched for broken bones, grinding his teeth as he found them: three ribs, two fingers, the left arm at the wrist. He went to the phone and dialed 911.

"This is Daredevil. I've got a woman badly beaten. Several broken bones and some blood loss, probably a concussion, too. She'll be fine as long as you get an ambulance here right away. Send the police as well, 'cause I've also got the scumbag who did it to her."

"You can't come in here!" the man began to scream behind him.

Daredevil turned, though his radar had already picked up the man rising to his feet. The bastard had finally caught his breath.

"Well," Daredevil said with a sneer, taking a step toward the man who was up against the wall already, "I guess this really screws up your alibi, huh?"

"Don't touch me! Don't touch me! You can't do anything to me, the cops are coming!" the man was practically raving. "I'll get off anyway, though. The bitch deserved it. She was a cheating slut. Don't you understand that? I gave my wife everything she wanted, and she was sneaking around! What kind of man does that make me?"

Daredevil had seen them before, men like this. Some women too. More than likely the guy had been raised by violence, and so that's all he'd ever learned. Daredevil wanted to feel sorry, but it was all too common. For some people, the wounds never healed. They could be helped. The others grew hard callouses over their wounds, their souls. They became monsters. And they had to be spoken to in the language of monsters.

He tried to run as Daredevil reached for him, but he was too slow. The monsters always were. Daredevil grabbed him by the back of the neck, his grip uncompromising, and dragged him over to the ravaged form of his unconscious wife. He shoved the man's face down to where the carpet was sodden with blood like he was showing a dog its business, then held his head above the woman's swollen face.

"You would have beaten her to death," Daredevil said.

"No," he cried. "No, man, I was going to stop. She just needed to be taught a lesson."

"*You* need to be taught a lesson," Daredevil shouted, pulling the man up to face him. "I suppose you're wearing gloves because it's cold in here?"

The idiot tried to bolt then, slamming both hands into Daredevil's chest. But when he tried to pull away, he found that he could not. Daredevil held his wrists in a vise-like grip. The guy uttered a bizarre noise, somewhere between a growl and a whimper, and headbutted Daredevil. Their skulls collided with a crack, and Daredevil felt slightly dizzy, but he held on with his left hand while his right cocked back.

One punch, hard, to the side of the head, and the man crumpled at his feet.

"The language of monsters," he whispered, shaking his head as he knelt by the woman again. Her breathing and heartbeat were still steady, and he could hear the ambulance a couple of blocks away. He looked back at the husband, and wished he never had to speak the man's language . . . wished he had never had to learn it.

"Daredevil . . . ?" a tiny voice said, and he spun around. A small boy, perhaps seven years old, stood in the shadows of the hall. He'd been so wrapped up in dealing with the would-be murder, with the fading life of the woman, that he hadn't noticed the other heartbeat in the place, hadn't heard the soft padding of the boy's footsteps as he came out of his hiding place, probably a closet or a bathroom, and approached along the hallway.

"I'm sorry, son," he said soothingly. "I didn't see you back there."

"I was hiding," the boy said, and Daredevil nodded as if he hadn't known.

"Are you okay?" the hero said as he knelt by the boy.

"Uh-huh. Are they, DD? Are they okay?"

"What's your name, son?" Daredevil asked.

"Kevin," he answered, and Daredevil could hear the fear and uncertainty in his voice.

"Kevin, your Dad hurt your Mom pretty bad," he said, sadly accepting that the truth was the only way for the boy, that he'd probably seen it all before. "Your Mom is going to be okay. The ambulance is on the way, and . . . and so are the police."

"They're going to take Daddy away?" the boy asked, his hands clasped tightly in front of him.

"Yes, I'm afraid they are," Daredevil answered.

The boy started to cry, sucking in air as he broke down, sniffling and wiping at his runny nose almost immediately. He threw his arms around Daredevil and held him tight.

"Oh, thank you," the boy sobbed. "Thank you thank you thank you."

After a moment, he stood back and looked at Daredevil, wiping the last of his tears away.

"We'll be okay now," he said, and then the police were knocking at the door.

It was long past closing time for the Spotlight Costume Shop, but when Daredevil tried the door, it swung open without a squeak.

"Hello?" he said. "Melvin, I'm here."

"Go the hell away!" a voice cried from the back.

"Can't you read? We're closed!"

Daredevil wasn't surprised, but this bit of information was a useful reminder that, regardless of the enhancements his senses had undergone, and despite his incredible internal radar, he was and always would be blind. It wasn't that he could ever forget the fact of it, but sometimes he did lose track of the ramifications.

He stepped through the opening in the counter and walked into the back room. Melvin stood leaning over a worktable, his elbows on the wood and his hands propping up his chin. On the table there was clothing of some kind. Given that it was a costume shop, Daredevil had to guess that was what was on the table. Given the intensity with which Melvin stared at that costume, he thought he knew which one.

"I'm sorry I took so long," he said, and Melvin looked up suddenly, tense, then back down at the costume on the table.

"I tried to kill you in this," he said. "How many times? A dozen? More?"

"That wasn't you, Melvin," Daredevil said. "Not really. You're no more responsible for the deeds performed by the person who wore that costume than you are for the actions of . . . well, Bullseye, for starters."

Melvin turned away from the table now, facing him, throwing his hands up in dismay.

"You say that, Betsy says that," he let his hands flop back down at his sides. "Even the judge said that. And maybe it's even true, but there's something you'll never be able to understand, Daredevil."

The hero said nothing. Just waited.

"I remember," Melvin said. "Don't you see?"

He turned and picked up one of the gauntlets he'd worn as the Gladiator, upon which sat a razor-sharp titanium steel circular sawblade, whose internal circuitry made it spin with deadly speed.

"See this?" he asked, his voice revealing his pain. "My heart doesn't want to hurt anyone or anything. I can't even watch a lot of movies because the violence upsets me. I'm a good man, Daredevil. A good man. I know that. But I remember every single thing I did in this costume, with my hands and with these blades. Do you understand what I'm saying? I remember it all and it makes me nauseous! I killed people! Sure, not many, not like some of the real nutjobs out there. But enough!"

Melvin hung his head. Daredevil walked closer and laid a hand on the big man's shoulder.

"We've got to get moving, Melvin," he said. "If we're going to get Betsy back, we've got to . . ."

"I know what I have to do!" Melvin snapped. "Don't talk to me like I'm stupid. I may be a little slow at times, but I am not an idiot!"

Daredevil didn't move his hand.

"I'm sorry," Melvin said, and Daredevil could feel the fury rush out of him with the next breath. "It's just all of this, weighing on me."

"Don't apologize," Daredevil said. "I've been working out a plan. It's pretty shaky, but I think it's the best we can do on such short notice and with just the two of us . . . I don't know what kind of effect wearing the costume will have on you, but you're going to need to put it on, just this one last time."

Melvin looked down at the costume laid out on the table, and didn't look back up.

"It isn't the Kingpin, Melvin. That I'm certain of. He may have been in it at the beginning, but it isn't him now. I say that for a lot of reasons, but it would be enough just to know that the whole thing is too low-class for him. He thinks too much of himself to operate this way. I told you about this new player in town, this Gary Wiezak. I think it's him. I think he wants to send you back into that mental abyss that Betsy saved you from, maybe hoping he can use you when he's through.

"I think Wiezak has your wife, but I don't know where. Hopefully, if these guys don't bring Betsy with them, and I don't think they will, we'll be able to either track them back to her, or take them down and force them to give up her location."

"You don't think they'll have Betsy?" Melvin asked, incredulous, as if it had never occurred to him that he might be double-crossed.

"That's what I'm trying to tell you Melvin," Daredevil answered. "I don't think this is about Betsy. I think it's about you. Or, rather, I think it's about the Gladiator."

"I love her more than anything in the world, Daredevil," Melvin said with a quiet anger. "I want Betsy home. Let's hear your plan."

"Okay, the meet is for midnight at Battery Park. I'll be there before you, and once I spot the kidnappers, I'll hide out and look for Betsy. If I find her, I'll get her out, but if not, I'll wait until you arrive. Then we'll see where it takes us."

"But they wanted me to kill you!" Melvin said. "What happens if they have Betsy with them, and I show up with no corpse?"

"That's the key," Daredevil said. "In fact, it's the only intelligent thing about this plan."

He walked back toward the front of the store and Melvin followed. When he stopped by the mannequin wearing the copy of his costume, he heard Melvin take in a quick breath.

"We use the sawblades to cut it," Melvin muttered quickly, grasping it now, "bloody it up good with some stage makeup . . ."

"And we've got ourselves one dead hero," Daredevil finished for him. "I just hope they go for it. It will at least get you close to them. Beyond that, we may have to wing it."

"It really isn't much of a plan," Melvin said, "but it's the only thing we've got, isn't it?"

Daredevil realized there was nothing he could say to soothe Melvin's nerves, and if he was honest with himself, he had to admit that he was feeling terribly anxious himself. He was the man without fear, true, but that only applied to his personal safety. When it came down to the life of a woman and the fate of a gentle man on the brink of tragedy, he was no stranger to fear. And when Daredevil, the man without fear, thought of what might have already happened to Betsy Potter, he was indeed afraid.

"Let's get moving," he said after they'd stood silent a moment. "We don't have a minute more to spare."

"You get going now," Melvin said, a weak smile playing over his lips. "I'll take care of murdering the mannequin."

"You sure?" Daredevil asked.

"It's what I do, DD," he answered.

Daredevil walked toward the front door, but turned back at the sound of Melvin's voice.

"Daredevil," he said tentatively, "whatever happens tonight, I want you to know that everything Betsy and I have, in some ways we owe to you. You don't need to say anything, I just wanted you to know. Thank you."

Daredevil couldn't help thinking of Bullseye, then, and the Kingpin and Gary Wiezak and the man in the apartment, monsters all. In the presence of Melvin Potter, Daredevil knew that there was always hope. Monsters were at least partially self-made, monstrous behavior a choice. But to choose goodness, to choose ordinariness, as Melvin had after being a monster so long, took so much more strength.

Daredevil swore that if Betsy Potter were still alive, she would be returned to her husband, no matter what the cost.

They had earned their shot at love and ordinariness.

Chapter 13

GARY WIEZAK WAS ON TOP OF THE WORLD. HE stared out at the lights of New York City and smiled to himself. He felt almost like a ghost, not invisible, but untouchable. As if at any moment he might walk through a wall.

"That's me," he laughed quietly. "Friggin' Casper."

That idiot Fisk had been so caught up in playing legit businessman, wanting everyone to like and respect him, he'd been thrown completely off guard when Daredevil had blown his cover. Wilson Fisk, the Kingpin of Crime. The mayor wouldn't be shaking his hand any time soon, and that really pissed Fisk off. Hurt him, too, in a lot of ways even Wiezak didn't understand.

And if anybody should have understood, Gary Wiezak was the man. He'd studied Wilson Fisk for years, and when he'd come back to New York, he'd walked into the Kingpin's office with a business plan prepared. With the profit margin he'd shown, there was no way the Kingpin wasn't going to bankroll his operation. And as soon as Wiezak had things up and running, he'd cut himself a bigger slice of the pie. And then a bigger one, and pretty soon, Fisk would be begging him to run the show.

That's how he'd planned it. Way it worked out, things happened a little faster than he might have liked. But hey, that was cool. He was a man who rolled with the punches.

What it came down to was simply a difference in style between Fisk and himself, a difference that was what made him better suited to be Kingpin than Fisk ever had been. Fisk was form over substance, more concerned with the show than the box office receipts. Not Gary Wiezak. Uh-uh. He had no pretensions to legitimacy, no pretensions to honor, nobility, honesty, courtesy, morality . . . none of the things that kept Fisk from international power. So maybe Wiezak came from the gutter. So what? Everybody had to start somewhere.

Wiezak had never tried to hide his criminal intentions. Why bother? A good lawyer and a lot of money could get you anything in the world, he'd always said. Now the cops thought they had him. Daredevil figured he was headed for jail. Idiots! He'd hired the best firm in New York, and they'd already figured out ten different ways to get him off. They hadn't found a single thing to really incriminate him except for the witnesses. Now Rodriguez and Mallory were dead, and Bullseye would take care of Karen Page just in case the cops ever identified Shane as the shooter who'd taken Rodriguez down.

Shane *was* starting to get on his nerves, though. He was so used to being the number two guy that his hackles were raised every time Bullseye showed his face. Wiezak didn't want to see Shane Cairns die. They were friends, had been for a long time. But if he kept getting up in Bullseye's face, Wiezak had no doubt the assassin would kill him. And Gary wouldn't stop him either. He needed Bullseye if he was going to usurp the Kingpin's throne.

It wouldn't be long before he would make his final play for Wilson Fisk's kingdom. And looking down on that kingdom, the darkened alleys of Manhattan, Wiezak could almost taste the power that he yearned for, that he would have one day soon.

Gary Wiezak was an ambitious man. But after all, he figured, what the hell was a man without ambition?

Melvin Potter had put the Gladiator behind him, he'd thought. But he realized now that the Gladiator was not behind but within him, deep inside his heart and soul. He wondered idly if an x-ray might show the beast's presence, a tumor laying dormant, waiting for the right moment to take complete control of his life.

An hour earlier, he had finally forced himself to put the costume on. The blue kevlar pants had not been terribly difficult, and the boots and jersey only slightly more so. The gauntlets, though, with their buzzing steel blades, had been nearly impossible. Only thoughts of his loving wife in some killer's hands had enabled him to put them on. On the drive downtown he had looked only at the road, his gaze never shifting down to the reflection of streetlights and neon bar signs on his blades. What would he say if a cop stopped him, he'd wondered. What could he say?

As he sat in the car in the blackness of Battery

Park, he reached into the passenger seat and picked up his blue titanium steel helmet. The empty eye slits stared at him with ominous intent, or so he imagined. The entire ensemble was forbidding, despite the brightness of the colors. It was a work he ought to be proud of, and might have been if it weren't associated with so many terrible things.

But it was the costume of a killer, and Melvin Potter felt only shame when he looked at it, and he felt far worse when it came time to put it on. In the costume, he was Melvin Potter, a man who'd once been ill, who'd once done terrible things in a fragile state of mind. But now, as he slipped on the helmet for the first time in oh-so-long, his face disappeared beneath another. His identity was buried under the cold steel gaze of the Gladiator.

The Gladiator stepped from the Ford with a heavy foot, a dangerous man, a man not to be trifled with. He looked around at the park and noticed that the moonlight did actually penetrate much of the lawn. It would not be terribly easy to hide here if you were being sought, or more accurately, hunted, but it was far from impossible, especially for a man like Daredevil.

"I am Melvin Potter," the Gladiator said quietly to the night. "I'm a husband and a businessman. I'm a good man."

I'm a good man, he repeated in his mind over and over as he went to the trunk, opened it, and lifted out the cold, lifeless, bloody form of a mannequin in a Daredevil suit. The thing was not light, weighing perhaps sixty pounds, but it was far from the two hundred odd pounds that the hero actually weighed. Still, the Gladiator's muscles rippled in the chill Atlantic breeze, the strain of his shoulders and back was visible in the moonlight.

It was all a part of the act. The Gladiator was certain that his hosts would be watching, and Betsy's life might depend upon giving them exactly what they expected.

Bearing his tattered burden, he turned toward the water and began to walk. Through the trees, he could see the light of the moon on Lady Liberty's face, and her presence there helped to calm his thoughts, to soothe his tormented heart. His brain sent out one word, *Betsy,* through the park, as though his wife might somehow sense his presence and call out to him, or at least know that she was no longer alone.

"Stop right there, Potter!" a gruff voice shouted behind him. "Turn around slowly, and let us get a real good look at your victim!"

The Gladiator turned as slowly as possible, hoping desperately for at least a glimpse of his wife. As soon as he was looking back the way he'd come, however, headlights snapped on, their brights shining in his eyes. He squinted, trying to get a look, but could see nothing more than silhouettes of two men standing in front of the car.

"Where's my wife!" he shouted.

"In due time," came the answer, in a voice that slid over his ear like a shoe stepping in something nasty. "Lift Daredevil up so we can get a better look."

He followed directions, being certain to keep the face turned as much toward him as possible. The goons wouldn't know what DD looked like anyway, so it probably wouldn't be important for them to see his face.

"How'd you do it, Melvin?" the disturbingly slippery voice asked. "You tried so many times before, how did you manage this time?"

This was not a question he had prepared an answer for, but it came to the Gladiator in a moment. He was beginning to think like a killer again, despite his revulsion at the mere thought, and it was easy to see right away how he might have been able to murder Daredevil if he'd been of a mind to.

"It was easy," he called out. "This time he trusted me! Once I was close enough, he had no chance. Now enough of this talk . . . give me my wife back!"

"Put the body down and back off!" the man shouted. "And let's stop pretending you're in any position of power here, shall we Melvin? You're beginning to annoy me, and you don't want to annoy a man who's holding a knife to your lady's throat, do you now?"

The Gladiator winced, but his eyes had grown somewhat used to the brightness, and he could see that the man was not holding Betsy at all. Either she was still back in the dark with the others, or they hadn't brought her . . . if they had her in the first place! Maybe he was speaking figuratively, the Gladiator thought, but realized that was desperate hope talking.

"How do I know you even have her?" the Gladiator called back.

"Just do as I say, and maybe she'll survive the next ten minutes!" the man said, and his voice was almost a snarl.

The Gladiator set the "corpse" of Daredevil on the ground and backed away a few steps. When the men behind the lights made no effort to come forward, he backed off another half dozen paces, but no more. He was going to stay within striking distance of the mannequin.

Now! he thought to himself as two men came forward in the light. Daredevil ought to attack them now, before they realized he wasn't dead, before they decided to kill Betsy after all. *Come on, DD, make your move,* his brain screamed, but still nothing happened. And suddenly the Gladiator was Melvin Potter again, a scared and angry husband who only wanted his wife back.

"Where's my wife, you bastards!" he screamed without moving from his spot.

And then the headlights went out, and the Gladiator's eyes, which had almost adjusted to their brightness, were practically blind once again. He heard the sound of footsteps pound the lawn as the two rushed toward him to pick up Daredevil's "body," and he knew suddenly that something had happened, that Daredevil had not gotten here in time . . . that maybe he wasn't coming at all. The Gladiator had to save his wife on his own, but that would mean he would have to really *be* the Gladiator, not just feel like him or act like him. It would mean the end for him, he knew, but at least Betsy would live.

If he could force himself to violence in the first place.

The sawblades on his gauntlets buzzed into deadly life, he set his feet wide apart, eyes wide to take in as much light as possible, trying desperately to adjust to the crushing blackness, and he snarled and rushed back toward where the bloody mannequin lay.

"You don't get the body unless I get my wife!" he shouted as loud as he could, to be heard over the buzzing of his saws.

"Jesus!" one of the men shouted. "Watch out for those blades."

Ah! he thought happily, *even if I can't force myself to harm them, I can make them believe I will!*

"Don't take another step!" he screamed, as his eyes finally adjusted enough to see them only a few feet in front of him, the mannequin on the ground between. Luckily the plastic face was turned toward him, so they still didn't know it wasn't a dead hero.

"Move and I'll kill every last one of you!" he screamed like a madman, and at that moment, he realized it might not be that far from the truth.

The two men turned back toward the darkness where the headlights had been, as if to get further instructions, and the slippery voice erased the need for any further inquiries.

"Kill him if you have to," the voice said, "but bring me Daredevil's corpse."

"*Melvin!*" another voice shouted, and this time it was one the Gladiator recognized.

"Betsy isn't here!" Daredevil yelled from somewhere in the night. "She isn't anywhere near here! We've got to immobilize these guys and make them tell us where she is!"

Raising the razor sharp blades buzzing at his wrists, the Gladiator let out a mad scream and hurled himself at the two men in front of him. They nearly dove from the path of his whirring blades, but he shut them off and disarmed both men. Then he lifted the two thugs as if they were babies and marched them forward as a human shield.

The headlights blazed on once again from the car in front of him. The Gladiator blinked several times, but that didn't keep him from seeing Daredevil do an aerial somersault, seemingly from nowhere though likely from the roof of the ticket building, to land on the hood of the car.

An energy shot through the Gladiator that he had not felt in years, adrenaline surged into his arms, making the gunmen even more weightless. He wanted to break these two men who would dare try to harm him, who had possibly already done harm to Betsy, the woman who was his whole world. The Gladiator wanted to kill them, and then to throw himself, blades slicing flesh, into the midst of Daredevil's battle around the car.

That's what the Gladiator wanted. But the Gladiator was also Melvin Potter, and Melvin Potter was a peaceable man. He wanted to save his wife, and keep Daredevil safe from harm. He didn't want to be hurt himself, but he was not willing to give in to the savage urges that had once been his undoing. He would not kill. More than that, though, he would not allow himself to hurt these men through rage.

The Gladiator would do no more than defend himself.

He watched intently as Daredevil flipped over a man and woman who'd leveled their guns at him. The pair tried to hold their aim, to follow him with their weapons, but his move disoriented them, and even as they looked up at him his feet came around to slam into their backs. They both went to their knees in front of the car, and Daredevil followed through by slamming their heads into the grill.

The Gladiator winced, but then two burly men, one black and one white, who looked like tag team wrestlers, approached Daredevil from either side, and a third, thin man wearing an expensive suit stepped out of the back seat of the car with a gun in his hand.

"DD, watch out!" he yelled, but the hero paid no attention.

He took a step forward, wanting to go to his friend's aid, but held back instead. If Daredevil needed help, he would ask for it. And then the Gladiator would have a real decision on his hands.

The tag team rushed him, and Daredevil had no choice but to jump forward at the one he was facing.

He drove his fists into the big man's belly like a boxer on the hunt, but he couldn't put the guy down. The dapper man targeted Daredevil with his pistol, and then the Gladiator couldn't stop himself, he did start to run.

"Gun!" he yelled.

He needn't have worried, he realized a moment later, as Daredevil did a back flip that put him on the other side of the car, where he crouched in darkness, almost invisible. For all intents and purposes, he had disappeared.

"Kill the Gladiator, now!" the dapper man yelled, and the Gladiator knew that this was the voice he had heard before. The man and woman who had been first to attack Daredevil were unconscious in front of the car, unable to respond to this call to action, but the tag team moved in the Gladiator's direction, and he kept moving in theirs.

No rage, he told himself. Not even hostility. He was merely protecting himself and his friend, and trying to get his wife home safely.

"Where are you, Daredevil?" the dapper man screamed in a high pitch, panicked because he could not find the hero he'd expected to see dead. "Come out now, or the Potter woman dies!"

The huge black man on the left took the first swing at the Gladiator, and despite the temptation the dapper man's threats inspired, he did not turn on his blades as he blocked the blow and threw a punch of his own. He heard the crunch of bone in the man's nose, but instead of feeling satisfied, he

DAREDEVIL

felt nauseous. His tag-team partner reached around the Gladiator's neck, attempting to get some kind of stranglehold. The Gladiator drove an elbow back in the guy's chest, grabbed him by the hair, and flipped him onto the ground.

The Gladiator looked at the two big men, struggling to rise for more punishment, and his mind revolted at the sight. He had done this. He had lashed out in anger, no matter how nicely he attempted to disguise it. He was in the costume, the armor. He was the Gladiator again.

"No!" Melvin Potter screamed, and tore the Gladiator's helmet from his head. It landed on the grass with a quiet thump as he took several staggering paces toward the nearest tree, leaned over, and threw up.

Melvin fell to his knees, tears streaming down his face as he attempted to keep his sobs silent. His stomach convulsed again, and he bent over but nothing came. To his left, a gun landed in the grass, followed by another, and then two more. He had given up on his own safety and Daredevil's as well, but now, even as he battled his tears and his sick belly, he heard Daredevil speak.

"Get out of here, now! I don't want to see any of you again, not working for Fisk, or Wiezak, not even in New York. Be grateful I don't have time to wait for the cops."

Several pairs of feet beat a hasty retreat across the grass.

"What about me?" the dapper man's shrill voice

asked. The man had sounded dangerous before, and now his voice was a frightened squeak. It should have been gratifying, but it was only more upsetting.

"You're not going anywhere," Daredevil answered, and finally Melvin started to turn around.

"Look at him," the dapper man laughed. "Jesus, what a loser! Who ever thought he was some kind of stone killer?"

Melvin said nothing, but shivered as Daredevil grabbed the man by the jaw and squeezed his face so that his lips puckered involuntarily. Violent preparation for a kiss, it looked like, but it was nothing of the sort.

"Where is Betsy Potter?" Daredevil asked, his voice calm, reasonable, belying the danger in his face and stance.

The man smiled.

Daredevil slapped his face.

"Where is Betsy Potter?" he asked again.

"I don't know," the dapper man answered, and Daredevil turned away and seemed to curse under his breath.

"Get out of here," he said to the dapper man, and Melvin gaped in astonishment as the man set off across the lawn toward his car. Daredevil was going to just let him walk away!

"DD, what are you doing? This guy's got Betsy!" Melvin yelled, incredulous. He had started after the man when Daredevil took strong hold of his shoulder.

"No, Melvin," Daredevil said. "He has no idea where Betsy is."

Melvin's jaw dropped in astonishment.

"Wait," he said, his voice nearly hysterical, "you mean that just because this guy tells you he doesn't know where Betsy is, you're gonna believe him. Just like that!"

His face was only inches from Daredevil's now, and Melvin felt his fists clench and unclench of their own accord. After what he'd just been through, how close he'd come to letting the Gladiator take over his life again . . . but no, this was just giving in, wasn't it? He'd defended himself from Wiezak's goons, and from the violence that was inside of him. He wasn't going to give in now.

"Melvin," Daredevil said softly, reasonably, "you just have to trust me. He was telling the truth. I'm certain Wiezak has Betsy. I just don't know where. But I promise you, I won't sleep until I find her."

All the breath went out of Melvin then, and he turned his back on Daredevil, his hero, the man without fear. He had so many fears himself, and he did not want Daredevil to read them in his face. He stared south, where somewhere in the dark, Ellis Island sat, a quiet stone testament to courage in the face of adversity. He wished for even an ounce of that courage for himself, but felt sure whatever allotment he'd once had, it was gone.

Daredevil laid a hand on his shoulder before disappearing into the night, and Melvin wanted to turn and thank him, to say that yes, he did trust the man. But he didn't do that, because he was ashamed.

Melvin Potter didn't want his hero to see him cry.

Chapter 14

K AREN PAGE SAT, SIPPING TEA, IN FRONT OF HER small television set. Images flickered by, limp sit- com jokes barely registered on the amusement scale. Karen had far too much on her mind to force an amusement she did not feel. The situation with Wiezak was insane. Here was a guy who had clearly hired one of the world's most infamous assassins to murder anyone who might possibly incriminate him on trial, and the cops couldn't do anything about it! It was madness.

The worst part of it was that Karen hadn't even been scheduled to testify yet. Wouldn't have any- thing to testify about if the police couldn't identify the sniper, the man who had threatened her the night before. What did Wiezak want with her? She was no real danger to him. Karen could only assume that the man was so vicious, so power-mad, that he wanted a trail of dead bodies behind him when he made his final play for the Kingpin's throne.

Either that, or he was certain the cops would iden- tify the sniper before the trial. Could be he had someone inside the force feeding him information. Karen had lived too long on the wrong side not to know there were plenty of dirty cops to be found if you looked hard enough.

In any case, she really didn't believe Bullseye would find her right away. Nobody but Sister Maggie and Foggy Nelson knew where they lived, and Matt would have known if they'd been followed earlier.

She wasn't afraid.

Still, better safe than sorry. The shades were partially drawn and the lights out. Her outer calm belied her inner tension. She was prepared to react to any attack, any invasion, instantly. To run if she could, and fight if she couldn't.

Karen Page didn't plan to die tonight. Or any night for a long time to come. And if that meant putting her life in the hands of Natasha Romanova, Matt's former lover and, as the Black Widow, Daredevil's former partner . . . well, she'd do whatever was necessary.

She nearly leaped from the couch when there came a knock at the door. Her heart pounded violently as she stepped lightly in her bare feet to a spot to one side of the door. Karen assumed it was Natasha arriving, but she couldn't be certain, and so must be extremely cautious. She had assumed the Black Widow would, like Daredevil, come through the window. But then, she had never taken the time to get to know Natasha very well.

Karen was afraid to speak, knowing an assassin like Bullseye might simply wait to hear a voice, and then shoot her through the wall. And yet, if she did not, and it were Natasha, the woman would not know she was inside.

She waited, but the knock did not come again. After a few moments, though, she heard a low voice on the other side of the door.

"Karen," the Black Widow said, "we don't have all night."

Rolling her eyes, Karen undid the double dead bolts and the main lock and pulled open the door. Natasha hurried inside, and Karen closed the door and locked up again.

"How did you know I wasn't already dead or something?" Karen asked.

"The light from the TV is visible under the door," the Widow answered as she slipped out of her long coat to reveal the gray bodysuit underneath. "When you walked to the door, your feet blocked the light. Bullseye would have known that."

There was a moment of silence as Karen tried to determine whether there was an arrogant dismissal in Natasha's tone, or if it was merely her jealous imagination. With a slight tinge of regret, she realized it was the latter.

"I'm sorry," Karen said, realizing the awkwardness of the moment. "I just never thought we'd get to know each other better under such bizarre circumstances."

"Well, bizarre or no, I'm glad we have the chance," Natasha offered.

"Can I get you something, a cup of tea?" Karen asked.

"That would be great. But why don't you turn off the TV, first?"

"It would be completely dark, then," Karen said, surprised.

"With New York outside the window?" the Widow

smiled. "I doubt it. Besides, this is a slumber party, isn't it?"

"I suppose," Karen said, then smiled mischievously. "At least one of us is already in her pajamas."

They laughed comfortably, and the ice melted.

It was just after nine o'clock. Bullseye sat on the roof of an old apartment building across from the one in which Karen Page had shacked up with her old flame, blind boy Matt Murdock.

Bullseye snorted and hung his legs over the edge of the building. He was really enjoying himself tonight. Normally, on a job of this nature he was much more serious, more circumspect. Even now, knowing that Daredevil had a special interest in Murdock and Page and might come by, Bullseye was not nearly as alert as he would usually have been. There was too much pleasure involved in this job. Hell, he ought to give Wiezak back his money, not take the rest of the payment. It just didn't seem right.

Someone passed in front of the window in the apartment across the street, and his face went blank, muscles slack, devoid of all emotion. He stared in silence, not breathing, as someone moved in the darkness of Page and Murdock's apartment. He was fairly certain the figure was female, apparently his target.

The night was breezy and cool. He was warm enough in his costume, but the chill felt nice on his face. Every breath was exhilarating. He scanned the neighborhood, appreciating for the first time its aesthetic value. Hell's Kitchen was one of a kind, a place that seemed to have barely survived its obsolesence. It hung on, a lonelier, more dangerous version of its youthful self, but it had character in every brick, every granite block. On top of Page and Murdock's building sat a water tower. More than likely it was no longer in use, but the simple fact of its presence was a comfort to Bullseye. Whatever you want to do, sir, go on ahead, it seemed to say. I'll still be here in the morning.

Not as if he needed its permission.

A flicker of movement brought his attention once again to the apartment window, but he could see nothing. Clearly, Page knew her number was up and was trying to stay alive. Bullseye didn't know if Murdock was home, but he wasn't terribly concerned. The guy was blind, after all.

A part of him, a broken part that had been shattered once upon a time by the devil of Hell's Kitchen, wanted Murdock there. He owed it to Daredevil to take the lawyer out. But Bullseye was a professional. He was being paid to kidnap Karen Page, and then, when Wiezak was through playing, to murder her. If Murdock wasn't home, he would have to take him out later, along with his old law partner, Foggy Nelson, another member of Daredevil's little protected circle.

Bullseye picked up his bag and went down the fire escape, not a single clank of metal to mark his passing. He ran across the street miraculously unseen, but he'd had a lot of practice. A trip around the side of the building, and he went up the fire escape there as quickly and silently as he'd descended the other. On the roof, he turned to gaze appreciatively at the huge water tank, and he nodded as if in response to a profound wisdom.

The fire escape was on the east wall of the building, while Page and Murdock's apartment was on the south. He crossed to that side quickly, reaching into his bag to pull out the grapple he carried with a nylon line attached. He wound the cord around one leg of the water tower then set the hook snugly between two steel support beams that crisscrossed under it. He walked to the edge and threw the cord over the side, wound it about his hands and let himself over. He pushed off the brick face and slid down a couple of feet, then did so again. The window was directly below him.

Foggy Nelson's mind was caught up in a whirlwind of self-recrimination. He'd been hoping to somehow regain the closeness he'd once had with his best friend, Matt Murdock. When they'd met that morning, Matt had invited him to dinner at the new apartment, the first time he'd asked Foggy to do anything in a long, long time. Eight o'clock, Matt said. It was now just past nine.

Foggy would have been on time, but just before he left home, the phone had rung again. Craig Barron, the firm's senior partner, demanded that he fax his latest comments on the Wiezak case over immediately. It didn't matter that it was long after normal human beings had forgotten all about work. Barron wanted it, and Barron always got what he wanted.

Problem with that was that Foggy, or "Franklin," as the stuffy old bastard insisted upon calling him, hadn't finished the draft he'd been working on. It took him forty minutes to complete the document, and he had to wait another ten agonizing minutes of busy signal before Barron's fax machine finally rang through.

Once again, he'd let his friends down. What made it even worse was that Foggy knew neither Matt nor Karen would say word one to him about it. But he would know. Where it counted, he knew he'd gotten his priorities crossed again.

He carried a bottle of wine in his left hand, and as he approached the door to their apartment, Foggy shifted the roses he'd brought for Karen to the crook of his left arm. Then he knocked.

Though their conversation was warm, Natasha Romanova could tell that Karen Page was distracted. And she couldn't blame the woman. There were a handful of people in the world who knew Daredevil and Matt Murdock were one and the same, but not many of them knew the man the way both Karen and Natasha did. Though she had no interest in a relationship with him, Natasha still loved Matt, would always love him in a way. She made no secret of that fact, though she could see it disturbed Karen slightly.

From where Natasha sat, though, Karen had nothing to worry about. She knew how much Matt cared for her. He always had. Karen had strength, energy and a savvy that the Widow envied, in a way. And yet, despite all she'd lived through, she still seemed to have kept some of her naïveté about the way the world worked. Natasha envied that as well.

"You're a good friend, Natasha, dropping your own agenda just to help us out," Karen said.

"Matt would do the same for me," Natasha answered.

For a moment she regretted it, as she saw the jealous look steal over Karen's face, but then the look was replaced by a bemused smile.

"He would, wouldn't he?" Karen said, shaking her head. "I guess that's one of the reasons I love him."

Natasha was about to reply when someone knocked a happy rhythm on the door. She shot a glance at Karen, and in the dim light filtering in from the neon city outside, saw her shrug and shake her head. A clear message: she wasn't expecting anyone.

The knock came again, and with the extraordinary stealth she had trained all her life to achieve, the Widow made a wide circuit of the room and crouched next to the door.

"Matt? Karen? Hello, anybody home?" a tentative voice called from the other side of the door, and Natasha relaxed. It was a voice she recognized.

"Foggy? What's he doing here?" Natasha heard Karen wonder aloud, even as she went to open the door. She looked over her shoulder at the other woman, to share the relief they both felt and turned the first of the deadbolts. Even as she looked at Karen, though, her gaze was instinctively drawn past her.

Movement at the window! Somebody's clothesline or . . . a rope!

Thump!

And that wasn't rats.

"Move!" Natasha hissed as she reached out and grabbed Karen's hand, even as she threw back the second deadbolt.

The window shattered as Bullseye came crashing through. He landed squarely, eyes darting around the darkened room. Natasha felt cold as he looked at her and smiled, drawing a sai from behind him.

"The Black Widow," Bullseye said gleefully, "what a pleasant surprise. You've saved me the trouble of hunting you down."

Natasha didn't know what he was talking about. She had no connection to this case. But it didn't matter, nothing mattered except . . .

"Karen, get out of here!" she shouted, and moved in on the assassin.

Bullseye launched the sai at her, but the Widow turned it aside with the thrust of her forearm and went on the offensive, keeping the assassin busy with blow after blow. He had gotten much better since the last time they crossed paths, and she was forced to wonder whether they were now evenly matched. Bullseye thrust out his foot in a sideways kick, and nearly connected. Natasha leaped up and over the kick, bringing her own foot around for a hard blow to the back of the assassin's head.

He stumbled, but did not go down.

"Oh, my God!" Natasha heard Foggy Nelson exclaim behind her, as Karen finally got the door open.

"Foggy, get her out of here!" the Widow yelled.

"Run, Karen, run!" she heard Foggy shout, and was relieved that the two of them were finally out of the way so that she could concentrate on this fight with Bullseye.

It was time the assassin paid for his crimes.

They faced off again, in the dim light from the street, and the Black Widow could see the gleam of teeth in Bullseye's wicked smile. He beckoned her with his hands, not bothering to take out another sai, or some other weapon. His aim was deadly, it was his greatest strength, and yet he was taking her on hand to hand. She realized that he must believe he didn't need his target skills to defeat her.

The Black Widow was insulted.

"Come on, then, Poindexter," she snarled. "This isn't some sparring match. It's over for you."

Then, seemingly from out of nowhere, Foggy Nelson charged the assassin, a lunatic frenzy of fear and hatred on the lawyer's face and in the scream of rage that bellowed from his lungs.

"Bullseye!" Foggy shrieked.

"Ah, Nelson too!" Bullseye cackled. "You people are making this much too easy."

Before the Widow could get between them, Bullseye had turned, thrust out his hip, and used the combination of his strength and the momentum of the overweight attorney to throw Foggy out the open top story window.

"No!" Natasha screamed even as she ran and dove out the window, snagging Foggy's leg as she fell with him. All thoughts of Karen and Bullseye were put on hold in her effort to save the man's life. She knew that was exactly what the killer wanted, but it couldn't be helped.

Falling. Maybe sixty feet to the street, if that. The Widow knew she didn't have time to throw a line up, get it to snag, and still swing to safety. The wind whipped past her face as she did the only thing she could. Holding tightly to Foggy, she pulled hard on his legs and used her extraordinary agility and acrobatic skills to flip them both around so that she was now below him.

Foggy Nelson weighed at least twice as much as she did, and the Widow knew that if they hit the pavement, she was likely to die. But she wasn't about to let that happen. Her body was moving faster than her mind could command it, and even as she flipped under him, she had spotted the second story ledge that jutted out of the front of the apartment building. It was a long reach, and hopeless, but she grabbed it.

The Black Widow cried out in pain as her arm was nearly wrenched from its socket. She held on a moment, letting Foggy fall past her again, but their combined weight was too much. Natasha was torn from the side of the building and their descent continued.

Mind reeling with pain, she spotted their only

chance. Already slowed somewhat by her actions, they might be okay if she could only aim for the yellow lobby awning below. She spun again, so that she was below Foggy, and stretched herself out so that they would not simply rocket through the plastic.

They struck. The awning stretched, and tore wide open. Natasha Romanova and Foggy Nelson struck pavement and did not move.

Bullseye didn't stay to watch Nelson and the Widow die. He was after Karen Page the moment he threw Nelson out the window. Half a dozen long strides took Bullseye across the apartment, and he yanked the door open as he drew three shuriken from the pouch at his back. These were not dipped in curare, though. Wiezak wanted Page as insurance now that Daredevil had become such a problem. Bullseye was glad. He would be able to torture the woman before she died.

He dove across the hall to the well of the opposite apartment door, just in case Page had a gun. The kevlar would protect him, but bullets still hurt. No gun, though, and when Bullseye peered down the hall to see Page disappearing through the door to the stairs, he began to get annoyed. Before he was consciously aware of it, the shuriken were flying from his hand, and two of them lodged in the woman's shoulder before the door could close completely.

*　　*　　*

Karen yelped in pain, then bit her lip, not wanting to give Bullseye the satisfaction. She grabbed the wooden block used to prop the stairwell door open, slammed it under the door and kicked it in with all the power she could muster. Then she was off again. At the first landing, she heard the pounding start on the door, heard it scrape open an inch or so even as she hurried down to the next floor.

At the landing, she paused by a door marked "MAINTENANCE," considering it as a hiding place. Then she heard the upstairs door slam open and gave up the idea, taking off down the steps again. The hall door opened behind her, but she didn't slow to see who it was. The janitor, most likely, and she prayed he'd be okay.

She breathed in through her teeth with a pained hiss and reached for the slashes on her shoulder, which had suddenly flared into a more severe pain, as if to remind her they were there and were not going away. She could have done without the reminder, and without the new pain as the razor edges of the shuriken punctured her hand, but she was glad they were there.

As delicately as possible, despite her pounding down the stairs, she pulled the deadly stars from her shoulder, and held them together between her thumb and forefinger.

"What the hell are you . . ." someone said above her, and then cried out in pain.

Karen leaped the last few steps to the next landing, nearly falling to her knees but grabbing the cement wall to keep herself up. She turned to head down the next flight, trying to remember how much further she had to go to reach the street, and glanced at the bloody path she had left behind her. It was a fuse, leading directly to her, and Bullseye the spark fast approaching.

"No," she snarled through gritted teeth, and kept going.

Bullseye was really getting pissed now, not that he had to exert himself, but that the Page woman actually believed she might be able to escape him. It was laughable. Surely the woman had heard enough about his exploits over the years to know his reputation.

Then he knew what it was. Daredevil! The vile horn-headed vigilante was tight with Murdock and Page, and so the woman obviously had not developed a respect for Bullseye's abilities because she was used to having Daredevil around. She knew that Daredevil had beaten him, by sheer luck of course, several times.

It always came back to him, to Daredevil. Yet another day was ruined for Bullseye. He ground his teeth together.

Bullseye was smiling as he saw the janitor step through the door onto the stairwell landing, and the man's eyes first glanced down the stairs. That's how close he must be to Karen Page, Bullseye realized; the old bastard can see her. The man, a thin, white-haired guy who Bullseye figured should have long since retired, looked up and saw the killer swooping down on him, smiling as though he were an old and dear friend.

"What the hell are you.. ?" the guy started to say, but then there was a sai through his heart, and he let out a dying shriek even as he fell, sliding off the blade. Knowing he would catch up to Page in moments, Bullseye took the time to wipe the blood off on the janitor's gray sweatshirt.

Blood was running freely down Karen's arm now, and the thumping of Bullseye's feet on the stairs behind her matched the beating of her heart. It was so close, now, so loud to her.

She knew she wasn't going to make it.

At the landing she turned . . . and waited.

Bullseye leaped down to the next landing. He looked up just in time to see that Page had stopped and was waiting for him, face burning with hatred. He began to smile, believing she'd given up. Maybe she was going to plead for her life after all?

Then her arm flashed out, the pair of shuriken he'd hit her with buzzing toward him. He jerked his body to one side even as the stars whispered past his head, one thunking into the cement and the other just glancing off his cheek, dragging a thin slice through his skin.

Astounded, Bullseye missed the next stair, and fell.

Karen couldn't believe her luck, and her surprise kept her at the bottom of the stairs for several seconds as the assassin tumbled toward her. Then she was off, nearly sliding on the banister in her attempts to reach the outside world, though what she would do then was beyond her.

"Bitch!" she heard Bullseye scream as he set after her again, but she had begun to think now that she might actually survive the night.

A man stepped into the stairwell from the hall even as she reached the landing, and she collided with him. They went down, and the man was scowling, looking to her for an apology or an explanation as he helped her up. Karen watched him as his eyes found the blood on her shoulder and arm, then looked up the stairs, back the way she had come.

Suddenly the man stiffened, and it took Karen a moment to register that the pommel of some kind of blade was snug up against his chest. He slid down the cement wall, leaving a bloody trail. Shock numbing her finally, Karen turned to run again, thinking she had perhaps one more flight of stairs to the lobby, then the street.

She launched herself across the landing, a flash of black in her peripheral vision, and there was a sudden, excruciating, burning pain in her head and her neck snapped back. Her legs flew out from under her and she fell hard on the cement, the breath leaving her in a burst. Bullseye bent over her, one hand wrapped in her hair. From her angle, he was upside down, but he quickly moved around and sat down hard on her stomach, straddling her like a playground bully.

"Are you through?" he asked. Karen noticed the gash in his face, the blood there, and she had at least one thing to be glad of.

"It appears I am," she said, and then the killer's face turned dark and twisted, like rotten fruit. His lip curled and his eyes narrowed under the mask as he leaned in close to her.

"You hurt me," he hissed, and slapped her hard, her jaws clacking together.

"Well," Karen said, smiling through the pain, "that's something at least."

She was prepared for another slap, but it didn't come. Instead, he held the point of a blade to her neck and whispered to her.

"It was going to be a pleasure to kill you just to get under Daredevil's skin," he said, intimate as an obscene phone call. "Now I'm just looking forward to hurting you."

And then he smiled. Karen knew that smile. She'd seen it on the man at St. Bridget's and on the sniper who'd threatened her.

Predators smile.

They enjoy their work.

Chapter 15

A S FOGGY CAME AROUND, HE HEARD POLICE SIRENS
in the distance, getting closer. The police cars
couldn't have been less than a block or two
away, the volume of their screaming blanketing the
darkness around him.

"Hey, buddy, you okay?" asked a kid in tattered
clothes whose lip and eyelid were pierced. The kid
was standing over him, but Foggy had just been listening to the sirens for a moment.

Then he realized he was not alone on the ground,
and it all came back to him in a rush: where he was,
what had happened, who was there with him.

"Oh, God, Natasha!" he cried, then crawled stiffly
to his knees.

The Black Widow was still unconscious. The left
side of her face was torn and bleeding, her right arm
underneath her body at an awkward angle—Foggy
thought it might be broken. He felt her neck for a
pulse, but couldn't find the right spot to press. Gingerly, he lifted her left wrist, and released a breath
he hadn't realized he'd been holding as he found a
beat. He was no expert, but it seemed strong.

"Natasha?" he said quietly, then with more force
as the police sirens wailed insanely close. "Natasha!"

"Foggy?" she asked weakly as her eyes flickered
open. Then she gave him a halfhearted smile.
"You're worse than the sirens."

"Are you okay?" he asked.

"I think I'll be fine," she said unconvincingly. "Go look for Karen, Foggy. It's her Bullseye wanted."

"Karen?" Foggy said in surprise.

He stood and pushed through the crowd of people who had gathered around them. Foggy didn't know what Bullseye wanted with Karen, but he was terrified for her. He had known her as long as Matt had, she was one of his dearest friends. If Bullseye had gotten his hands on her, it was only because Natasha had been forced to break off the fight to save his own life! It would be his fault, and he couldn't bear that.

Foggy went through the outer door of the building and found a knot of people inside the foyer. What were they looking at?

He turned around to look back at that outer door, and saw it, a smear of wet blood on the wood. His eyes and mouth went wide and his heart stopped in his chest.

"Dear God, no," he whispered to himself, tears already at the corners of his eyes.

"Let me in, quickly!" he pounded on the door. "Where is Karen Page? Somebody let me in!"

An older man, apparently reassured by Foggy's businesslike attire despite his panic, opened the door for him.

"Where's Karen Page?" he yelled.

"Well," the old guy said, "her apartment's on . . ."

"I know where it is!" he snapped, heading for the stairs. Obviously they had no idea whether Karen was involved in what happened. Behind him, he heard the old man mutter, "Then what the hell did you ask for?" but he was too crazed to even consider the comment.

He followed the trail of blood up the steps at a run, and at the first floor landing found the body of a man who'd been stabbed in the chest, the murder weapon standing straight up out of him. Relief began to sweep through him, but then he saw that the blood trail did not come from the man. There were splotches continuing on up the steps, and Foggy cursed and headed up after them.

Three flights later, his heart felt like it was going to explode from the exertion, but he kept on to the next corpse. The man, who lay on a damp mop, was apparently a maintenance person of some sort. He had also been stabbed, but Foggy immediately looked up the stairs and saw that the bloody trail continued up the last flight to the top, to the floor where Matt and Karen lived.

"Oh, dear Lord, I'm sorry," he sobbed suddenly, knowing that he was too late. He'd done more than let them down, he'd gotten Karen killed. "Oh, Karen, I'm so sorry. Oh, Matt . . . God help me!"

He stared at the trail of blood, and weighted down with the burden of his guilt like the condemned climbing the hill at Calvary, he started up the stairs. When he reached the top floor, he tried to ignore the wide open door down the hall. He knew whose apartment it was, of course, just as he knew it would be empty.

Foggy went to the window and watched as a pair

of EMTs loaded Natasha into the back of an ambulance. His heart sank even further. Not only had his helplessness probably gotten Karen killed, but Natasha had been badly injured while saving his life. She would never have allowed them to put her into the ambulance otherwise.

Foggy Nelson sat down to wait for the police. Amidst the shattered window glass were green shards that had come from the wine he had brought, the weapon he had tried to use against Bullseye. What a fool he'd been. He'd dropped it instantly. The roses he'd brought for Karen lay trampled near the door. He knew he should start cleaning up, but he couldn't move. Matt had invited him to dinner, a little reunion for the three of them, the team that had once made up the firm of Nelson & Murdock.

Now, because of him, Karen Page was dead.

Foggy had tried, desperately, to stay awake, but despite his best efforts, he nodded off in front of David Letterman. Daredevil shook him awake.

"Nelson!" he said sharply. "What's gone on here? Where are Matt and Karen? What's going on?"

The man sounded furious, panicked, and verging on the hysterical. He knew Daredevil cared greatly for Matt and Karen, but this was far from the reaction he expected from the usually super-calm man without fear.

"Matt went out hours ago to help Melvin Potter find you," Foggy said, repeating the story he'd gotten from Natasha when he phoned the hospital. "He got in touch with the Black Widow somehow, and she was here to protect Karen from Bullseye. But I'd had a dinner invitation from Matt, and I got in the way." Foggy buried his face in his hands. "Bullseye threw me out the window. Natasha saved my life. She'll be okay, but she's been hospitalized because of her injuries. Bullseye took Karen!"

He sobbed openly then, looking up at Daredevil, hoping for some kind of forgiveness.

"Two men were killed here," Foggy continued, "and Karen was hurt, bleeding pretty bad. But the cops think if he was going to kill her, he'd have just done it and left her like the others. They think he's holding her for something. One of the cops, a Lieutenant Bryce, said he'd be 'waiting up for you,' whatever that means."

Daredevil turned away then, as if in disgust, and Foggy only nodded, accepting the blame, accepting the hero's dismissal of him.

"Oh, God, if only I'd been here sooner, or not at all, the Widow might have beaten Bullseye. Karen might still be here," Foggy said, as if trying to convince himself.

Then Daredevil put a hand on his shoulder, and his voice was soft and comforting.

"Why don't you head home, Counselor? Don't tear yourself up over this," he said. "There's no way to know how things would have turned out if you hadn't shown up. Saving your life, the Widow may have saved her own life as well. We'll never know."

Daredevil turned, went to the window, and in a moment, he was gone. His words stung Foggy Nelson, despite the truth in them.

The thought of facing Matt with this news was almost more than he could bear.

Daredevil wondered if Melvin Potter hated him. Despite the fact that he had given every available moment to searching for Betsy over the past few days, it hadn't been enough. It wasn't enough until he brought the woman home safely. Now, with the most important person in his own life gone, her life in the hands of someone else, he realized what Melvin must be going through. Every second not knowing their fate was agony.

But unlike Melvin, Daredevil was equipped to do something about it.

Gary Wiezak was not in the apartment where he'd been arrested, that much was clear. But Daredevil had yet to figure out where he might be holed up. Certainly, the would-be Kingpin would not run his operations from a hole-in-the-wall Manhattan walk-up. There had to be somewhere else, his real headquarters. What Daredevil really needed to do was go see Fisk and get him to cough up the information, offer him anything for it, fight for it if necessary. That would be instigating a war with the Kingpin that Daredevil could not afford, but once he had exhausted the few leads he had, Fisk would be his only choice.

Foggy had said Bryce would be waiting up for him,

and when Daredevil reached the lieutenant's apartment, he discovered the cop was as good as his word. The window was even open a crack, and he slid it up the rest of the way, and dropped to the floor. Bryce sat in a high-backed chair, reading. From the way he slumped forward and to one side, canting the book so that its pages were right under a lamp next to the chair, Daredevil could tell that one feeble light was the room's only illumination.

"You'll hurt your eyes," he said ironically, "reading in this light."

Bryce looked up, not startled in the least. He'd been expecting Daredevil, had obviously been aware of his presence the moment the window had started to rise.

"I hate to be so cold," Bryce said, "but without witnesses, the Wiezak case is sunk. The DA will not pursue the charges if we can't turn up those witnesses. I've been given twenty-four hours."

Daredevil sighed and leaned against the window sill, arms crossed. He'd expected this, but hoped DA Tower would at least wait for Wiezak's attorneys to push him on the subject. And twenty-four hours? That was no time at all. Then again, if he hadn't found Wiezak by then, Karen would probably be dead. Betsy Potter was, in all probability, dead already.

"I'll find Karen Page, but you've got to identify that sniper or Wiezak is going to walk anyway," Daredevil said quietly.

"We're working on it. What else can I do to help?"

Bryce asked, no more squabbling over police jurisdiction or vigilantism. They'd moved past that.

"Any other addresses on Wiezak yet?" Daredevil asked. "Do you guys have any idea where he's been when he's not at his apartment?"

"Nothing," Bryce said. "It's been a dead end for us, and his attorneys only laugh at us when we suggest he has another residence. Obviously, he's got nothing else under his name."

"What about business associates?" the hero continued. "I mean, he's been doing business with the sleaziest people in New York, you've got to have his most common contacts down somewhere?"

"Nothing you don't already have, I'm afraid," the lieutenant answered, and Daredevil could see they weren't getting anyplace. Both of them were merely growing more frustrated.

"Can I use your phone?" Daredevil asked.

"It's two o'clock in the morning."

"I know what time it is."

"All yours," Bryce shrugged.

Daredevil picked up the phone and dialed the *Daily Bugle* office, let the phone ring six times, and would have let it go on several more, but a voice mail system picked up, and he hung up on it. Even if there were human beings there, the machine wouldn't ever let him reach anyone anyway. He dialed again, and this time a very sleepy voice answered.

"Ben, it's me," he said. "I'm sorry, but it's important."

"Go on," Ben Urich said, interest piqued. Daredevil could hear his wife complaining about the late call in the background, but he had no time for niceties.

"The one night you're home at a decent hour," Daredevil said, by way of apology. "Bullseye killed two people in Murdock and Page's building tonight," he began, and heard Urich gasp on the other end of the line. The reporter would immediately understand that Daredevil wasn't alone, or he wouldn't be speaking about Matt Murdock in the third person. "Karen Page was wounded and appears to have been kidnapped," he said. "The case is going to fall apart unless I can find Wiezak, and identify the sniper. Do you have anything that can help?"

"Thanks for taking the time to explain," Urich said, but the thanks were unnecessary. Ben was a reporter, and Daredevil knew that reporters had to have the facts.

"Yeah," he said. "I've been working on that, using the police sketch. I think I might have one slim lead for you."

"You're all I've got," Daredevil responded.

"The sketch looks a lot like a photo I acquired of Wiezak's right hand man, bodyguard some say. His name is Shane Cairns, and apparently he keeps pretty much to himself, so the cops might not have anything on him yet. He lives on 12th Street in the West Village. Here, I've got the address."

Bryce had been hovering around him during the phone call, and when Daredevil put the phone down, he wanted to know exactly what was going on. It was his job, after all.

"I've got precisely nothing," Daredevil answered.

"But whoever that was gave you some information," Bryce said. "Look, man, I'm here to help, but I don't want you withholding pertinent facts of the case from the police."

Daredevil nodded.

"He gave me the name and address of Wiezak's top man," he said. "I suspect he's our sniper. I'm going after him."

"Give me the information, I'll send a car down to pick him up. We'll get him to give up what we need," Lieutenant Bryce said, confident, his words containing a promise that legal procedure wouldn't stop him.

"No disrespect, Lieutenant, but I think I'll have a better chance of getting him to talk, if he's there at all," Daredevil said. "You have someone to answer to, all I've got is myself . . . and my memory of the people I've failed. I'll do whatever it takes, and I'll call with whatever I get."

Bryce paused a moment, about to speak, then nodded. He walked to the back of the apartment, and into his bedroom.

Thanks for not pushing, Daredevil thought, then slipped back out the window and into the night.

The apartment on 12th Street was a basement job, its window at the same level as the sidewalk. It was a nice neighborhood, the kind of place people made

buttons to find the one that said, "play," and pressed it. The sound of tape rewinding was reassuring, and the techno-voice said, "Hello, you have two new messages." One was from a woman Cairns was clearly involved with, wondering why he hadn't been returning her phone calls.

The other was a voice Daredevil didn't know.

"Shane it's Gary," the voice, Gary Wiezak's voice, played on the tape. "If you're home, pick up . . . Oh, forget it. Look, just call me when you get in. I'm at the hotel."

The hotel? What hotel?

"Damn," Daredevil shook his head and slammed a fist on the counter. He didn't want to think that an average New York City hotel would be a safe place for Wiezak to hole up with bodyguards and at least two prisoners. The guy probably had at least a suite somewhere that he used as a regular residence.

But where? There were hundreds of hotels in Manhattan alone. Cairns would know, and Daredevil was confident he could make the man talk, but he wasn't here now and wasn't likely to be coming back any time soon. He couldn't wait. The most important person in his life was out there, her life on the line. More than that, however, he would never be able to forgive himself if something had happened to Betsy Potter. He knew he had done everything he could, but that wouldn't matter. He shouldn't have left Wiezak to the police. He should have gotten the guy himself and forced him to produce the woman.

He was desperate now. Close enough to taste it,

but still much too far away. If he could find that hotel, he would find Cairns and Wiezak. If he found Wiezak, he would find Betsy Potter. If he found Betsy, he would find Karen.

And he knew Bullseye would be waiting. Bullseye would be counting on Daredevil's ability to find them all, looking forward to the confrontation. If he could live up to his old enemy's confidence in him, he might be able to bring Karen and Betsy home alive.

"You boys need a man with vision!" Turk proclaimed, and several people at tables in hearing distance groaned, but he went right on about his business. Luka and his brothers were planning an art heist, and though Turk had never been in on a museum job before, he knew he had vision, and that's what turned a so-so plan into a gem.

"I'm telling ya, fellas," he started, and then his mouth clamped shut and his eyes narrowed.

"We'll have to put this one on hold for a sec," he said, and began walking toward the bar near the front of Josie's.

He'd vowed to himself never to sit with his back to the door again, and tonight it had paid off. He still had stitches from his last run-in with Daredevil, and he wasn't ready for another. That meant he wanted to be as close to Josie herself as possible. Turk wasn't a man to hide behind a woman's skirts, no sir. But Josie, sometimes Turk wondered if she was a woman at all, the way she ran her place.

Daredevil stepped through the door.

"What's wrong with you, Daredevil," Josie yelled the minute his foot landed on her floor. "Can't you read plain English? The sign on the door says 'No Super Heroes Allowed,' and that means you!"

Daredevil smiled, just a little, but it was hard and grim and made Turk take a few steps back.

"Josie I'm hurt," the hero said. "But don't worry, I'm not breaking any rules. I'm not a super hero, just a man. A man who desperately needs help."

Josie didn't say anything, but Turk could see that she wasn't about to challenge Daredevil's presence again, despite the bullet she'd taken just days before. He waited, but the hero didn't approach him, just stood there a moment surveying the room. In the dark bar, the red of his suit was a purplish black, like an awful bruise, and the thought made Turk very uneasy.

"Most of you know Melvin Potter," Daredevil said loudly. "Or know of him. You also know that his wife is missing. I've been searching for her. Now I'm certain if any of you had any information about this, you would have come forward by now to help out old Melvin, if not me. But there's something else I need. I want you to spread this around tonight when you leave here. I'm looking for a shooter named Cairns, and for Gary Wiezak, who holds his leash."

"You the dogcatcher, now, Daredevil?" somebody said from the crowd. Turk didn't recognize the voice, but he flinched nevertheless. DD was in a hell of a mood, and the smart-ass was asking for trouble.

"You'll be seeing me later, Hugo," Daredevil said, all trace of humor gone from his face.

Turk heard Hugo whisper, "How the hell did he know it was me?" but Daredevil ignored his remarks.

"If you know anything, or find out anything, and don't pass it on to me, believe me when I say you'll be sorry. Whatever you've got, get it to Turk, here."

Turk stiffened, about to ask why him. But he knew why. Daredevil scared him, and fear could be trusted.

"Now wait just a . . ." Josie started, but Daredevil cut her off.

"Don't mess with me, Josie. There are lives at stake. And if that's not enough for you, you've got a lot of wanted men in here right now, not to mention you don't always close when you're supposed to. I could roust you every night if it came to that, your 'No Super Heroes' sign notwithstanding.

"Turk," he said, "wait by the pay phone. I'll call."

"How long do I wait?" Turk asked, not pleased by the assignment.

Daredevil turned without responding and walked out the door. Turk shook his head, muttering curses and false threats under his breath, but he went back and took a table by the phone. He looked for Luka and his brothers, but they'd seen that Daredevil knew Turk, and they weren't interested in his vision anymore.

Chapter 16

DAREDEVIL HAD BEEN ROUSTING PUNKS FOR HOURS, but hadn't come up with any leads on what hotel Wiezak might be staying in. He'd begun to realize that the crimelord had even less of a chance at the Kingpin's throne than he'd originally thought. If his fingers were deep enough into Manhattan's criminal pie, Daredevil would have been able to find a lead.

In despair, Daredevil realized he needed to go home. He knew he would find Wiezak, but he didn't know when. And with Wiezak, he would find Bullseye. If he was going to be prepared for Bullseye, who was probably sleeping like a baby at that very moment, the least he would need was something to eat, a two-minute shower, a fresh costume, and two Tylenol. After all, fifteen minutes wasn't likely to make much of a difference. Bullseye wasn't about to let Wiezak kill Karen until Daredevil showed up to rescue her.

He stopped at a pay phone on the corner of 9th Avenue and 49th Street to call Turk. For a moment, he considered not calling. He doubted the man would have any leads, and it would give him pleasure to let Turk sit there all night, afraid to leave or go to the bathroom. It would serve as a lesson, and he'd drum it in next time he saw the man . . . for it was an order Turk was bound to disobey eventually.

But no. He had to call.

"Turk," the man answered.

"Anything?" the hero asked.

"Zip. Can I go home now?"

Daredevil paused, heart sinking lower, then answered: "Get some sleep, and stay out of trouble."

Morning was still several hours away, but Daredevil could feel its approach. Surprisingly, he wasn't sleepy, but he could feel exhaustion creeping into his body limb by limb, into the muscles of his back and shoulders. His head ached and his empty stomach felt like a wound.

He stood atop the building directly across from his apartment, and wondered if Bullseye hadn't stood here as well. It was by far the best vantage point for surveillance, if the killer bothered with such things. His radar sensed that the shattered bedroom window had been boarded up, which could only have been Foggy's doing.

What a friend! How he got anyone to come out in the middle of the night to board it up was a mystery, but Daredevil was sure it had cost a bundle. He wondered if Foggy was still inside, perhaps asleep and awaiting his return, awaiting news of Karen, feeling guilty still, Daredevil imagined, for letting himself be used by Bullseye.

He could relate.

An enormous heave landed the grappling end of his billy-club tether on the fire escape that jutted from the building's left side. He checked it every week or so to see that it was secure. He swung then, diagonally across the street, and his momentum took him into the alley between his building and the one next to it. He dropped silently to the fire escape, halfway down from the roof and began to climb up it, certain to stay out of sight of the hall windows.

He had a change of clothes hidden there and a key to the roof he had "borrowed" from the landlord and duplicated. He tried to come into the apartment as Matt Murdock, or at least to use the roof when possible. The window was too conspicuous to be used frequently.

Instead of stripping on the roof, he pulled the gym bag from its hiding place, removed the pants and sweatshirt and slipped them on, then tied his Reeboks. He slid mask, gloves and boots into the bag, put his spare glasses on, and headed down to his apartment.

From the hall, he could hear Foggy's heart beating, and its steady, peaceful rhythm was reassuring. The man was a great lawyer, intelligent and sincerely caring, but useless in a fight. Still, he was a good friend and a stand-up guy. Ironically, Foggy Nelson was probably everything Matt's father had wished for in a son.

From time to time, Matt had considered revealing to Foggy that he was Daredevil, but he never had. Instead, he had actively kept it from him. They had had their problems over the years, as friends do. These problems had created a certain distance between them. If Foggy were to discover that he was Daredevil, Matt had always believed that distance would grow to be insurmountable. Foggy would not know how to deal with it. And every year older that the lie became, the more drastic the repercussions were likely to be if the truth were revealed.

In the end, he had put himself in a position where only chance would ever reveal his secrets to his best friend.

Matt entered the apartment quietly, the only sound the tumbling of the lock. Sprawled on the futon-bed, Foggy was blissfully unconscious. Matt went directly to the bathroom. He peeled off clothes and costume, burying the latter at the bottom of the hamper, which Foggy would never delve into. He showered quickly, but scrubbed himself well, and let the water go cold at the end, its freezing spray bracing his body and waking him up completely.

He dried off in a rush, popped two Tylenol from under the sink, and didn't bother with a shave. No time. In the apartment's single room, he listened carefully for any change in Foggy's heartbeat as he opened his armoire and jiggled the false back to get at his spare costume. He dressed quickly, pulling jeans and a sweatshirt over the costume and once again putting the mask, boots and gloves in his gym bag. Several times he bumped the wall, and at one point shut a drawer rather loudly, but Foggy didn't stir.

He went to the little cubbyhole his landlord had the audacity to call a kitchen and poured himself a bowl of Raisin Bran. He followed the cereal with a quick glass of orange juice and an apple-cinnamon

Pop Tart whose smell alone, he thought, would normally have woken Foggy from even the deepest slumber. He must have been completely wiped out.

Finally, Matt was ready to go out again, and hit every hotel in the city if necessary. He was weighing a difficult decision. He could narrow his search by visiting the Kingpin first, but getting in to see him would be time-consuming enough. If he attempted to force the information from the crimelord, there would be blood, much of it likely his own, and as tired as he was, he had little hope of winning. Really, searching the hotels was his only practical choice.

But first . . . he knelt by the bed and shook Foggy awake.

"Ugh," Foggy said, tongue clicking inside a dry mouth. "What, huh, Matt?"

Foggy sat up.

"Oh, man, you're home," he said. "How long was I sleeping, what time is it? Never mind that, what's up with Karen?"

"I was with Melvin most of the night," he said, knowing the lie was safe, that Melvin Potter would never speak to Foggy Nelson socially. Despite Foggy's liberal mind and Melvin's rehabilitation, the lawyer had never been quite able to forget that Melvin Potter had once kidnapped his sister Candace.

"Betsy is still missing," Matt said. "Daredevil found me there. He's out searching for Karen right now, and I'm heading down to the police station. I guess that's where I can do the most good. I'm hoping they pull in Wiezak soon, but I just don't know."

329

Foggy ran both hands through his hair and sighed.

"Matt, I'm so sorry, y'know. I was late getting here. If I'd been here earlier, maybe things wouldn't have happened the way they did. I just wish . . ." he said, surrendering his ego to his guilt.

"Foggy, don't beat yourself up, okay?" Matt said, trying to console him. "I could just as easily say I never should have left. I should have put Karen first, before Melvin, but I just didn't expect it all to happen so fast. I was a fool. You couldn't have known what was happening, and I'm just glad Natasha was here. Bullseye's almost killed Daredevil a few times, and if he's capable of that, what chance would a couple of sharks like us have?"

Foggy nodded.

"That's pretty much what Daredevil said, though I gotta say he was pretty arrogant about it."

Matt smiled, trying not to let Foggy see it.

"Listen," he said, "I've got to go. If you want to just stick around here, keep an eye on the place, that's great. But don't feel like you have to."

"Not at all," Foggy replied. "I couldn't go home now if I wanted to."

"Great," Matt said. "I'll see you in the morning, and hopefully we'll all be fine."

Matt went to the door.

"Matt, wait a minute," Foggy said, getting up to follow him. "I wanted to tell you something. I know you're in a rush, and I don't blame you, but this will just take a minute."

"Okay," Matt said, nodding for him to continue.

"You're my best friend, Matt," he said, and his voice hitched with emotion. "But more than that, you've always been my conscience. Without you around, it's hard sometimes to know what's right and wrong, especially with our society becoming grayer every day. But tonight has made up my mind."

"You're going to quit?" Matt guessed.

"Not yet," Foggy answered. "Eventually I'm sure, but not for a while yet. No, what I am going to do, though, is nail Wiezak."

Matt was stunned.

"But Foggy that's . . ."

"Unethical? Maybe. But it's also right. Oh, I'm not going to make anything up, I'm just going to make sure that we don't hide anything either. No matter what the law says, it isn't right for the firm to help Wiezak substantiate false alibis, to hide foreign accounts and shell-companies, to maintain connections to shady businessmen. Oh, I'm not going on record, but you can bet that new ADA, Marcia Martinez, will be receiving a large, anonymous package.

"He's going down, Matt, and every penny he's got will end up seized by the government. Maybe it's wrong, and maybe it goes against everything we stand for, everything you've always been so eloquent in defending, the word of the law. But it's also the only thing I can do and still live with myself. The guy's a monster, and I have a chance to get him. If the Kingpin weren't so well protected, with so many people in his pocket, I'd wish for the opportunity to do it to him as well."

There was a moment of silence between them, and then Matt reached out to embrace his friend. He hugged Foggy tight and made a vow to see him more in the weeks and months to come.

"You're a good and courageous man, Counselor," Matt said. "I don't think people tell you that . . . I don't think I've told you that often enough."

Foggy said nothing, but his silence held sufficient meaning.

Matt was about to turn for the door again, when Foggy's words came back to him. If Wiezak was hiding property as well as accounts . . .

"Foggy, you said Wiezak has shell-companies," Matt said excitedly. "This is a long shot, but do you remember if any of those companies own a hotel here in Manhattan?"

Foggy's heartbeat quickened.

"Well, not exactly, but . . ."

"But what?" Matt pushed.

"Well, he has a half sister," Foggy said, thinking aloud. "Hamlin is her last name I think. She owns the Wilmington Hotel by Central Park."

"Old friend," Matt said, rapping him on the shoulder, "you may have just saved Karen's life after all."

"Do you want me to call the police?" Foggy asked.

"No," Matt answered quickly. "Bullseye would only kill Karen, and probably Wiezak as well, and take off. Only Daredevil can handle this."

Matt rushed out the door, nearly forgetting to act blind. Outside the door, his incredible hearing picked up Foggy's whispered words: "I just wish you could rely on me the way you do on DD."

Matt felt a twinge of sadness at Foggy's words, but the friendship would have to wait. Karen's life, and Betsy Potter's as well, hung in the balance.

Melvin Potter had barely slept since Betsy had been kidnapped, and this night was no exception. Instead of sleeping, he worked in the shop on new costumes for Halloween, or sat in the living room staring out the window, or up on the roof in the cold night, clutching his wife's nightshirt close and searching the stars as if they might hold a clue to her whereabouts.

The phone rang, startling him as he stitched a new costume, and he looked at the clock as he answered it. Three-forty-three A.M. *Who the . . .*

"Hello?" he asked, the question, and his displeasure, obvious in his voice.

"Melvin," a male voice said, "This is Daredevil."

Oh, God no! Not bad news.

"What's happened?" he asked, every muscle tense.

"I think I know where they're keeping Betsy," Daredevil said, and Melvin's heart leaped. "But Melvin . . . I don't think we should get our hopes up until I've gone in there. We can't know . . ."

"I know all that, DD," Melvin said. "I know. But I know she's still alive. I know she is. I think I'd feel it if she died, y'know? Maybe you can't understand that, but I think I'd feel it."

"Believe me," the hero answered. "I understand."

Silence.

"Daredevil?" Melvin said. "Bring Betsy home."

He hung up without waiting for a reply. What could Daredevil say?

Chapter 17

THE WILMINGTON HOTEL HAD TWENTY-TWO STO-
ries, not including the penthouse. It was a
unique building, and therefore old. Nobody
built anything unique anymore. Its stone face would
have allowed many handholds, but Daredevil didn't
even consider trying to climb it. Oh, he'd reach the
top just fine, but he'd be pretty exhausted by the
time he got there.

Despite the hotel's age, if Wiezak was up there in
the penthouse, and Daredevil was certain that he
was, the lobby and elevators were certain to be video
monitored. They'd be expecting him, perhaps looking for anyone who might be Daredevil in disguise,
and there weren't too many people to choose from
this early in the morning. No doubt they'd have
guards at the top of the stairs. They would certainly
have considered an approach via the service elevator,
in the back of the hotel.

But it was four o'clock in the morning.

If he had to bet, based on his previous run-ins with
the kind of talent Wiezak had working for him, Daredevil would have to say most of the guards would be
half-asleep at best. And despite Wiezak's precautions,
there was a good chance there wouldn't be a camera
in the service elevator. Wiezak would never expect a
real assault on his little fortress. That was why Wilson
Fisk was the Kingpin, and Gary Wiezak would never
be anything but a gutter rat.

337

There was a small wire-mesh reinforced window on the service door, which didn't stand up to his billy club for more than fifteen seconds. Snapping the two portions of his billy club together to form a long cane, which could easily pass for a blind man's walking stick, Daredevil slid it through the window and bent his arm around and down. He planted the straight end of the "cane" on a metal bar and pressed down hard, popping the door open from the inside.

The kitchen was deserted, as expected. Room service didn't care *what* you wanted at four in the morning.

Silently, he rushed through the kitchen area and found the service elevator on the left. He pressed the button, and there was a *ding* immediately, a sound he knew, and though he couldn't see it, he assumed a white plastic arrow had lit up to show the elevator was there.

If he was wrong, if Wiezak wasn't as cocky as he thought, and there was a camera inside, he'd be tipping them off by getting in the elevator. They'd all be wide awake, alert and waiting when he reached the upstairs. It would go down a lot harder than necessary. Karen and Betsy's odds of living would be dramatically lowered.

Daredevil stepped into the elevator, scanned with his radar, and breathed a sigh of relief when there was no visible camera, nor an obvious spot to hide one. He snapped the cane into halves again and used his billy club to push up the trapdoor on top of the car, jumped up and pulled himself far enough through to see that there was nothing on the exterior of the elevator either, at least nothing obvious.

Dropping back into the car, he reached out and scanned the buttons with his fingers, easily "reading" the indented numbers and symbols. As expected, the top button said "P," but when he pressed it, the elevator did not move. *At least Wiezak was that intelligent,* he thought. *You must need a key to get the elevator to reach the penthouse.*

No problem. Daredevil pressed the button directly below "P," which was for the twenty-second floor.

Still, the elevator did not move.

He pressed twenty-one. The doors slid shut, and the elevator began laboring to raise him up through the hotel's gullet.

A key was necessary to reach the twenty-second floor as well as the penthouse. The only reason Daredevil could conceive of for this precaution was that Wiezak lived on that floor as well as the penthouse . . . or perhaps *lived* was the wrong word. Perhaps Wiezak merely used the twenty-second floor for his business purposes..

And if so, that could very well be where Betsy Potter and Karen were being kept.

The elevator stopped on the twenty-first floor, and Daredevil pulled himself up through the trapdoor to stand atop the car. He wrapped his hands around the elevator cable and began to climb. Above and to his left, two male voices whispered quietly to one another, both speaking in a tone that implied arrogance and bragging, even if the words were unclear. Daredevil paid little attention to the words. It was enough to know that they were there, and at ease, expecting nothing and likely grumbling about being handed the early morning watch.

"Shane still up?" one of the men said, and Daredevil listened intently. This had to be Shane Cairns.

"Don't know," the other replied. "He was pretty pissed at the boss for making him baby-sit the woman. I wouldn't be surprised if he sacked out in one of the guest rooms."

Daredevil didn't know if Cairns was awake or sleeping, but he was on the twenty-second floor, that was fairly clear. That left only Bullseye and Wiezak upstairs, and who knew how many armed guards. But down here, it was these two bozos, maybe a few more, and Cairns.

Elevator doors were heavy, and not intended to be easily opened unless the elevator was behind them. There was every possibility these two thugs would be quick enough to alert their boss or cohorts that their sanctum had been compromised. But he had no other choice. He would simply have to move as fast as he could, hope the element of surprise would work in his favor long enough to take them out.

His radar perfectly sketching the shaft around him, Daredevil reached out and grabbed a parallel cable, then pulled himself over to stand on the inner threshold of the elevator door. It was extraordinarily narrow and offered very little purchase. Even if he had the strength to pull the door open quickly, he would probably fall back into the shaft. Luckily the elevator was only one floor below. The fall wouldn't kill him. On the other hand, the hail of gunfire that was nearly guaranteed to follow him down would do the job just fine.

Daredevil pinpointed the two preoccupied watchmen, one on either side of the elevator door. He squatted on the threshold, feet pointing away from him, chest and pelvis nearly resting on the door. His hands gripped the right side of the elevator door, burrowing for purchase and finding it, sliding around to the inner wall of the door.

And then he pulled.

Every muscle in his body was tense as he put all his strength into one massive heave and hauled the door open. As predicted, he lost his balance. He might have saved himself from falling, but Daredevil had other plans. He let the fall turn into a backward somersault, reaching under himself to snag the bottom of the threshold with his hands.

"What the hell?"

"What's going . . ."

The two guards, drawing their weapons, rushed to the open door, expecting an elevator, expecting an enemy, a target, a victim. Pushing off from the shaft wall with both legs, Daredevil reversed the move he had made only seconds before, flipping up and back, each guard getting the heel of a boot in his jaw. They fell back, and Daredevil was on his feet immediately.

One guard, shaking his head with disorientation, stumbled forward only to be met with a right hook.

The man crumbled to the ground in a heap, but his friend was alert now, and his gun was pointed directly at Daredevil's face.

"Blink and you'll miss it," the guy said, and Daredevil could hear his heartrate increase as his brain told his finger to pull the trigger.

Can't have that, he thought, even as he reached forward, yanked the guy's arm toward him, flipped the guard over his shoulder and onto the marble tile floor; and suddenly the man found his own gun staring him in the face.

"Get up, and not a word," Daredevil said, silence of the utmost importance. "Where's Cairns?"

The guard stood and faced him, and Daredevil heard him give a small chuckle. The hero wouldn't shoot him. The goon knew that and drew a breath to shout an alarm. Daredevil's left fist flashed up and took him down for the count. He tossed the gun through the open elevator shaft, then grabbed the other guard's weapon and did the same.

Still on alert, he let his radar give him a complete picture of his surroundings. Visible down the hall was the double elevator bank that came up from the lobby. There were no guards there, so he had to assume these two were for all the elevators, and that there were probably other guards on the stairs. Fortunately, they didn't seem to have been alerted by the noise . . . not yet, anyway.

The twenty-second floor was made up, as far as his radar could determine, of a number of large hotel suites and a conference room, likely where Wiezak gathered his goons to plot his next crime against civilized society.

And that's when it hit him. Wiezak, Cairns, Bullseye . . . it wasn't simply that they were uncivilized. It was that they could not be civilized. Certainly, they were cunning, particularly Bullseye. But he was insane. And come to think of it, Wiezak didn't seem terribly rational either. And then there were the things they did, unnatural, antisocial, uncivilized. Inhumane? Yes, that was it. They were not human beings, they were animals. And rabid at that. And there was nothing to be done about rabid animals.

You had to put them down.

Daredevil listened intently, picking out two heartbeats on the floor, in two different rooms. One was so slow that the person must have been asleep. The other was awake, but not beating abnormally fast, not pumped full of adrenaline. He guessed the sleeper to be Betsy, hence the guards. It wouldn't be Karen, he knew. Bullseye would have her upstairs with him. The other had to be Cairns, awake, but probably trying, hoping, to get some sleep before morning arrived.

He was in the suite at the far end of the hall, past the room where Daredevil thought Betsy Potter lay sleeping. But first things first. The man was awake; there would be no sneaking Betsy out until he'd been taken care of.

As silently as he could, though the rooms must be relatively well insulated if Cairns hadn't heard the fight in the hall, he padded to the door where Cairns struggled with the sandman, turned the knob, threw the door open and rushed in. Cairns lay on a king size brass bed, arms crossed behind his head. He was more alert and faster than Daredevil had anticipated. On the bedside table was a sharply gleaming throwing knife, and it was flying toward him from the bodyguard's fingers before he'd taken his third step into the room.

Daredevil did the only thing he could. He fell. Like a base stealer sliding for home, he went down on his side and then his back, his momentum carrying him across the hardwood floor and under the bed. Cairns was up already, surely about to jump on the man he thought was on the floor at the end of his bed, but he'd miscalculated. Daredevil reached out from under the bed, grabbed his legs and pulled, but Cairns kicked him in the jaw, hard enough to turn his head, splitting Daredevil's lip.

Daredevil slid out from under the bed and was up to meet Shane Cairns, who was unarmed for the moment at least, but whose eyes showed little or no worry that he was facing the protector of Hell's Kitchen, the man without fear.

Perhaps he wasn't aware of Daredevil's reputation? In which case, of course, he would have to be instructed in its many facets. Daredevil moved in quickly, ready to deal Cairns a breath-stealing blow to the gut, then put his lights out with the second punch. But the stocky brute surprised him, sidestepping his punch and hammering his forearm across the side of Daredevil's skull. The hero tried to shake it off, but Cairns brought a knee up into his solar plexus, and Daredevil went down.

Too angry, too hyper, too cocky, he scolded himself, and rolled out of the way before Cairns, in only his socks, could kick him in the head. The man moved away, going for his knife, and Daredevil was up and lucid when he came back with it.

"I'm glad you came to me first, Daredevil," Cairns said. "I always knew you were nothing but headlines."

As he drove the knife forward, Daredevil brought up his billy club to parry the jab, hooked its curved end around the man's wrist and twisted, not hard enough to break it, but wrenching it painfully. The knife clattered to the hardwood as Daredevil continued his turn and kicked Cairns in the breastbone. The man stumbled backward, began to lose his balance, and as he attempted to regain it, his feet got caught up in the sheet and blanket that trailed onto the floor from the bed.

Shane Cairns fell hard against the window, which shattered, his momentum carrying him straight through. Daredevil dove forward, right hand reaching for the man's legs as his left found the wall above the window, anchoring him there. He strained, his head and right shoulder out the window, hanging over the city, and snagged the big man by the left ankle.

He had a moment to wonder how he would ever hold Cairns up with one hand, and then the weight was there, yanking him further out over the abyss.

The muscles in his neck, shoulders and arms stretched to their limit, legs braced to attempt to stop Shane Cairns from falling. After that, he'd worry about pulling him back up. It happened in a heart-beat, the weight pulling on him, Daredevil worrying that he wasn't going to be able to hold on, that he'd be pulled through the window behind the man.

"No," he said quietly, refusing to give in, pulling with all his strength, and hauling Shane Cairns's body back through the window, then dumping it somewhat unceremoniously onto the floor.

Daredevil looked down at Cairns, determined that he was still alive but unconscious, probably from the impact with the window. A small mercy. It had the advantage of not alerting the people upstairs, if the shattering window had not done so already, and he doubted it had . . . the rooms were soundproof after all.

But not completely. As he stepped into the hall, checking to see how badly he was bleeding, Dare-devil's radar picked up a form to his left and he spun to defend himself. Betsy Potter stood in the hall star-ing at him. He breathed a sigh of relief and put his hand to his side again.

"D-d-daredevil?" she asked, incredulous. From the way her head moved he could tell that she looked from his face to the blood at his side.

And then it came back to him, painfully, that Betsy was here as Wiezak's prisoner. He had no idea what she might have been through, but with the lessons he had learned through the life he had chosen to lead, on the streets of New York City, in the alleys of Hell's Kitchen, he could imagine the most repulsive, horrifying things.

"I'm here Betsy," he said as she crumpled in his arms. "I'm here to take you home."

Betsy backed away from him, heart speeding again. "Please tell me Melvin isn't with you?" she asked, and to Daredevil it sounded like a prayer.

"He's not."

"Oh, thank God," Betsy sighed.

"He's at home waiting for you right now," Daredevil said. "I want to get you to him as quickly as I can. We're going to go to the stairs. It's a long walk down, but I want you to move fast. As soon as you leave the stairwell, I need you to pull the fire alarm, wait until the guests start to leave the hotel, then mix in with the crowd and stay with them, out in front of the hotel, until the police and firefighters arrive. The first police officer you see, tell him I'm upstairs, and he should call Lieutenant Bryce right away. Lieutenant Bryce, got it?"

"Got it," she said. "But where are you going to be, Daredevil?"

"Wiezak has another friend of mine upstairs. I'm going up to get her. You can ask a policeman to drive you home, or wait for me," he said, and his heart went cold. "I won't be long."

"Are you going to kill him?" Betsy asked, the psychologist coming out in her, even here.

"No," Daredevil said immediately. "I'm going to send him to jail."

"Even though you know he'll get out eventually?" she asked.

"If that's what the system has in store for him, that's what will happen," he answered. "The justice system is flawed, but it's what we made it. Anything else is anarchy."

Betsy paused for a moment.

"There's something to be said for anarchy," she said grimly, then turned and headed for the stairs.

"Wait," Daredevil said. "There are probably guards."

Betsy stopped and waited for him to catch up, to pass her. He didn't have to listen for heartbeats this time. There were three people, two men and a woman, talking on the other side of the door. He smelled cigar smoke, a trace of perfume and somebody's leftover meal, tuna on wheat, sweet pickles. One voice was further up the stairs, and he listened more carefully now. A male and female on the landing, another male on the steps up to the penthouse . . . and who knew how many inside the penthouse itself. A dozen? Two dozen?

Fingers drummed a military march on the cement wall next to the door. Daredevil knew that whatever these low-rent mercenaries expected, it wasn't the wrath of an exhausted and disgusted hero. And it wasn't from behind them, it was from below. He was pleased to disappoint them.

"Stay back," he said to Betsy, turning the knob, then pushed the door open as hard as he could. It slammed into the man tapping on the wall before he could even pull his pistol, smacking his forehead and crashing his skull against the wall. He slumped back and began to tumble down the steps.

Before the man had begun to fall, Daredevil launched himself across the landing and slammed his female partner into the wall, yanking the AK-47 from her hands. She fell to her knees, reaching for the pistol at her belt, and he kicked it from her hand, then hauled her up in front of him, even as the guard up the stairs leveled a pistol at him.

"You'll kill her," Daredevil warned.

"Yeah?" the guard asked. "So?"

The man's heart raced, and Daredevil knew he was not bluffing. Arms around the woman who'd tried to kill him moments before, he threw himself back through the open door to the twenty-second floor, landing heavily and grunting with pain from his punctured side. It had gotten numb, but now the pain returned. Unfortunately, he couldn't spare a moment to tend it.

"Piers!" the woman yelled. "You bastard! I'll kill you myse . . ."

Daredevil chopped her hard, flat-handed on the neck, and she went out like a burnt bulb.

"You're a dead man, Daredevil," the final guard said, dry amusement in his voice. "That gunfire is going to bring a lot of reinforcements from upstairs."

His radar and hearing focused completely on the guard coming down the steps, Daredevil could pinpoint his every move, breath, heartbeat, knew when he was going to take a step, open his mouth to speak. He hefted the straight half of his billy club in his hand, testing its weight, and concentrated on the approaching gunman. One more step, he calculated.

Daredevil moved across the open doorway and threw the club with incredible accuracy. The gunman squeezed off another shot, but his head turned to follow the club, which was way off the mark. A laugh had begun to burst from his mouth, but it died there as the club slapped the concrete wall and ricocheted back to strike him broadside across the forehead.

He went down with a thud.

"Go, quickly, before more guards come, and pull the alarm as soon as you get to the bottom!" Daredevil said, and Betsy leaped past him and down the stairs.

Daredevil watched her go, hearing the growing sound of the alarm from the stairwell above him. Seconds later, there were voices coming down, calling names, one of which was Piers, the man he'd just knocked out. Betsy was at least three floors down when he heard footsteps, and he picked up his billy club and ran back into the twenty-second floor, back into the room where Shane Cairns had tripped on his bedding and almost fallen to his death.

Daredevil went to the window and looked out. A stone ledge, perhaps three inches wide, ran around the building. Looking up, he saw that there was a much larger one on the outer wall below the penthouse. That was the way to go, for certain. He removed what little glass was left from the bottom of the windowframe, then stepped up onto it. He turned carefully, his mind not even considering the drop that loomed behind.

He couldn't reach the ledge, even standing on the windowframe. It was several inches beyond his greatest reach. There was a great commotion inside; he had only seconds. Blood was dripping down onto Central Park West from the wound in his side. Hands bent into claws to grab hold of the ledge above him; he jumped up and out of the window.

Daredevil, the man without fear.

Chapter 18

SLEEP. THAT'S WHAT KAREN PAGE WANTED MORE than anything in the world. Well, more than anything except to keep living. But at the moment, it seemed that neither wish was likely to come true.

Since Bullseye had brought her back to Wiezak's penthouse, weak from loss of blood, her arm had been bandaged, but precious little else had been done. Blood had dried to a crust on her shirt and pants, and she'd been allowed precisely two trips to the bathroom, during neither of which had she been inclined to waste the little time given her by trying to clean herself up.

Bullseye had seemed impatient throughout the night, with time itself, and with Wiezak's power trip. Karen had come to realize that the crimelord was nearly as unstable as the assassin he'd hired. Bullseye stood at the sliding glass doors that led out onto the penthouse patio, barely paying attention, never speaking to her. He was waiting, she knew. Waiting for *him*.

The night had been long, the coffee hot and strong. She had defied Wiezak at first, refused to drink it, and he had poured it on her lap fresh from the pot, scalding her thighs. So she drank. Wiezak taunted her, caressed her. She ignored him as best she could.

From time to time, she would hear murmuring and look over to see that it was Bullseye. He was apparently singing, or humming to himself, nonchalantly whiling away the time until his greatest enemy, the man he so desperately wanted to kill, would arrive. And Bullseye said Daredevil would come. Wiezak appeared uncertain and unconcerned. If the hero came, his men would kill him, simple as that, he bragged. And then they could move on, the way clear to the Kingpin's throne.

Just past three in the morning, Wiezak had tired of the game.

"It's over now, Karen," he had said, smiling all the while. His breath was bad and the stubble grown over his chin. He wore sweatpants and a Harvard University t-shirt, both of which had stains. Bloodstains, she'd thought then. Probably her own.

"You shouldn't have told the police what you saw," he'd said. "Shane tried to tell you to stay out of it, and you hurt him. You should have listened. Only because I have a lot of respect for Bullseye, have I waited this long. He figured Daredevil would come after you. But I guess you're not as important to ol' DD as we thought, are you? Now it's all over."

He picked a long, flat case up from the table, opened it and showed her its contents. A long, flat, shining blade.

And that was when Bullseye had stepped in.

"Put that away," he'd said sternly.

"What?" Wiezak said, taken aback. "What the hell are you . . . ?"

"I said put it away," the assassin had insisted.

"She's bait, you idiot. When Daredevil is dead, you can kill her. Not before."

"You work for me!" Wiezak had declared.

"You can't pay me if you're dead. Put it away for both of us."

Wiezak had looked as if he were about to argue, and then Bullseye slapped him. Gary Wiezak's head rocked back, his eyes wide with shock even as he went for the gun at his back. Bullseye held the sharp point of a sai to his chest and said, "Don't even think about it."

Wiezak's hand had come back around to rest at his side.

More than an hour had passed since then, and Wiezak had done nothing but feed her coffee, and glance smirkingly, promisingly, down at the case that held her ultimate demise. Bullseye had stood by the sliding glass doors and stared down at the park below, humming quietly to himself.

"Drink, damn you," Wiezak was saying now, and Karen was ready to collapse from exhaustion.

"I have to go to the bathroom again," she complained.

Before Wiezak could reply, two of his bodyguards burst into the room.

"Boss," said one. Karen thought his name was Rico. "There's gunfire on the stairs."

"Well check it out," Wiezak snapped. "Bullseye, go with them."

"I stay with the bait until the fish bites," Bullseye said without even turning to face his employer.

Rico's eyes widened at such insubordination, but he said nothing.

"Go!" Wiezak shouted at the two bodyguards, who went back out into the front room and headed for the stairs. Several minutes later they were back, redfaced.

"All the guards down there are out cold, and the Potter woman's gone," Rico admitted.

Karen thought she might be able to die happy after seeing the look of frustration, disbelief, and utter rage that transformed Gary Wiezak's face at that moment.

His voice rising to a shout, he said, "scour both floors, find out what the hell is going on here. Find the Potter woman, find her rescuer, and kill him."

Rico and the other man started to leave the room, but Rico turned back toward him, a final thought reaching his lips.

"Gary," he said, "if that is Shane down there, the cops will be here any second. If the woman reaches the street, the show's over."

Wiezak slammed a fist onto the top of the television set.

"Three of you stay on this floor. Send two down to search twenty-two again and then stay by the stairs and the elevator. The rest, what's that, three? They go down after the woman. Get her before the cops do."

The two men left, and Karen heard orders shouted in the other room, people scrambling to do as their employer had instructed. Thirty seconds later, there was silence, but Karen knew that three well-armed guards stood outside that door.

Then the fire alarm went off.

Wiezak whipped his gun from the rear waistband of his pants and clicked off the safety, eyes darting nervously about the room. Bullseye turned to look expectantly at the door the guards had gone out only minutes before, and the sliding glass doors at his back exploded into the room in a blur of red.

Daredevil slammed hard into Bullseye's back, forcing the assassin to the floor as his momentum carried him further across the room. Wiezak took a shot at Daredevil, but the bullet struck Bullseye in the shoulder, making him wince. Wiezak reached for Karen, but his eyes were glued to Daredevil, and she took advantage of the moment, hugging him close, holding the gun away, and ramming her knee up into his groin.

Daredevil was four feet from the door when it opened. Two guards burst in as the hero threw his weight against it, knocking the two men together and down. The door was kicked open again as the third man came through, gun leveled at Daredevil's chest, but he moved much too quickly for the thug. Arm flashing out, he grabbed the man's wrist behind the weapon and drew him forward and past his body.

And two of Bullseye's shuriken sliced into the gunman's flesh, so sharp they nearly disappeared within him. The shuriken had to be poisoned, because the man slipped to the ground, dead. Bullseye pulled out some other weapon then, as the two men on the ground were recovering themselves enough to take aim, though they had yet to rise to their feet. Three steps and Daredevil launched himself into the air, arcing over the pair, who twisted wildly to try to get a shot off at him.

Karen let Gary Wiezak fall to the ground; he sucked in air as he tried to recover from her knee to the groin, and dropped his gun. She reached down to grab it, but as she did, Wiezak slammed a fist down on the back of her skull and she nearly blacked out from the pain. The next thing she knew, she was standing with Wiezak behind her, and he had the gun to the side of her head.

Daredevil was behind the two guards and they were up, blocking Bullseye's aim. They were about to turn their weapons on Daredevil again when he moved in close. Crossing his arms, he grabbed the barrel of each weapon with his opposite hand, then yanked the two guns apart. The men slammed together, heads cracking hard. Daredevil hit them simultaneously with their own weapons, and they were falling even as Bullseye flung two heavy metal balls at Daredevil. The weapon flew through the air so quickly that the wire that attached the balls was nearly invisible.

Daredevil lifted an appropriated AK-47 into the air and allowed the bolos to wrap around it, scoring the metal and actually beginning to cut into it. The weapons fell harmlessly to the floor.

Bullseye and Daredevil faced one another across the room. The assassin was grinning, despite the bullet in his shoulder, and Daredevil was bleeding badly from a wound at his side.

"Daredevil," Wiezak screamed, his voice hurting Karen's ears, "back off now or I kill her."

"You won't kill her right now," Daredevil said with confidence. "She's your only insurance once I've dealt with Bullseye."

"I will," Wiezak shouted at him. "I'll blow her head off!"

Karen was convinced. She thought at any moment the gun would go off and she would cease to exist. But Daredevil never even turned in Wiezak's direction. Karen knew that Daredevil, that Matt, could tell when somebody was lying by the rhythm of their heart, that he must know whether Wiezak was telling the truth or not. But that didn't make her any less afraid.

" 'Dealt with Bullseye'?" the assassin was saying. "You can barely stand, how are you going to deal with me?"

And Karen saw that there was something to what the madman said. Daredevil was standing and doing quite well at it, but he looked exhausted, and he was still bleeding from a wound he'd gotten who-knew-how-long ago. With all the action he'd seen in the past few minutes, it hadn't had any opportunity to clot.

"Kill him, Bullseye!" Wiezak nearly shrieked. "Kill him and I'll double your fee!"

"Oh, I'll take your money," Bullseye said, inching closer to Daredevil now and drawing a pair of sai from behind him. "But this kill isn't for the cash, it's for the pleasure."

And then the hero and the madman clashed.

Rico had just started searching the twenty-second floor with Dave Trebor when the fire alarm went off. The two men looked at each other, and Rico knew that Dave was thinking exactly what he was thinking.

"There's no way Gary's getting out of this one," Rico said, and the relieved smile that crossed Dave's face was signal enough that the man was in agreement with him.

"So what do we do?" Dave asked, relying on Rico's greater experience and his seniority in Wiezak's employment.

"What do you think we do, Trebor?" Rico laughed. "Only the captain goes down with his ship, we're out of here!"

Rico wiped the prints from his weapon, unsnapped his holster and left the works in the marble hallway. Dave followed suit and they went for the stairs. One floor down, they were joined by a stream of hotel guests evacuating the building, and they knew that the team that had already gone down in search of Betsy Potter would have no luck finding her in the crowd.

They shuffled calmly along with the nervous tourists and businesspeople that had always been the Wilmington's typical herd of cattle, and when they reached the bottom, continued on out to the street. The sirens were already wailing, and not too far away at all. Rico knew he'd made the right decision.

"Rico!"

He whirled at the sound of the voice, and saw the three guards that had been watching the prisoner. The woman among them, who called herself Isis, had yelled to him. He waved them over.

"What are you doing down here?" Isis asked him.

"Did you find the woman?" Rico asked, ignoring her question.

"No."

"Didn't think so," he shook his head. "Look, you guys want to go down on the kind of charges being involved with Wiezak will get you?"

They all looked worried.

"Didn't think so," Rico smiled. "Why don't we all melt away?"

"But Piers and the others are still upstairs!" Isis complained.

A police car, siren wailing, rounded the corner followed quickly by the first of the firetrucks. Rico looked over at them curiously, then turned back to Isis.

"You can find another boyfriend, or you and Piers can look lovingly at one another across the prison yard in Ryker's," Rico said. "I'm outta here."

The others all agreed, and had started to move away before Isis finally accepted the truth. Rico watched her take one last look up at the penthouse, and then she followed him and Dave.

"It's almost dawn," Rico said. "Who's up for breakfast?"

*   *   *

Betsy Potter saw a tight knot of people, all of whom she recognized as Wiezak's guards, standing outside the building with the hotel guests. The guards split up and walked away, clearly not intending to return to the Wilmington Hotel any time soon. That made up Betsy's mind. She headed back inside. She thought of using the stairs, but there were still people streaming out the door and she didn't want to fight that rush. You weren't supposed to use the elevator during a fire, but since she'd been the one to pull the alarm, she knew it was a false one.

She stepped inside the elevator, saw that there was a switch placed in the "stop" position, and flipped it back to run. As she pressed the button for the twenty-first floor, a man in the stuffy uniform of a hotel employee started toward her across the lobby, yelling for her to stay out of the elevator, there was a fire! The doors closed long before the man could get to her.

On the twenty-first floor, Betsy ran to the door that opened onto the stairs and started up them. On the next landing, there were several guns, and she picked up a big one before deciding it was too heavy. She settled for an automatic pistol.

Betsy Potter had shut herself down several days earlier, cut off all her emotions. But that had not stopped them. Instead, they had simmered there, hate, anger, humiliation, and now they were boiling into a raging fury. She let them all flow back into her at that moment, all of those feelings, and the tears came to her eyes.

She knew it was wrong, that it was everything she and Melvin had worked to overcome in *his* past. She was his therapist, for God's sake. But Gary Wiezak had ordered her taken from her home, had humiliated and abused her, and would have killed her without a second thought. And her death would have destroyed Melvin, murdered any hope he had of living a normal life.

The gun felt sweet and just and powerful in her hand.

Daredevil's battle with Bullseye had moved onto the penthouse patio. The hero's head was ringing from several blows he'd been unable to avoid, but he'd had better luck with his enemy's sai. Bullseye had tried half a dozen times already to feint in one direction and stab in the other, and each time he'd received a kick in the gut or head or a tumble to the ground for his troubles. With his senses completely focused on Bullseye, despite his nearly twenty-four sleepless hours, it was nearly impossible for the assassin to fake Daredevil out.

His knuckles were sore, several possibly broken, from hitting Bullseye's face. The bones there, like much of the assassin's skeleton, had been reinforced with adamantium and were nearly unbreakable. In a sense, though, that factor was incredibly freeing for

Daredevil. He could hit the assassin as hard as he wanted.

And he did.

Daredevil backed up to the hot tub, and Bullseye must have imagined he saw an opening for he thrust then, left hand up to parry and right hand slashing a sai toward Daredevil's heart. Daredevil sidestepped, the sai sliced through his costume and the skin of his side, just above where the glass had punctured him earlier. The hero reached out and laid hands on Bullseye, forcing him to continue his momentum, straight into the side of the hot tub.

"You're trying to make a fool of me!" Bullseye screamed. "You've done it before, but no more! You hear me! It's time for you to die!"

The assassin moved in, feinted several times, then kicked Daredevil's chest hard enough that the hero heard two ribs crack as he fell, rolled and sprang back to his feet. But Bullseye gave no quarter, that one moment he had caught Daredevil napping was all his ego needed to convince him that he could beat the man without fear. As far as Daredevil was concerned, the big problem was that he might be right.

Fists and feet lashed out, with Bullseye on the offensive and Daredevil parrying his every attack, yet getting little opportunity to launch a counter. Slow as his mind was from exhaustion, however, it was only a matter of time before he noticed that in his rage, Bullseye was relying almost exclusively on Taekwon-do, likely the first hand-to-hand martial style he had learned, and thus the most natural to him.

Daredevil, on the other hand, used no single style. He had long since mastered everything from boxing to Judo, Ninjitsu to Capoeira, and had developed his own personal style, completely unique, as a synthesis of all the training he had done. As tired as Daredevil was, Bullseye's use of Tae-kwon-do had driven him into automatically responding with that form as a defense.

Well, no more.

Bullseye aimed a kick at Daredevil's face. In the moment that his leg began to rise, Daredevil ducked and moved forward, under that raised leg, slamming into Bullseye's groin. He flipped himself into a forward aerial somersault, dragging Bullseye with him into the air and, landing on his feet, slamming the assassin hard onto the cement patio.

All the air left Bullseye in a huff, but he twisted from Daredevil's grasp and stumbled away. He pulled his remaining sai from behind his back and hurled it at Daredevil's face. No tricks, just a straightforward, panicked throw with deadly perfect aim and a speed a normal man would not have been able to notice, much less avoid.

Daredevil didn't duck. He faced the sai head on and clapped his hands together in the air around it just before it reached his face, its pronged hilt latching onto his hands and stopping its flight. With one smooth motion, he stopped it and turned it back toward its owner, who had begun to move forward again hoping to take advantage of the moment in which Daredevil would be busy evading the blade. The sai took Bullseye in the shoulder, directly beneath the collarbone, piercing the flesh and carrying all the way through to poke through the skin of his back and the kevlar costume there.

Bullseye cried out in pain and stumbled away, sitting down hard as his legs hit the hot tub. His searching arms found two abandoned champagne glasses, and despite the wound in his left shoulder, the assassin brought both arms around in a quick flick of the wrists that sent the glasses sailing for Daredevil's eyes.

The hero was closer than before, but he didn't feel as tired as he had. His body was exhausted, yes, but he felt as if he'd gotten a second wind. He whipped the straight part of his billy club from his hip and spun it in front of his face, shattering the two glasses before they had a chance to reach him.

He heard a click, and his radar scoped ahead to find that Bullseye had unsnapped his holster and was pulling his gun.

Daredevil got angry.

"What's wrong, killer?" he asked, venomous sarcasm in each word. "Can't win a fight man-to-man, can't even win with hand held projectiles? You've got to have a gun, eh? I always knew you were a loser!"

"Loser!" Bullseye shrieked, pulling the gun and beginning to take aim. "Loser?"

Daredevil dove forward, making himself a much smaller target should Bullseye get off a shot, but Daredevil's move had spooked him, and he pulled the trigger without aiming. Daredevil slammed into him, wrapping his arms around the killer's waist and taking him down hard. Then he was kneeling, like a schoolyard bully, sitting on Bullseye's stomach, feet behind him preventing Bullseye from using his legs to pull him off. Under other circumstances, Bullseye probably would have thrown Daredevil off easily, but the assassin was obviously too tired, or too angry, or both. With his billy club, he batted the pistol from Bullseye's grip, and as the man fought him, Daredevil simply started punching.

It was just like a schoolyard fight then, a particular one. Daredevil hadn't been the bully then, but the kid everybody picked on, the butt of every joke. He never fought back, his father had made him promise. But that day, he fought back and won, he beat the bully bloody, and it felt fantastic. That was the night his father hit him for the first and only time.

That had been different, though. The stakes had been so petty then; they were so much larger, so morally complex, now.

Daredevil stopped punching. Bullseye was not unconscious, but he was disoriented, even delirious. Despite his adamantium laced skull, he could be knocked out. Daredevil's radar scanned the face of his opponent. He couldn't see the blood, but he could smell it. He couldn't see the bruises, but he could feel how raw his knuckles were and knew Bullseye's face must feel the same.

He realized that, despite the differences, this fight wasn't all that different from the one in that old schoolyard years before. And completely unlike that day, for no reason he could think of, or perhaps one or two he would not have liked to think of, Daredevil felt ashamed of himself.

Maybe he had enjoyed that a little too much.

"Oh, well done, Daredevil!" Gary Wiezak's voice came to him as he got up from Bullseye's mumbling form. "Well done."

He turned to face the bogeyman, the monster of children's nightmares, and knew that no matter how devious and insane a killer Bullseye was, Wiezak was by far the worse of the two criminals.

"Why didn't you shoot me?" Daredevil asked.

"Well, up until just now I didn't know you were going to win," Wiezak said, trying to sound amused through his obvious anxiety. "Now the hotel is probably full of cops. I'll never get out of here on my own, so you're going to get me out. Or I put a bullet in her head." He fitted the barrel of his pistol tight against Karen's temple.

"One question," Daredevil said quickly, stalling while he tried to decide upon a course of action, and also genuinely looking for answers. "Why did you take Betsy Potter?"

"It wasn't my idea, but it *was* a good one," Wiezak said offhandedly.

"Fisk?"

"I think you know the answer to that, Daredevil. Shall we go now?"

"But why did Fisk want the woman?" Daredevil pushed.

"The Kingpin hasn't had the best of luck with his bodyguards and hired assassins," Wiezak said, cockier by the minute because he thought Daredevil was going to get him out.

"That doesn't make sense," Daredevil shook his head. "Even when Melvin Potter was the Gladiator, sure, he committed crimes and unfortunately a number of people died at his hand, but he was never the kind of cold-blooded killer Fisk has used before!"

"You overestimate your friend Potter," Wiezak laughed. "Fisk didn't really think he could turn the guy into the next Bullseye, but he figured what the hell, right? It was an experiment, that's all. One I was happy to continue when I left the Kingpin's employ."

Daredevil was stunned. What they had done to the Potters had been nothing more than an experiment! The family had been irrevocably scarred for the sake of Wilson Fisk's curiosity! Daredevil felt sick and vowed once again that the Kingpin's day of reckoning would come.

Now this fool Wiezak, the lowest of lowlifes, had put him in a very familiar situation, two men, one gun, one hostage. But this time it was different. This time the hostage was the woman he loved, the person who had become his lifeline in the darkest hour of his existence. They were returning to the sunlight together, and he wasn't about to let Wiezak take that away.

But he couldn't let the son of a bitch escape, either.

Daredevil was overwhelmed by his hatred of Wilson Fisk, of Gary Wiezak, of Bullseye, all of those predators who had set out to destroy people he cared a great deal for. No, Wiezak wasn't getting away.

A change came over him, and he knew it was a visible one, for the cockiness went out of Wiezak like a burst balloon. He felt the scowl on his face but could not control it. And as he spoke, he also listened, and listening, he heard Wiezak's heart speed up in terror of the man in front of him, the protector of Hell's Kitchen. Gary Wiezak was an evil man, but perhaps his greatest weakness was that he was rational.

"You will never get out of here," Daredevil growled through clenched teeth. "You won't shoot her, because then I'd have you, and the cops downstairs would put you away for life."

Daredevil heard Karen's heart, already speeding with fear, begin to flutter as she listened to his words. After a moment though, her heart not only calmed, but began to slow. She loved him, and obviously had faith that he was doing the only thing he could do.

"If you turn the gun on me," Daredevil continued, "even if you somehow manage to shoot me— and you know your odds on that are pretty slim—I'll be able to take you down before you can do anything to Karen. One way or another, Wiezak, you're going to prison. You've just got to decide how you're going to go."

Wiezak was silent for a moment, trying to cope with the truth in Daredevil's words.

"You've left out one contingency, Daredevil," he said after a moment. "I don't plan to go to prison at all. They wouldn't treat me very nicely in there. Too many cons still loyal to fat-man Fisk."

Daredevil had to agree. Fisk had influence everywhere. Wiezak wouldn't last long. But what did the man have . . .

"No!" Daredevil yelled as Wiezak turned the gun on himself, but he knew he'd never get there in time.

Luckily, he didn't need to.

Karen slammed her elbow back hard in the man's sternum, stomping her heel down onto his foot and pulling his gun hand forward, flipping him onto his back on the floor. She disarmed him easily after that. She had clearly been waiting for a moment when the gun, and Wiezak's attention, turned away from her.

"You bastard!" she screamed, and began pummeling him in the face. "There's no easy way out for you . . . you've got to pay!"

Daredevil kicked the gun away and lifted Karen off Wiezak, who was groggy from her blows. She hung on to his hair a moment, and Daredevil tugged her away, paying no attention to the pain it caused Wiezak.

And then he heard, behind him, a soft footstep, a heart hammering, and the sound of a pistol's safety clicking off. Everything was happening too fast!

"Betsy, don't do it!" Daredevil said as he turned.

Betsy Potter stood there, gun in hand, tears streaming down her face.

"Karen's right," she sobbed as she aimed at Wiezak, who lay on the floor in stunned silence. "He has to pay for what he did."

Betsy took a couple of steps forward. Daredevil knew that he could easily disarm the woman, but Betsy might be hurt. More importantly, though, if she were ever to lead a normal life again, it had to be her choice not to shoot. Otherwise, the question of what she might have done that day would haunt her forever and could well destroy her life with Melvin.

"Not this way," Karen said before Daredevil could open his mouth. "Killing him is too easy, Betsy, don't you see. He'll be in prison most of his life, might even die there."

Betsy's heart slowed some, but her aim was still dead on. Daredevil knew she was teetering on the edge of murder.

"Betsy," Daredevil said, "listen to me. Your husband was a violent man once, but he's changed. He's a good man now, and so few bad men ever get the chance to change. He's fought to become someone you can look up to, be proud of, someone you can love. It will destroy him if he thinks that you have become what he's tried so hard not to be!"

The sobbing overcame Betsy then, and she dropped the gun. Karen went to her and held her close.

"I want to see Melvin," she said through her tears, and Karen assured her that she would.

Daredevil picked Wiezak up from the ground, and he must have known he had lost finally, for he did not struggle. Daredevil's radar searched the room, but the three guards were still unconscious and the cops would be up to retrieve them momentarily, he was certain.

The patio, on the other hand, was empty. Twenty-three stories up, Bullseye had somehow escaped.

Daredevil was not surprised.

Epilogue

"I F WE CAN GET ONE OR TWO OF THOSE BODYGUARDS upstairs to turn state's evidence, we can probably put the bastard away for life," Lieutenant Bryce said, and Daredevil nodded grimly.

The two men turned and watched as a police cruiser carried Gary Wiezak away to meet his fate. Daredevil felt the sun on his face, and could not remember the last time a morning felt so good, despite his injuries and his exhaustion.

"You should let a doc take a look at you, Daredevil," Bryce said.

"Eventually," Daredevil agreed. "I've got some things to take care of first, though."

"You going to take the Potter woman home, then?" Bryce asked.

"You mind?" the hero replied.

"Not at all," Bryce allowed. "But tell me, where did Page get off to?"

Daredevil smiled. Karen had slipped past the police immediately upon their exit from the building. Natasha Romanova was in the hospital, with injuries she received trying to save Karen's life. Karen wanted to thank her for that, and Daredevil thought the experience might have formed a bond of sorts between the two women.

Right now, his thoughts were of Betsy Potter. The woman had been through a terrible ordeal. She was a strong woman, who had likely helped others deal with similar situations in her practice. But this was different. This was her own life.

But for all his strength, all his special abilities, there was nothing more that Daredevil could do for Betsy Potter than to bring her home.

It was not yet seven o'clock in the morning when Daredevil knocked on the door of the Spotlight Costume Shop. He could hear Melvin puttering around in the back and was fairly certain the man had not slept a wink all night. Who could blame him?

A bell above the door rang as Melvin jiggled the lock and swung the door wide, and Daredevil cursed his blindness once again, wishing he could see the look on the big man's face.

"Betsy?" Melvin gasped, a harsh whisper. "Oh, God, Betsy!"

Betsy didn't say anything as Melvin swept her up and hugged her tight. Both of them were crying, and Daredevil did his best to turn away, to allow them some privacy. At first, Betsy didn't say a word, and Daredevil could only assume that she was humiliated that she'd been made so vulnerable. It was possible she thought that Melvin would think less of her.

"Oh, Betsy, thank God you're all right!" Melvin said. "I love you, honey, I was so scared for you!"

And then, finally, reassured of her husband's love, Betsy finally spoke.

"Melvin," she said softly enough that anyone but Daredevil would not have heard. "They hurt me."

"Hush," Melvin said, his gravel voice choked with emotion. "I know they did. But it's over now, and I'm going to make sure nobody ever hurts you again."

Daredevil saw that Melvin had been a drowning man, life leeching from him with every day that passed while his wife was missing. He had been offered a lifesaving hand, and Daredevil knew too well what that was like. Karen had been there to save him very recently.

He slipped away, not waiting for thanks or praise, not wanting his own emotion to intrude on the reunion of husband and wife.

Back at the apartment, the answering machine was beeping to let Matt Murdock know he had a message. Foggy had long since gone home, which was a relief, though he wanted to spend some time with his best friend very soon. Get back in synch with Foggy's life, with their relationship.

Matt pressed the play button, and heard the tape rewinding.

"Hey Murdock," the voice began, and he knew it instantly as Bullseye's. "Just wanted you and your ladyfriend to know that it's not over. You can pass that on to your horn-headed buddy as well. This time was just target practice. So keep looking over your shoulder. I'll be back."

Matt erased the message, fell into bed, and was asleep almost immediately.

A short time later, when Karen finally made it home, she climbed in next to him fully clothed and drifted off with her head on his chest.

CHRISTOPHER GOLDEN is the author of eight novels, including *Of Saints and Shadows*, *Angel Souls & Devil Hearts*, and the upcoming trilogy *X-Men: Mutant Empire*. Golden has recently entered the comic book field with work on such titles as *Wolverine*, *Vampirella Strikes!* He has written articles for *The Boston Herald*, *Hero Illustrated*, *Flux*, *Disney Adventures*, and *Billboard*, among others, and was a regular columnist for the world-wide service BPI Entertainment News Wire. His short story appearances include *Forbidden Acts*, *The Ultimate Spider-Man*, *The Ultimate Silver Surfer*, and *Gahan Wilson's The Ultimate Haunted House*. Golden was born and raised in Massachusetts, where he still lives with his family.

BILL REINHOLD started drawing comics professionally in 1981 with the Noble Comics title *Justice Machine*. He drew Mike Baron's *Badger* at First Comics, then joined Marvel in late 1987 with the Punisher graphic novel *Intruder*, and also drew the monthly *Punisher* comic for a year. His other art credits include the Silver Surfer graphic novel *Homecoming*, *Clive Barker's Hellraiser*, *Spyke*, *The Prowler* miniseries, and *Punisher: The Empty Quarter*. He has also inked *Spirits of Vengeance*, *Venom: The Mace*, *Phantom 2040* (over Steve Ditko's pencils), and he currently inks the monthly *Daredevil* comic over Ron Wagner's pencils. He is married to his favorite colorist, Linda Lessman; they live in Evanston, Illinois, with their two children, Leanna and Michael, two cats, and a turtle.

SPIDER-MAN

__**SPIDER-MAN: CARNAGE IN NEW YORK** by David
Michelinie & Dean Wesley Smith   1-57297-019-7/$5.99
Spider-Man must go head-to-head with his most dangerous enemy,
Carnage, a homicidal lunatic who revels in chaos. Carnage has been
returned to New York in chains. But a bizarre accident sets Carnage
loose upon the city once again! Now it's up to Spider-Man to stop
his deadliest foe.   *A collector's first edition*

__**THE ULTIMATE SPIDER-MAN**   0-425-14610-3/$12.00
Beginning with a novella by Spider-Man cocreator Stan Lee and Peter
David, this anthology includes all-new tales from established comics
writers and popular authors of the fantastic, such as: Lawrence Watt-
Evans, David Michelinie, Tom DeHaven, and Craig Shaw Gardner.
An illustration by a well-known Marvel artist accompanies each story.
Trade

__**SPIDER-MAN: THE VENOM FACTOR** by Diane Duane
1-57297-038-3/$5.99
In a Manhattan warehouse, the death of an innocent man points to
the involvement of Venom—the alien symbiote who is obsessed with
Spider-Man's destruction. Yet Venom has always safeguarded
innocent lives. Either Venom has gone completely around the bend,
or there is another, even more sinister suspect.

The Epic Fantasy Series Based on the #1 Bestselling Computer Game

KING'S QUEST®

♦♦♦

__KINGDOM OF SORROW 1-57297-033-2/$5.99
by Kenyon Morr

A dark, frigid winter has descended on Daventry, a blizzard that will not stop. Yet beyond the boundaries of the kingdom, it is spring. Dark forces are at work, and the mighty King Graham must find out who—or what— is behind the treachery.

♦♦♦

__THE FLOATING CASTLE 1-57297-009-X/$5.99
by Craig Mills

On the clouds of a vicious storm, an ominous black castle appears in Daventry, ushering in a reign of terror which claims both the kingdom and its ruler. To save his father's life and the kingdom, Prince Alexander must penetrate the dark forces surrounding the castle...and face the very heart of evil itself.

® ™ & © 1992 Sierra On-Line, Inc. All Rights Reserved. Used Under Authorization.

Payable in U.S. funds. No cash orders accepted. Postage & handling: $1.75 for one book, 75¢ for each additional. Maximum postage $5.50. Prices, postage and handling charges may change without notice. Visa, Amex, MasterCard call 1-800-788-6262, ext. 1, refer to ad # 552a

Or, check above books	Bill my:	☐ Visa	☐ MasterCard	☐ Amex	
and send this order form to:				(expires)

The Berkley Publishing Group   Card#_____
390 Murray Hill Pkwy., Dept. B
East Rutherford, NJ 07073   Signature_____ ($15 minimum)

Please allow 6 weeks for delivery.   Or enclosed is my: ☐ check ☐ money order

Name_____   Book Total $_____

Address_____   Postage & Handling $_____

City_____   Applicable Sales Tax $_____
                                      (NY, NJ, PA, CA, GST Can)
State/ZIP_____   Total Amount Due $_____